"One more shot and you're a dead man," Spur barked.

The runner stopped suddenly, turned and pulled the trigger. His weapon didn't fire. He pulled the trigger five more times as Spur walked up to him, his Colt trained on the man's chest.

"Enough," Spur said. "Drop it and keep your hands in sight."

The gunner wilted, let the six-gun fall to the grass and shook his head. "Didn't seem so tough when he told me about the job."

"Killing a man is always harder than it looks, especially for a rotten shot like you. Who hired you?"

"You know I won't tell you that."

"How would I know something dumb like that? You look halfway smart. I might just as well shoot you right here and let the buzzards have their afternoon meal."

The man's eyes grew wide. His hands jiggled around at the end of his arms. He stared hard at Spur. "You wouldn't just kill me in cold blood."

"Tell me now or I'm going to start shooting."

Other *Spur Giants* from *Leisure Books*:

WILDERNESS WANTON
KLONDIKE CUTIE
HIGH PLAINS PRINCESS
DENVER DARLIN'
MINT-PERFECT MADAM
TALL TIMBER TROLLOP
PHOENIX FILLY

SPUR

SOILED DOVE

DIRK FLETCHER

LEISURE BOOKS ⬛ NEW YORK CITY

A LEISURE BOOK®

June 1995

Published by

Dorchester Publishing Co., Inc.
276 Fifth Avenue
New York, NY 10001

SPUR

SOILED DOVE

Chapter One

The big Topeka and Santa Fe engine with a string of 30 freight cars behind it rolled through the northern Arkansas green hills and shallow valleys. The workhorse engine poured its power onto the rails through its eight, red-painted drive wheels.

From his position in the locked express car, Clancy Steffens wasn't exactly sure where the train was. It was against regulations to open either the vestibule doors at the ends or the side loading door, but he moved deliberately to the side opening. Clancy unlocked it and edged it along the tracks two-inches. He stared through the slot until he was sure he knew exactly how far the train was from Fort Smith, then closed the door, locked it and returned to his chair in front of the small desk where he finished the paper work for the run from

Fayetteville to Fort Smith.

He checked his watch, then took out the two sacks of registered mail from the locked steel storage bin and left them on the floor. He twirled the knob on the Railway Express safe, unlocking it. He pulled the heavy door open to check and pushed it back making sure he didn't lock it.

He looked at his watch again and trembled. He was average sized, about 35, with fading brown hair and a widow's peak. Clancy squinted slightly but was damned if he'd get spectacles. He wore the required white shirt and tie. His jacket hung on its usual hook. He set his jaw, took one more look at the locked sliding side loading door and then hurried to the far end of the express car putting a high stack of mail sacks and merchandise between him and the side door.

He sat on the floor with his back to the rest of the car behind a solid shield of wooden crates. He had done too much planning to get killed at this late date. He waited.

Outside the train on a wooded ridge, three men also waited near the steepest uphill grade on the run south of Fayetteville.

"She's a comin'" one of the men said. He was the shortest of the three with pale eyes that sparkled and a mask over the bottom of his face. "By damn, this is my fifth train job, but I still want to piss my pants ever' time. So damn exciting I want to hold me up a train ever' day."

The older man, Russ Dolan, was tall and slender with a slouch hat and red suspenders. He snorted through his kerchief mask. "You wait till we through with this one, Sully. Then you can piss your pants all you want. Now get down to your spot and pull the damn string when I give the signal."

Sully ran 30 yards along the side of the ridge and picked up a piece of sturdy cord letting it hang slack in his hand. In front of him, seven loaded rifles had been staked securely to the ground, aimed at the tracks and the triggers cocked ready to fire.

A string ran from each of the triggers through screw eyes in the stakes in a way that a pull on the one long string held in Sully's hand would trigger the seven rifles at the same time firing them all.

They had tested the set up an hour ago and it worked perfectly. Now the rifles were reloaded, cocked and aimed.

Sully tensed as he heard the engine coming closer. It probably would be a big freight engine, maybe a Matthias Baldwin built 0-8-0, for this tough uphill grade. It came pounding along the hill, dragging a long string of cars behind it. In another two or three minutes he should be able to see it.

Sully glanced at the other two men. They were spaced down from him and each held a string in his hand that would trip the hammers on his own line of seven rifles staked to the ground in front of him. Twenty-one rifles would fire almost at the same time at the railroad train.

Now he saw Russ, the middle man of the three, put down his string. The plan was to first get the attention of the railroad crew. Russ picked up a

Spencer repeating rifle and waited. When the train was 300 yards down the tracks from them, he'd start firing his hand held weapon.

Sully grinned and felt a little wetness in his pants. He struggled with all his might and strained to hold it in. Damn, but this was a wild, wild time for him. This was the big one, a huge payday for all three. After today, he'd take his share and go to Kansas City and live it up with all the forty rod he could drink. He'd have two or three naked girls at a time in his fancy hotel bedroom. Yeah.

He looked north. There she was! He could hear the laboring engine, see the steam and the cinders spewing with the thick black smoke from the stack. The big engine charged around a small bend on the upgrade. Russ said that point was 400 yards down the track. From their position they were only 100 yards to the rails. Fish in a barrel. Sully held his breath as Russ aimed the Spencer at the moving train. He'd try for the engine and then the passenger car windows. Only one passenger car on this mixed lashup.

Russ aimed the Spencer and squeezed off the first shot. The jolting sound of the rifle fire lanced into the soft green stillness of the Arkansas hills. Quickly, he levered another round in and fired. He sent eight rounds into the engine and the passenger car. By that time the laboring Baldwin had the string of cars almost across from them. Russ lifted his left hand, picked up his heavy cord and swung down his left arm.

Sully pulled the cord exactly the way he had the

first time. His eyes glowed as all seven rifles in his line fired. The rifles were close enough to the small line of brush on the little ridge so the white smoke from the black powder in the cartridges would be easy to see from the train. His rounds hit the end of the passenger car and three empty cattle cars.

He only half heard the other rifles going off down the line. His were first. Then the others blasted just the way they had planned it. Knute Safire, the third man in their group, dropped his cord, leaped on board his bay mare and spurred hard for the train.

Sully grabbed his own Spencer then and popped rounds at the crawling train a few seconds apart to give a longer firing pattern. Russ pushed a new tube of rounds into his Spencer and alternated shots with Sully to drag out the attack.

Knute spurred his mount across the 100 yards to the train. As soon as Knute got to the train, the two on the ridge stopped firing. Knute raced along the right of way until he could swing up on the slow moving Railway Express car. He had a packsack on his back and climbed to the top of the express car.

He stood for a moment, swaying with the motion of the train. He dropped to his knees once, regained his balance and moved cautiously along the rocking train to the middle of the car. There he bellied down and took a bundle of dynamite from the packsack.

He had tied a string to it and now let the bomb down on the string over the side of the express car until the dynamite hung directly over the latch on the sliding side door. He tied off the string keeping the bomb in place. Then he pulled up the bomb, inserted a prepared fuse and blasting cap and lit the two-foot long fuse. He gently lowered the bomb back to its position against the sliding door.

He watched a moment. The six sticks of powder remained in place and the fuse burned fiercely. It had a two-foot-long fuse that burned a foot a minute. That allowed Knute time to get back out of the way of the blast and lie down on top of the car.

Right on time, the explosion blasted into the quietness of the Arkansas countryside and blew the express car door inward. The sound of the explosion echoed in Knute's ears as he walked carefully along the top of the car, laid down in the smoke coming from the blast, and then swung down into the railway express car.

The inside of the car was filled with lung searing smoke. Knute waved it aside and saw most of the smoke pulled out of the car through the half open sliding door.

As soon as the two men on the ridge stopped firing at the train, they mounted their horses and rode hard for the struggling train. By this time it was at the steepest part of the uphill grade crawling along at no more than ten miles an hour. They hung back until the bomb went off, then rode up beside the slowly moving train.

Inside the express car, Knute fanned away the acrid smelling smoke and fumes from the dynamite blast and found the safe. He had to make this part look like a real robbery. He taped two sticks of dynamite from the packsack to the safe dial and lit the foot-long fuse. Then he ran to the end of the car and sat down across from Clancy.

They eyed each other a minute, then Knute motioned. Clancy leaned forward and Knute slammed his big fist into Clancy's eye knocking him against the wooden boxes, scraping his cheek and bringing up a gout of blood.

"Sorry, Clancy, but you know this has to look good."

When the two sticks blasted, Knute had his hands over his ears. The sound in the closed car was like a dozen strikes of lightning on an outhouse with you inside.

Knute shook his head to clear it, then stood and ran for the safe. A moment later the two riders from the ridge came alongside the half open sliding door, with Russ leading Knute's horse.

Knute tossed the two registered mail sacks to Sully who took them, turned and rode away to the north. Knute used a leather glove and pulled open the hot, blackened handle of the safe door and grabbed the two small boxes marked with green tape. They were five inches tall and just the size of a $20 Federal banknote. Nothing else of value was in the safe.

He pushed the boxes of money inside his backpack and ran to the side door. Russ handed him his horse's reins and he stepped down to the walking horse's saddle, and dropped on board. They rode to the rear of the passenger car. There they swung from horses to the steps and pushed open the door into the parlor car with their six-guns held high in warning.

"Nobody move and nobody gets shot," Knute barked.

He saw the person he wanted halfway down the aisle. As Russ covered the angry conductor and worried passengers, Knute caught the arm of a blonde girl sitting on the aisle.

"Miss, you got to come with us. There's someone who wants to see you."

The girl screamed. "No, no. I won't go with you. Leave me alone."

Knute laughed, pulled the blonde girl from the seat, tossed her over his shoulder and ran with her up the aisle. The girl wailed and cried and bellowed at him, but Knute kept going.

Russ sent one .45 round into the wooden trim at the top of the car and everyone ducked.

The girl wailed again. "I won't go with you. Put me down. Put me down this instant!"

The two men ignored the girl and stepped into the vestibule between cars. Russ jumped off the slow moving train, hit the dirt and rocks but maintained his feet. By then the train labored along at less than five miles an hour up the steep grade.

Knute stepped down with the girl still on his shoulder. The girl screamed again, beat at his back with her small fists and screeched as they walked along the side of the passenger car. They saw their horses grazing on bits of green grass on the right of way, and hurried in that direction to the north. There were only empty cattle cars in the train beside them now. The popping of two six-guns was well behind them and way out of range.

Two minutes later, they were at their horses.

14

Soiled Dove

The girl screamed. "What the hell do you think you're doing?"

"Giving you a free ride on my horse. You want to sit in front of me easy or do I bend you belly down over my saddle and haul you along that way?"

The girl grinned. "Hey, how did I do? Did we convince them?" She was a little over twenty, Knute figured, pretty, with a slender build and good sized breasts. He always looked at a woman's hooters first.

"I'd say you did damn fine," Russ said coming up behind them. "Everyone on that train is gonna think you was taken off there against your will."

The girl smiled. "Still wish you'd brought a horse for me. This means one of you gives me your horse and then two of you guys have to ride double. Which horse do I get?"

Russ nodded at her and handed over the reins to his chestnut mare. She stepped into the stirrup as if she had done it before and swung up to the saddle. Her dress billowed showing a shapely leg almost to her crotch.

She grinned. "You like that leg show, don't you?"

Knute grunted. "Hell, you know we do. We just ain't allowed to show it or we get our asses kicked. We best get moving."

Russ mounted behind Knute and they rode north, away from the direction of the train. They galloped along the right of way for a quarter-of-a-mile, then eased the horses down to a walk and headed deeper into the hills and woods to get out of sight. Soon they couldn't even hear the hard working engine on the tracks now far to the south.

"Told you it would go smooth as Tennessee sippin' whiskey on a hot afternoon," Russ said. The others yelped and agreed.

The woman's pretty face took on a questioning look. "You sure you got everything right? You know what to do and where to go?"

"That we do, pretty lady. They just didn't tell us that you'd be so beautiful."

"Let's hope that my father will be as easy to convince as those passengers were back there. Do you men know who I am?"

"Exactly. You're Amy Hellman. We know exactly who you are. Do you know who we are?"

She turned and stared at Knute who still hadn't taken his mask down. "I don't know your names yet, but you can take your masks down. It would look suspicious if anyone happened to see us, a hunter or somebody on the run."

They dropped their masks and she looked at each one. "Sully—you're the one with the mailbags, youngest one of the three. I can't figure out which one of you is Russ."

He held up his hand.

She smiled. "Pleased to meet all three of you. Now let's make a little better time so we can get where we're going. Riding this horse isn't my most favorite activity."

Amy Hellman rode well. She had soft blonde hair cut short and sassy around her face. Her brown eyes sparkled and dimples dented her soft pink cheeks. She was five-three and weighed no more than a hundred pounds.

She shook her head and looked over her shoulder at Knute again. "I was so relieved when I heard those first rifle shots. I didn't know when it would happen. How long until we get to where we're going?"

"A while yet," Russ said. "We have to find a nice quiet spot to check our mail for today."

They found a spot of dense brush half an hour later and stepped down from their horses. Amy went up to Sully and grabbed him by the shoulders and kissed him. He was so surprised he nearly fell down.

She caught one of his hands and pushed it under her blouse on her bare breasts.

"Sully, riding that damn horse has got my little cunnie so hot she just won't wait another minute. She needs a good quick poking and I don't care what they told you. Right here and right now Sully, before I just explode."

Two days later, Spur McCoy dropped off the Atcheson, Topeka and Santa Fe passenger coach in Fort Smith, Arkansas. He had been in Kansas City finishing a case when his boss, United States Secret Service Assistant Director General Wilton D. Halleck, sent him a telegram.

As usual, the man responsible for assignments and operations of the Secret Service worked quickly. The senior U.S. Senator from Arkansas had received a telegram two days ago detailing a serious train robbery that involved loss of government money, two sacks of registered mail, and a kidnapping. He requested immediate federal help.

Spur McCoy, one of the best Secret Service men in the West, drew the assignment and had a telegram to that effect later the same day.

The wire was short and direct:

TO: SPUR MC COY, HOTEL CLAYMORE, KANSAS CITY, MISSOURI. TRAIN ROBBERY YESTERDAY NEAR FORT SMITH, ARKANSAS. FEDERAL MONEY AND REGISTERED MAIL STOLEN FROM EXPRESS CAR, DAUGHTER OF ARKANSAS GOVERNOR KIDNAPPED. TRAVEL AT ONCE TO LOCATION. CONTACT JUDGE ISAAC PARKER FOR DETAILS. REPORT SOONEST. SENDING, GEN. WILTON D. HALLECK. WASHINGTON, D.C.

Spur McCoy had grinned when he saw the name of Isaac Parker, the famous hanging judge of Fort Smith and the terror of the Indian Territories 100 yards across the Arkansas river. He'd never had much to do with the hanging judge, but now it looked like he'd have the chance to work with him.

He found a hotel, the Wentworth, that was right on the river and had a private dock where small craft could tie up and discharge passengers from downriver and the state capitol at Little Rock.

Spur McCoy was a big man, standing taller at six-feet two-inches than most of the men he met. He kept his weight to a slender and tough muscled 185 pounds. He was well tanned from spending so much time in the outdoors, had dark hair, no beard or moustache, and green eyes. He usually wore a flat brimmed, low-crowned black hat with a string of Mexican silver pesos around it.

He had first been assigned the western section of the country by the Secret Service since he was the only field agent who could ride a horse and had experience on a cattle ranch. He was a crack shot with hand guns and rifle, an excellent horseman and had a smattering of skill with the oriental martial arts. He was also a graduate of Harvard University near Boston and had done his duty for the North in the Civil War as an army captain.

He wore his working clothes: brown town pants, a tan, long sleeved shirt, doeskin vest, and a black string tie. His cowboy boots were battered and worn, but the most comfortable he had ever owned. On his right hip rode a worn leather holster housing a .45 Colt. The bottom of the leather was always tied down with a thong around his thigh.

Spur pushed the door open at the Federal Court building where Judge Parker had sentenced so many killers to be hanged. It had once been an army barracks, two storied and made of stone as part of the original U.S. Army's Fort Smith built in 1817. He looked around, saw an office and stepped toward it.

Inside he found a large desk with a small man behind it wearing half glasses, a dark suit, tie. The man had large jug handle ears and almost no hair on his slightly misshapen head. He looked up and his disfavor showed plainly on his face.

"All deputies are to use the side entrance and report to the Chief Deputy Marshal."

"You keep the riffraff and rabble out of your office that way, I'd figure," Spur said walking to the front of the big desk and staring down. When the clerk made no comment Spur went on.

"My name is Spur McCoy. General Halleck sent me and I need a word with Judge Parker. I'm a United States Secret Service agent here to clean up your railroad robbery."

"Oh. I'm sorry, these deputy marshals—"

"This is a courtesy call, to let the judge know I'm in town and working on the robbery case. I don't actually need to stare at him face to face."

Before he finished the sentence a door to the left opened and a large man came through it. He had on the flowing black robes of his office. His dark hair was parted on the right side and he had bushy brows, a black moustache and a bountiful, untrimmed goatee. His face was set in a stiff, formal, impartial mask.

His dark eyes concentrated on Spur a moment, then he stepped forward and held out his hand. Spur shook it.

"Spur McCoy, good of you to come. I saw you once in Washington with General Halleck. I received word you would be coming. My deputies here have little experience in actual investigation work. The court stands ready to offer you any assistance you may require. Tell Percival here what you need and he'll provide it."

"Good to meet you, Judge Parker, I won't be

needing much. Just wanted to say hello."

Parker nodded, handed Percival a paper and without another glance or word, strode back through the heavy doors to what Spur figured was his courtroom. Spur watched him leave then looked at Percival.

"Anything you need, Mr. McCoy?" the clerk asked.

Spur shook his head, waved at him and walked out of the court house and down the steps to the baked dry ground around the building. He knew the jail was in the basement. The place had not been designed to be a jail and was dark and he figured damp. He turned to the street and asked someone how to find the county sheriff's office.

Sheriff Booth Grimm looked about 50, wore a serious full black moustache, had soft blue eyes that always seemed to be running, and offered a firm handshake.

"Heard you was coming, McCoy. We need lots of help on this one. Got a report for you here. Bastards made out like they had twenty rifles. Which they did actually, but fired them with a string and the trainmen thought an army was up there on the ridge. Caught the train going up the Deadhorse hill grade where she slows to about five miles an hour sometimes depending on how long the string of cars is she's toting."

"How many men hit the train?"

"Near as we can tell, just three. Blew in the express car side door with an outside bomb, then blasted the safe. Knocked out the express man and beat him some, but he ain't hurt bad. Reckon

21

you'll want to talk to him. His name's Clancy Steffens."

"Be good to talk to him." Spur read the two hand written reports the Sheriff handed him. Not much there. Little more than the lawman had told him. One porter had been wounded from one of the rifle shots but it wasn't serious.

"So it's not just robbery, but we can charge them with attempted murder as well," the sheriff said. "Makes it a bit more serious."

"I'm thinking the kidnapping might be more important," Spur McCoy said.

The sheriff stood and walked to the window. The lawman was average sized and had a generous belly flowing over his three-inch wide belt. "The young woman they snatched is Amy Hellman, only child of our governor Wild Bill Hellman."

"The governor's only child? How old is she?"

"Twenty-one. Common knowledge around the state that she's never got on well with her parents, her pa especially. So far there hasn't been any reward posted for her return. We've had a flock of letters and wires from the capitol down in Little Rock. Newspapers are screaming headlines.

"Governor Hellman is saying all the right things, but somehow it has a false ring to it. We haven't heard if there's been a ransom demand. Governor don't like to talk much about Amy usually. Now he has to."

"I'll stay in touch. Where can I find this Railway Express clerk, Clancy Steffens?"

"Family man. This is his home base. Lives at 210

Third Avenue. I've known him for several years. Good man."

Spur pondered the reports again. "Twenty thousand in Federal greenbacks, and two sacks of registered mail. Any complaints yet about what was in them?"

The sheriff shook his head. "Not yet. We'll have a mess of them soon. I sent out two of my deputies, but they ain't much at tracking. Lost the three horses about half-a-mile from the spot of the shooting. They found the rifles. Twenty of them all tied down. All old weapons, not worth much. They brought them in. Probably sell them off sometime."

"Then nobody's found the registered mail yet?"

"Not hide nor satchel full."

"Lots of times on a robbery like this they dump out the registered mail and rip it open looking for cash, diamonds, that sort of thing."

"Like I say, my deputies ain't too good at tracking, and Judge Parker can't spare a man right now, he tells me. I figure Post Office people will be in town soon. Hope you can find them letters before the postal folks get here foaming and frothing at the mouth."

"See what we can do." Spur thought about it a moment. "The mail and the cash can wait. They won't go anywhere. The girl might. I better concentrate on her first."

"Sounds reasonable. You want a posse? This is a hard town to get up a posse, but I can try."

"I work better alone, Sheriff. But thanks. I might need somebody to back my play later on.

The robbery took place about five miles north of town?"

"About the size of it. The railroad men left two small red flags there as a marker."

"I'll check it out from that end."

It was just after noon when Spur picked up a horse from the Anderson Livery Barn on the north side of town and took the old North Road. The livery man told him the road paralleled the tracks for two miles before it veered to the right. He could ride over and follow the tracks the rest of the way.

Spur McCoy had eaten at a small cafe before he left and carried a canteen. He didn't have any food or camping gear. Spur had a feeling this tracking wouldn't take long. Either the outlaw's tracks would be gone after three days, or they would fade out somewhere. There was a chance these robbers were new to their trade and might lead him right into their camp. He could use a simple case for a change.

An hour later, Spur came to the two-foot square red flags on stakes pounded into the side of the right-of-way. One of the eyewitnesses said that two men had ridden along the tracks and swung on board the slow moving train. He found the hoofprints along the tracks for some distance. A short way beyond the flags, he saw that one set of prints had penetrated deeper into the soft dirt.

Riding double. One rider must have taken the girl on his horse, probably in front of him. That could mean the kidnapping was a spur of the moment idea. If they'd planned it, why wouldn't they bring an extra horse for the kidnap victim?

He turned and followed those deeper tracks. They changed direction and rode north, now veering away from the tracks into the small valley and toward the brushy ridge to one side.

In the soft ground and across the brushy hill, the tracks were easy to follow. Soon a third horse joined the first two. Only one of the sets of prints showed double riders. About three miles north of the attack site, the tracks petered out on some sheet rock. He circled the half acre of bald rock but couldn't find where the tracks left the stone.

Spur sat on his horse a minute thinking. This was how they had fooled the deputies. What would he do in a case like this? Lead the horses across the hardest ground available. Yeah.

He moved out a quarter-of-a-mile from the rock and made a circle around the place, leading his horse, watching the ground for any resumption of the trail.

He found it on the far side but now the tracks headed south again. A mile on he found where they had stopped in some tough to penetrate, dastardly thick brush. The two mail sacks and registered mail of all kinds lay scattered around. Half of it had been ripped open, evidently examined to see if there was anything valuable in it.

He picked up every piece he could find and stuffed it all in one mail sack, pushed the other sack inside, pulled the ropes, and tied the sack behind his saddle.

Then he followed the trail again. Now it

switched back north. A half-mile later, the tracks entered a small stream no more than a foot deep and ten-feet wide. He went across but could find no spot where the tracks came out of the water.

North. He took the near side of the creek and worked his way north along the soft banks. It would be obvious when the three horses left the water and got back on their right route to wherever they were heading.

He rode the bank for two miles, but nowhere did he find any sign of the tracks leaving the water. He crossed over and rode back south expecting to locate some sign of the riders on that side.

By the time he got back to the original entry point, he had found nothing. That meant they had reversed their direction again and rode south in the stream covering their tracks.

Spur repeated his search routine, this time to the south. Nearly a mile downstream he found where three sets of prints came out of the water. One set sank deeper into the soil than the other two.

No change, double weight still on that horse. Now he had an easier trail as he worked along the horseshoe prints. The riders didn't seem to be trying to cover their tracks. Why?

Three miles later, he found out why. The tracks veered to the left to the North Road and kept moving south toward Fort Smith. In places, he had trouble finding the three sets of prints due to other traffic on the road. Two farm wagons with wide steel wheels had rolled into town since the trio of horses had passed nearly wiping out all sign of the tracks.

Soiled Dove

He found enough to keep on the trail.

Near the town of Fort Smith, the tracks faded completely as dozens of horses and wagons had used the road in the three days. The object of their ride was now plain. Spur had tracked them to within a quarter-of-a-mile of Fort Smith before the sign was blotted out.

Why would the robbers ride deliberately into Fort Smith where they must know that the search for them would have its headquarters?

Chapter Two

Spur McCoy rode on into Fort Smith, found the Post Office in the Mallory General store and handed the mail sack to the postmistress.

"What's this?" Mrs. Mallory asked.

"My guess is that's the registered mail that was stolen off the train two days ago as it headed into town."

A man in a trim brown suit, matching vest and gold watch chain came forward at once. He held out a card.

"Bret Hardy, United States Postal Inspector. I've been sent here from our regional office in Kansas City to investigate this matter. May I ask who you are?"

Spur told him and he relaxed a little.

"Where did you find this registered mail?"

Soiled Dove

Spur explained where he found it and what he did.

"Good, excellent. We'll deliver all registered mail that hasn't been tampered with," Mrs. Mallory said.

"No, Mrs. Mallory. I'll have to determine that. No one may touch that mail but me until I make a determination," Inspector Hardy stated.

Spur watched the officious little man. Obviously, he was a person who liked his work which he thought was the most important in the world.

"Oh, Mr. McCoy," the Inspector said. "I'd like you to sign a receipt that you retrieved this registered mail giving the time and place. We need it for our records."

"Afraid I can't do that, Mr. Hardy. Then I would be swearing that I received everything that the rail clerk signed for previously. I know how your system works. Then I'd be liable for anything missing. I won't sign any such receipt."

Hardy looked concerned. "You won't sign for what's here?"

"No. I don't know what's here and what's missing. Have you been notified that some valuable items were on that particular train?"

Hardy squirmed, moved from foot to foot, looked out the window and pushed one hand in his pocket, then brought it out.

"Actually, we have. There were three valuable parcels in these sacks, signed off by the expressman in Kansas City, received by one Clancy Steffens, and now it would be my guess that all three will be missing when I go through the sack."

"Which leaves either me or the train robbers, or anyone else who happened along that same area, as the felons with the valuable goods. Mr. Hardy, if I were going to steal something from the registered mail, why would I then conveniently bring you the rest of it?"

"Yes, yes, that's reasonable."

"Hardy, I want to know what's been reported missing. My office outranks yours considerably. Do you want the Secretary of the Treasury to instruct your boss to tell you to inform me about the missing items?"

Hardy wiped a line of sweat off his forehead. He blinked several times and his hands went behind his back and stayed there. At last he shook his head.

"No, I guess I don't want that kind of pressure. Let me make a quick check on what's in this bag, then I'll tell you and the Sheriff and the District Attorney all at the same time."

A half hour later the four men gathered in Sheriff Grimm's office. District Attorney Zane Hawthorne overflowed the chair he sat in. Fat arms bulged his black suit jacket and his white shirt struggled to cover a huge belly. By contrast his face was hard and lean with gray eyes that were always on the move gathering information every second.

Spur had heard that the man had a photographic memory and could repeat conversations word for word that he had had with people ten years ago. His eyes were close set with a narrow, small nose between them and thin lips below. He had almost no chin, then his body ballooned. His hands and fingers were fat as well.

Hardy looked at the Sheriff who nodded. Hardy stood and paced the end of the office a moment, then held his hands behind him.

"Gentlemen, we have a delicate matter here. There has been a kidnapping of your governor's daughter. The safe on the express car was blasted open and $20,000 in new Federal banknotes heading for banks here and on south were stolen." Harding watched for a reaction. Sheriff Grimm wrote down the figure and looked up.

"There also was a large envelope filled with bearer bonds. These bonds are unregistered by owner, only by amount and number, and can be sold at any stocks and bonds firm or brokerage house with no questions asked. They are as good and as negotiable as paper currency. The value of these bonds changes, but when they were sent by registered mail from Kansas City three days ago, they were worth a little over one-hundred-thousand dollars."

The District Attorney also took notes on the first page of a small leather bound pad.

"The other item missing is a fully negotiated Bill of Sale for the Triangle T ranch, north of here, owned by Dylan Teasdale."

"The Triangle T?" the D.A. asked. "That's the biggest ranch in most of Arkansas. Worth a great deal of money."

"There was ten-thousand in cash in the envelope as a good faith payment, along with a signed agreement to purchase the ranch and cattle for four-hundred-thousand dollars, to be paid over a period of time.

"My problem is, how do we find and reclaim the bank money, the bonds, and the stolen legal papers," Hardy said. Then he sat down.

The four men looked at each other. Spur had not told them that he had followed the robbers back to town. He figured it better not to let them know that right now.

"I'm sure that my office and that of the Sheriff will put every resource at our disposal in trying to find the perpetrators," the District Attorney said. "The trouble is, we have very little to go on. The expressman said the two men he saw both had masks over their faces and wore hats. All he saw were the men's eyes and a little of their foreheads. Nothing to work with."

"Mr. McCoy," Hardy said. "When you found the mail sacks, did you continue to track the culprits?"

"I did. They moved to the North Road, but after several miles of following their sign, I lost the tracks in a maze of farm wagon wheel prints and other horse traffic. Remember, it was almost three days after the deed when I had a chance to trace the robbers."

"Damn," Sheriff Grimm said. "That means we don't have a God damned thing to go on. No starting place."

"Sheriff, I noticed two or three small settlements between Fayetteville and Fort Smith when I came down on the train," Spur said. "You might send a man up that way and see if anyone saw the four people pass by, or stay all night anywhere."

Sheriff Grimm nodded. "Good. I'll have a man catch the next train through. Faster than riding a horse."

"I've sent a telegram to the Director of Currency at the Bureau of Engraving and Printing in Washington," Spur said. "He's going to wire back to me the serial numbers on those twenty-dollar bills that were stolen. They keep such records. The bills are new and all in sequence, and should be easy to spot in town if the robbers spend any of them here or nearby.

"We'll supply every merchant in town with a list of the serial numbers and ask him to check every twenty-dollar bill he sees. Could be productive."

"You don't think they would come back here, do you?" Hardy asked.

"How many residents in town now, nearly three-thousand, thirty-five-hundred? Best place in the world to get lost in and not stand out."

"What about the hostage?" District Attorney Hawthorne asked.

"She could be the key," Spur said. "They have her. They have to house and feed her. What do we know about her? She was riding the train alone, evidently. Is she a free spirit or a Sunday School teacher?"

"I've had a wire or two about her in the past," Sheriff Grimm said. "When she was sixteen she ran away from home. It was all kept quiet. My guess is that by now she's a real rebel, not taking kindly to her father's tight reins."

"Sheriff Grimm, could I ask you to wire the governor telling him you've found no trace of his daughter and asking what kind of a search he wants you to launch?" Spur asked. "We might learn something from his reaction and instructions."

The sheriff indicated he would.

"Gentlemen, I have twenty pieces of damaged registered mail that I must hand deliver here in town and try to get releases signed," Hardy said. "Then I have thirty-five more damaged items I must deliver on down the tracks. I'll contact Sheriff Grimm when I get back." He stood, waved at them and walked out of the office.

Sheriff Grimm looked at McCoy. "You didn't say which direction on the road those robbers rode, north or south."

McCoy grinned. "Caught me, Sheriff. I lost the tracks maybe a quarter-of-a-mile outside of town. The robbers and their victim all came back to town the same day the train was robbed."

The sheriff sat up straight in his chair. "So they're in town right now?"

"Maybe, maybe not," Spur said. "They've had two days to catch a train. With the money they have they can travel anywhere in the world and go first class all the way."

Hawthorne heaved his bulk straighter in his chair. "I'd guess they are still here in town. Too hard to travel with a woman. If she's a kidnap victim, how could they get her on a train? She would be screaming and kicking all the way. If she's a kidnap victim they need a base of operations to negotiate from with her father. I'd say they're still in town."

"This local ranch, the Triangle T," Spur said, "how could it fit in? The robbers would steal the ten-thousand in the envelope, but why the signed agreement to sell the place? Doesn't seem natural."

Spur looked at the other two men who shook their heads.

"Could it be that something is going on at the big ranch most people don't know about? What's its reputation? Does it have a clean slate? How does Teasdale get along with his neighbors, with the town people? How far is the ranch from Fort Smith?"

"Don't see where you're going, Mr. McCoy, or how you can connect this up, but I'll give you some of the answers," D.A. Hawthorne said. "Lots goes on at that ranch, not all of it good. As a ranch, it has the reputation as a tough customer; takes care of its own, solves problems on the ranch, sells a lot of steers it drives to stock pens on the railroad from a siding the ranch paid for.

"Old man Teasdale is Dylan, a Welsh name. He's tough as just tanned buffalo hide. He's got two grown daughters, no sons, no wife anymore. Some say he had a small stroke about a year ago, but nobody knows for sure.

"He fights with his closest neighbors, is seldom seen in town anymore, and his two daughters have married and both of them live in separate houses on the ranch while their husbands are supposedly trying to learn the cattle business. His ranch buildings are about eight miles north of town. Edge of his property extends down to within two miles of the Fort Smith city limit."

Spur chuckled. "I'd say you have quite a file on Mr. Teasdale. Thanks for the information. It could be a place to start. He was probably the first one to wire the Post Office Department about his missing contract."

The district attorney moved in his chair again and the wooden structure creaked from his weight. He rubbed one hand across his face and then frowned at Spur.

"What?" Spur asked. "What's the problem? Is Teasdale an untouchable or something around here?"

Hawthorne shrugged and slowly shook his head. "No, not at all. I just think it would be a waste of time to concentrate a lot of work on him."

"I need to start somewhere, you have any other ideas?"

"I'm afraid not," the district attorney said. He lifted himself out of the chair with his massive arms and the move showed Spur that there was a lot of muscle in his arms that didn't show.

Hawthorne held out his hand. "Mr. McCoy, let me know what you uncover. I'll be trying to figure out some way to help, but I only have one investigator in my office and right now he's got three cases he's working."

Spur shook the hand and found the grip firm. "I usually like to work by myself, anyway, Counselor. I'll keep you informed."

When the district attorney left the room, Sheriff

Grimm studied Spur. "Looks like you upset Zane."

"He have a special relationship to the great man at the Triangle T spread?"

"Not that I'd known before, but he was irritated for some reason. Usually Zane holds his feelings inside that big body of his."

"Can't be helped. If it bothers him too much, he'll probably tell us why. Oh, no need to send a man up north. You were right, the bounders are right here in town. Wish to hell we knew how to find them."

Sheriff Grimm nodded. "Let me know when those serial numbers come in. I'll have my people write out the notices and take them to the store owners. We'll keep it as quiet as we can so we don't tip off the robbers."

Spur thanked the sheriff, shook his hand and went out to the street. He stopped at his hotel and checked with the room clerk. He showed him his identification. The clerk gulped and his eyes went wide for a moment.

"Nothing is wrong, so relax. I'm hunting a party of four that probably came into the hotel two days ago. Three men and a woman. You have any groups like that?"

The clerk lifted his brows. "Oh, boy, you had me going for a minute there. Let me check the register." He turned it sideways so they both could read it and flipped the page over where the previous two days were annotated.

They found two sets of two men each, but they were all salesmen. No cowboys that the clerk remembered.

"Any single women?"

There were three. "Two of them are still here," the clerk said. "Both are in their fifties. The third one is maybe fifteen. She's waiting for her uncle to come pick her up. She's from Boston."

Spur went down the street and talked to two more hotel clerks before he went for supper. None of the three hotels had any groups of four.

Maybe the robbers didn't stay at a hotel. If they had planned this out at all, the ideal way would be for them to have a rented house to use. One could go for groceries and supplies, the rest stay in the house, keep out of sight and most important, keep the woman hidden.

Supper was fair. He decided to try a different eatery the next day. On a sudden impulse he went down to the train station and found the telegrapher still on duty. He showed his identification and then told the man what he was working on.

"So, if you get any telegrams being sent to the governor, I want you to handle them as routine, but keep a copy of the wire for me."

"Can't do that, sir. Against regulations."

"I think you can. Ask your supervisor or the stationmaster. We're trying to solve a railroad problem here. I'm sure he'll say it's all right since this is a criminal investigation."

"All right, I'll ask him, but—"

"I'll check back later to see if there's anything coming either way," Spur said, cutting him off. "Copy any of those messages for me."

He turned and walked out of the telegraph office and toward the hotel. He pondered the strange re-

action by the district attorney to the talk about the
Teasdales. The man would bear watching. Nothing more he could do tonight. He decided on a
good night's sleep. Might be a while before he had
another one.

Early the next morning, Spur picked up a horse
at the livery and asked for directions to the Triangle T spread. It was a little after 9:00 when he
rode into the ranch yard. A cowboy from the bunk
house met him and asked what he wanted.

A short time later Spur stood outside the
kitchen door of the two story ranch house.

"I'd like to talk to Mr. Teasdale," Spur said.

The man who faced him had on range clothes
but no hat. He looked as if he'd just finished a late
breakfast.

"I'm the foreman here. We don't need no riders."

"Good, I'm not looking for work. I want to talk
to Mr. Teasdale about the papers he lost in the
train robbery."

A smaller man came out the kitchen door and
pushed the foreman aside.

"I'm Teasdale. You find my papers and the
money?"

"Not yet, Mr. Teasdale. I'm Spur McCoy with
the U.S. Secret Service. I want to talk to you about
that robbery."

Teasdale was short and heavy, in his fifties and
pale faced like a towner. He wasn't on the range
much anymore, Spur figured. He swiped at the
remains of dark hair on a balding skull and
scowled for a moment, then he waved.

"Come on in out of the hot sun. Reckon I can

spare you a few minutes. Why the hell ain't you caught them train robbers yet?"

"Why haven't you caught them? The robbers set up their guns on your property."

Teasdale turned and stared hard at Spur, then he chuckled. "I'll be damned, there is one man left in this country with a little bit of spunk. McCoy, wasn't it? Come on in and we'll have some lemonade and maybe some cookies the galley slave just finished. The secret is to get them before they cool off too much, and still not burn your fingers."

Twenty minutes later in an elaborate den, they had chewed over the President, then Congress, refought the Civil War and agreed that Judge Parker was the best thing that had ever happened to Arkansas and the Indian Territories.

"Now, what about my papers and that ten-thousand in cash?"

"Wish I knew, Mr. Teasdale. All we know is there were three men. They hit the express car, blew open the side door, blew the safe, took twenty-thousand in new twenty dollar bills from the safe and the two sacks of registered mail, and then kidnapped the governor's daughter from the passenger car and vanished."

"You look like a tracker. You follow them?"

"I did. Lost their tracks on the North Road when they were trampled out by wagon wheels and horse's hooves."

Teasdale's shoulders slumped. "Holy damn. I was hoping maybe your help would do some good. What the hell can you do now?"

"Keep on digging, hoping and waiting for some

kind of a break to give us a lead."

"You know the serial numbers on those bills?"

"I'll know some time today." Spur frowned. "What about that ten-thousand from the ranch buyer? Was it all new money?"

Teasdale downed the last of the lemonade and shook his head. "Don't know, I never saw it. My guess is that it wouldn't be. So, whoever hired these men would be smart enough to use the old money to pay off the three robbers."

Spur looked up, a nervous tremor riding the back of his neck. "You said whoever hired the robbers. You think they were working for somebody else, some third party?"

"Figures. Only two people knew that signed contract and the money was coming from Kansas City in that envelope and mailed that day."

"You and the buyer?"

Teasdale nodded.

"Mr. Teasdale, maybe you're forgetting one other person who knew. Your lawyer, the man who drew up the contract and helped you on the sale of the ranch."

Teasdale looked up sharply. Then the fire in his eyes faded and he shook his head gently. "Oh, well, yes, I guess you're right."

"Is Zane Hawthorne your lawyer?"

Teasdale shrugged, started to speak but stopped. He took a deep breath and let it out. "Yeah. How did you know? Zane is the best lawyer in this end of the state. Just because he's the D.A. ain't no reason he can't have some private clients."

"Even if only three people knew about the timing, your goods may not have been the primary object of the robbery."

"Heard there was some other items in those registered mail sacks beside my papers. Something valuable?"

"True. Don't forget the kidnapping. Witnesses told the sheriff that the two robbers went directly to the passenger car, picked out the blonde Miss Hellman and carried her off the train like a sack of wheat."

"Holy damn! Why is everything so complicated these days?"

"I keep trying to simplify them, Mr. Teasdale. Are you sure that your two sons-in-law didn't know about the timing on the contract coming?"

"Hell, no. I don't let them know anything about my business. Both a couple of lazy-assed, nogoods. Only thing they do well is poking my daughters and knocking them up. Two grandchildren already and another one in the oven."

"Would you mind if I talked to them while I'm out here?

"Why not? Can't hurt a damn. Let them see how it feels to have somebody pounding buckets stuck over their heads. Might do them some good. I'll send somebody to bring them over. Both got houses of their own. Houses I paid for, of course.

"Holy damn. Wish to hell them girls of mine had done better in the marrying business."

He called and a young boy about 12 came running in. He gave him the message and the boy scurried out the far door.

"To have that kind of energy again," Teasdale

said and slumped in his chair.

They had more iced lemonade and in five minutes the boy was back shaking his head.

"Both Mr. Emerson and Mr. Chandler are gone today."

"Gone where, child?"

"The ladies didn't say, Mr. Teasdale."

"No, they wouldn't. Scat, get out of here."

The boy grinned and hurried out of the den.

Teasdale picked up his empty glass and threw it across the room into the den's fireplace. The glass shattered.

"Holy damn. I kept it a secret, my selling the ranch. Wanted it to be a big surprise for those two sons-in-law. Now everyone will know."

"Will the sale still go through?"

"Hell, not now. I was supposed to wire my acceptance the day I got the cash and the contract and send him a receipt for the ten-thousand. Now I'm sure he'll want his money back and slither out of the deal." He rubbed his face with his hand and let out a sigh. "So, if the robbers weren't trying for my papers and the ten-thousand, what was the prime target?"

"Could have been the Federal greenbacks. They took the mail sacks on the chance something might be there."

"Or how about they blew the express door and the safe as a cover up for their real target, the governor's daughter?"

Spur got into the spirit of it. "Maybe somebody knew about the other valuable things in the registered mail sacks and went after those, and the rest of it was all a diversion."

"So, Mr. smart man detective from Washington D.C. What the hell you going to do next?"

"Mr. Teasdale, I wish I knew."

He thanked the rancher, left the house and mounted up. He was halfway back to town when he figured out what he would do next.

Chapter Three

As he rode toward town, Spur worked out his next steps. High on his list was to meet and talk to the two sons-in-law of Dylan Teasdale. Since he couldn't do that today, he would look up the railway express man and have a session with him. There was always a chance of some kind of collusion with a "banker" type man that a railway express agent automatically became inside his car.

Spur should be able to tell if the man was hiding anything. Then he'd take it wherever that led. Next, he wanted to see Judge Parker. There was a chance the robbers had come back to town, changed clothes and horses and went across the river into Indian Territory as a sanctuary until things cooled down.

Judge Parker and his people would know the most likely spots nearby where outlaws were offered board and room and protection for a price. This bunch would be able to pay the going rate. He wanted the Judge's help in running a quick sweep of those close-by areas.

It was just past noon when Spur rode back into the livery and left the horse. He found a better restaurant, The Clinton's, and had a satisfying dinner of a bowl of beef stew and two slices of garlic sprinkled toast. He'd never had toast like that before and decided he liked it. The place was on a side street but had a steady stream of customers. It sported a dozen tables with red checkered oil-cloth covers and small vases filled with dried flowers on each table. His meal cost fifty-five cents with the coffee.

When he left the restaurant, he decided to go to his hotel room and clean up a little after his 16 mile ride out to the ranch and back. In his room, he had just stripped to his waist and begun to wash in the crockery bowl, when he heard the key turn in the door lock.

Spur was halfway to the bed post where his Colt hung, when the door pushed open and a woman stepped into the room carrying a bucket, a mop and a broom. She saw him, smiled, turned and closed the door and locked it.

She left the cleaning materials by the door and walked toward him as she unbuttoned the top of her calico dress.

"Spur McCoy. I've been waiting half the morning for you to come back." She stopped three-feet from him and shrugged out of the top of her dress and let it fall to her waist. She wore nothing under it. Her full breasts swung out with a little sag from their weight.

"See anything that you like?" she asked, smiling.

"A good deal, at least three things," Spur said.

"You don't know me. I got your name from the clerk. I've been watching you. Not much for a girl to do in this town for excitement."

Spur grinned. "There's always the old slap and tickle game between the sheets."

She smiled and rubbed one breast. "Oh, yes, there's that, and then there's fucking, too. I hope you have some spare time."

She walked up to Spur and pushed hard against him from crotch to breast and reached up and kissed his mouth. Her lips lingered, then came away.

"Oh, yes, I think this is going to be fine."

He reached out and fondled her bare breasts. "You don't happen to be married, do you?" he asked.

"I don't happen to be, and I ain't. Not since my old man left me for some chippy. I do need some loving now and again and I ain't had none for nearly six months and my little cunnie is just getting so hot and juicy I can hardly stand it."

"You assault men in their rooms this way often?"

"No, not for six months. Don't you like me and my bare boobies?"

"They're wonderful, but sometimes a man likes to take the lead."

"So go ahead, lead. You want me face down or face up?" She giggled. "Whoa, there I done it again."

Spur caught her hand and led her to the bed. He sat down and she sat beside him.

"I don't know your name."

"Lillian. That make you feel better? Hey, I ain't no whore."

"Good."

Spur bent and kissed her breast. She nodded.

"Oh, yeah, now that I like."

He kissed the other one, then licked both her nipples until she squirmed. He bit them gently, then harder until she yelped and dropped flat on her back on the bed.

"Do me quick, Spur McCoy, before I explode."

He pulled her dress up, found her pink cotton bloomers and gently lowered them off her legs. She helped.

"Lordy, lordy, lordy," she whispered. Her legs came apart and her knees lifted showing him how wet and ready she was.

Spur didn't even take off his pants. He opened his fly, brought out his whanger and eased between her white thighs.

"Do me now, now, now," Lillian chanted softly.

He bent and eased into her ready slot. She jammed her hips upward to take in more of him faster until their pubic bones grated together.

Her legs went up and around his back and she began rocking back and forth. Spur reached between them, found her hard node and rubbed it back and forth.

"What the hell you doing?" she barked.

"Wait and see."

Ten strokes later with his finger across the node, she writhed and moaned and yelped and then keened high and long as her body went into a series of vibrations. Her spasms shook her like a rabbit caught in a dog's jaws. She wailed and moaned and shivered.

Suddenly she stopped but only to start again and slam through the whole sequence as the spasms rattled her from her toes to the top of her dark-haired head.

Four times she went through the jolting climaxes before she sighed and dropped her legs, going limp under him. Spur watched Lillian. She peeked open one eye and looked at him.

"O mi' God but that was fantastic. I never knew . . . I mean I wasn't sure . . . oh, damn!"

She revived slowly. When she did she felt him still inside her and began to grind her hips under him.

"You now. Fast and furious, or slow and easy, however you want it. However, or wherever. You earned it."

Spur thrust slowly at first, then eased it up a notch and a moment later he drove so hard and fast that she couldn't keep up with him. Before he wanted to, he felt the start of it and then the roaring, smashing, plundering ecstacy of his own release. He was panting and wheezing and sweating like a railway track layer in August. At last he gave a big sigh and dropped on top of her.

She clamped her arms around his shoulders pinning them together.

"I like it this way, close and joined and nobody in any rush to get up and leave. But then it's your room so you wouldn't be leaving." She laughed softly. "I get a lot crazy when I've just been done good. Damn it to Frisco but you done me good, Spur McCoy."

It took him five minutes before he could see straight and get his breathing under control. He took one more deep breath and let it out slowly. Then he lifted away enough to get her in focus.

"Lillian, you know what goes on in town. Who is bedding who, who shouldn't be and whose wife is a little bit on the wild side?"

"I know some of the wild ones. Mostly the up to thirty-five group. There's these two couples who play cards every Thursday night. At least they start out by playing cards. The men always play the women. When the pinochle game is over they swap marriage partners and spend two hours making love, all four of them in the same bedroom. How is that for kind of wild?"

"Wild enough for me. You ever hear anything about either one of the sons-in-law of old man Teasedale?"

She laughed and grinned. "Oh, hell, yes. Doug Chandler and Nate Emerson. Are you kidding? Their escapades are all over this little town. Nobody has any secrets here. I've even done Doug once. He gets liquored up and starts grabbing women off the boardwalk. One of the ranch hands comes along and steers him off Main Street when he gets too drunk. If he can't find an uptown woman, he goes down to the soiled dove bedrooms on Front Street."

"Doug the wildest of the two?"

"Oh, yeah, by far. He's in town nearly every Saturday night leaving that cute little pregnant wife of his at home. He don't, you know, like to pay money or nothing like that, but time I did him he give me a present. Kind of like a gentleman, a gift."

"A nice gift?"

"Oh, my yes. A lady's watch, the kind that can go on a necklace. I know for certain that it cost over ten-dollars."

Spur loosened her hands and they sat up on the side of the bed.

Lillian laughed. "Hey, you never even took off your fucking britches."

"You didn't give me time. You still almost have your dress on."

They both laughed. She pulled the dress up, pushed her arms into it and buttoned it.

Spur reached over and caressed one of her breasts. "You hear anything more about Doug Chandler? Did he talk about his father-in-law, Teasdale?"

"He was half drunk and mad about something. Didn't take it out on me. He was gentle and fast. Four times in two hours. But he kept swearing at Old Man Teasdale, as he called him. Called him a skinflint, and a miser and all sorts of bad names."

Spur stood and she lifted up beside him standing close. He bent and kissed her breast through her dress.

"Again, right now," Lillian said. "You ever done it standing up? I can show you how."

"Love to, Lillian, but I have work to do. I was just getting cleaned up to go see a railroad worker. It's important."

"Maybe I could come back, sometime. How about tonight around nine? Then we'd have lots of time for an all nighter."

"You work here in the hotel?"

"Supposed to. Part time when they need me. No way to make enough money to get by. So how about tonight?"

Spur shook his head. "I'll be working until midnight talking to folks, then I'll need a good night's sleep. But maybe tomorrow night."

Lillian nodded, checked her dress, then picked up her mop and pail and broom. She unlocked the door and went into the hall after giving him one big wink.

Spur went back to the basin, finished his half bath and put on a clean shirt and a pair of town pants. He added the brown vest and his black hat and checked himself in the wavy mirror on top of the chest of drawers.

He found the express clerk right where he was told his house would be.

"Clancy Steffens?" Spur asked the man who came to the door.

The man shook his head and cupped his hand around one ear and leaned forward. "What?"

"Are you Clancy Steffens?" Spur said twice as loud.

"Oh, yes. Who are you?"

"Questions. I have some questions."

"Told the road people and the sheriff. No more answers."

Spur showed him his identification as a United States Secret Service Agent and Clancy's eyes went wide. He nodded and waved Spur inside the modest home. He saw a woman vanish through a doorway and could hear a small child somewhere.

In the living room they sat down on mismatched furniture.

"You were the Railway Express clerk on the train that was robbed, correct?"

"Yes. I'll tell you what happened. Save you a lot of questions. Same thing I told the sheriff. I was working my station when the explosion went off slamming the side door partly open. The explosion almost deafened me and pitched me to the floor. A masked man came inside, held me under his six-gun while he put a charge on the safe.

"He pushed me to the end of the car where we crouched down as the second bomb blasted the safe. That really deafened me. I haven't been able to hear right since."

"Thanks. Now, did you recognize the masked man?"

"Recognize? No. Never saw him before in my life."

"How did he get the registered mail sacks?"

"Registered? Oh, just finishing my logging and the paper work when the blast came. The two mail sacks weren't even locked up yet."

"Could you recognize the man who robbed the car?"

"Only saw his eyes. Not much to go on."

"Your hearing seems to be getting better."

Clancy nodded not looking nervous at all, Spur noted.

"It comes and goes. Sometimes worse than before. I think it's a little better each day. They told me to take the week off and get my hearing back."

"Did you know what was in the registered mail sacks?"

"Sure, knew who sent it and who it was going to. It's all down on paper. I had no idea what was inside the envelopes and packages. I had to sign off on the whole batch before the other agent in Kansas City would release it to me. That's why it's called registered mail. Everyone who handles it signs off."

"Notice anything unusual about the robber? Did he have an accent, a cough or a limp, any hair hanging out of his hat? See what kind of a horse he rode? Did he have on strange clothes. Anything that would identify him?"

Clancy shook his head slowly. "Nope, can't say as I saw anything unusual or different. He was a good sized white man. About all I can say. I was scared after that dynamite went off at the sliding door. Thought the whole damn train had crashed. Stunned me a little and sent me to the floor. I guess that's when I scraped my face."

Spur moved toward the man, looming over him. "How much did the robbers offer you to have the safe open and not remember a thing? Five-thousand dollars?"

"What? What are you talking about? Nobody offered me nothing. I got a good job, don't want to lose it. You're crazy? Get out of my house right now. Go on, get out. That makes me mad."

Clancy walked to the door and held it open. Spur sat down again in the chair and waited for Clancy to come back. He did so a minute or two later but he didn't sit down.

"Glad your hearing is better, Mr. Steffens. That line about being offered part of the money is one of our usual tactics. Sometimes it works. Thanks for talking to me."

Spur stood, walked out the front door and down the three steps to the dirt path leading to the street. He still hadn't made up his mind about Steffens. The man could be lying like a professional, or he could be as innocent as he seemed.

Spur checked his pocket watch. Five minutes after three. Maybe the Judge was through with his work for today. Spur walked up the street, down a block to the old army fort and went up the broad steps into the court building.

The same small clerk sat at his desk in the room outside the big double doors.

"Is court in session?" Spur asked.

"Mr. McCoy, it is. Hard telling when it might be over. This is not the last case of the day, I'm sure. You might wish to observe." The balding man pointed to the big doors and Spur slipped inside and took a seat on a chair at the back.

Judge Amos Parker sat on his elevated bench

behind a large cherrywood desk. He wore his black robes and a stern yet curiously blank expression that would not seem to favor either side. The county prosecutor was summing up the charge against the defendant to a jury of twelve men from the western part of Arkansas.

"So, gentlemen of the jury. Charlie Smith did and without remorse, shoot his partner on the night of January twenty-fourth while the two were camping in Indian Territory after fleeing from a robbery in the state of Arkansas. He shot him not once, but five times, then took his coat and his blankets as well as his six-gun, rifle and sheath knife, and moved down the trail to a known haven for criminals and spent the night 'sleeping like a baby,' as the defendant himself testified. He is guilty of murder in the first degree and of inhuman behavior so atrocious that he is no longer fit to participate in polite society. I ask that the court find the defendant guilty of murder."

The jury was out of the courtroom only 20 minutes. Judge Parker had not permitted the defendant to leave the courtroom. When the jury foreman read the verdict, Judge Parker nodded and asked the defendant to rise.

"You, Charles Smith, have been found guilty by a panel of your peers of murder in the first degree in Indian territory. It is my duty to sentence you to hang by the neck until you are dead. The sentence will be carried out at ten o'clock tomorrow morning. May God have mercy on your soul."

"But your honor," the defense attorney shouted

rising to his feet. "That doesn't give me any time to prepare my appeal."

Old timers in the court gasped. The lawyer looked around at the stunned jury and the surprised prosecutors.

Judge Isaac Parker looked at the speaker with patient surprise and a touch of anger.

"Sir, you are out of order. This matter concerns a crime committed in Indian Territory. Congress has given me exclusive powers to judge such crimes, and to pass sentence. No appeal is possible, except a direct appeal to the President of the United States. In this case there is no chance that the President would soil his hands by even considering your appeal.

"Mr. Smith will be hung tomorrow morning on schedule." He stared at the offending lawyer. "Sir, in my court you are allowed one mistake. If there is another one you will not be permitted to appear again for any cases tried in the Federal Court of the Western Jurisdiction of the State of Arkansas."

The lawyer wilted in his chair, his client was led off to the jail below the court room and the next case was called by the clerk.

Spur slipped out of the room and went to the clerk just outside.

"When will court be finished today?" The clerk shrugged. "Sometimes at five o'clock, sometimes not until seven. At least there is no evening session scheduled for today." The clerk looked thoughtful for a moment. "May I make a suggestion?"

Spur nodded.

"Judge Parker always walks to his home about a mile away right after court is adjourned. You might walk along with him. That would be a good time for an uninterrupted conference."

Spur agreed and sat in on two more trials before the Judge ended the session with his gavel. The clerk had told Spur that the Judge always stopped by his desk before leaving, so Spur took up his post on the polished wooden bench across the hall.

A half hour later, Judge Parker came from the court room wearing a black suit, a gold watch fob hanging by a heavy gold chain from his top vest button hole and the other end vanishing into his vest pocket. He looked as if he had just combed his dark hair but his goatee flared in its usual disarray.

Spur stood and Judge Parker looked at him.

"Yes, Agent McCoy. Is there something I can do for you?"

They talked the 15 minutes it took for the briskly walking judge to travel the mile to his house. At the end of that time, Spur had received the Judge's permission to attach himself to a special six man team of deputy U.S. Marshals to sweep four or five places near the border in Indian Territory where felons, criminals and outlaws were known to hide out between quick thrusts into Arkansas towns and villages.

"I'll have the Marshal deputize you, to give you full authority there," the Judge said. "There's a six man team going out in the morning with a wagon for hauling prisoners. Your trip should take about three days."

Spur thanked the judge, turned and walked to the downtown section of Fort Smith which had grown to just over 3,500 souls. It was not a Wild West town, neither was it a staid midwestern village. It was in-between somewhere.

He watched children playing on the dirt streets. There were no sidewalks, no concrete used at all. The houses were mainly wooden, with a few of bricks and an occasional one of native rock and mortar.

The town had begun as a trade center for the surrounding area, with flat bottomed boats plowing up the Arkansas River from the capitol some 150 miles to the east and slightly south. A few cattle were raised to the north, but the area was mainly light agriculture and some hardwood sawmilling. Much of the small growth hardwood trees on the flats and on the low rising hills looked useless to Spur.

He went back to the Clinton Restaurant for supper, and treated himself to a pound-and-a-half steak seared on the outside and blood red inside. He paid 95 cents for the meal, left the nickel as the tip and hurried back to his hotel.

The room clerk gave him his key and a message sealed in an envelope. It had not come by mail. He looked at the clerk.

"Sir, I have no idea where it came from or from whom. I found it on my desk here but saw no one leave it."

Spur thanked him and went up the stairs to

room 212 that faced front. He took off his gunbelt and hung it on the bed post, then looked at the white envelope. He shrugged and opened it. A single piece of white paper was inside with one line written on it and the message was not signed. It said:

McCoy. Get out of town by tomorrow noon or you'll be dead before sunset.

Chapter Four

Spur McCoy stared at the handwritten threat he had just opened. It was in pencil in what he figured was a man's hand. Written, not printed, so the man must have some education. The words were spelled correctly. That cut down by about half the men in town. He had only a thousand suspects.

He sat down on the bed. Sure, he'd be out of town by noon tomorrow. In fact he'd be out long before that going with the posse of U.S. Deputy Marshals across the river into Indian Territory.

Who could have sent the threat? He had made no secret that he was in town. He had told a dozen people who he was and why he was here. He had been seen going in and out of the sheriff's office and Judge Parker's court room.

It had to be someone connected to the train robbery. Who else would want him out of town? But who could that be?

Somebody he had met? Probably not. He thought of changing rooms in the hotel. He should be safe enough tonight. When he came back, he'd get a different room and wouldn't tell the clerk downstairs.

Now his move was to get some sleep. It had been a strange day. Tomorrow might be even stranger, especially if he could find the four he hunted. He had the feeling that the girl might not be an unwilling captive by now. She could well be a part of the gang who hit the train. So was it a serendipity or did they know she was on the train?

They had to know. They evidently went to the passenger car hunting the girl.

He gave up thinking about it. Let his subconscious work on it. He undressed, blew out the lamp and went to bed.

The next morning he was at Judge Parker's courthouse by six o'clock. The six deputy marshals were talking when he walked up, but fell silent as soon as saw him. One came forward.

"McCoy, with the U.S. Secret Service?"

"Right, and who are you?"

"I'm U.S. Deputy Marshal Jules West. I'm head deputy on this little mission. We was getting ready to make a deep penetration of the Territory, but understand you need a sweep of the close by spots where your train robbers might be."

"It's a chance I need to cover," Spur said shaking

the man's hand. "I understand you men get two dollars a head for every felon you bring back. If we can bring these three wanted men back, there's a hundred dollar bonus for you boys. I know you don't get paid much, so if we can connect, this will make it worth your time."

West grinned. "Oh, yeah, that sounds damn good. The boys will appreciate it. We'll work extra hard. What's the odds they're out there?"

"Can't figure it. Don't know these people. But I think the robbery and everything that's behind it and goes with it are all centered right here in Fort Smith somehow. Just how I haven't worked out yet. I brought a sack of grub. Figured we'd be cooking out."

"You're right there. We can't afford the prices they charge for food out there in the Territories. Most of the outlaws have more money than they know what to do with."

"Until you catch them," Spur said.

West grinned. "Yeah, until we nail them to the wall of some log fort in the willies out there." West looked at the others. "Everyone ready? Get the wagon moving and we'll get underway. Don't want to miss the first run on the ferry."

Ten minutes later they waited at the banks of the Arkansas river. It was wider than Spur had guessed. A horse pulled ferry on a rope made the trip from one side to the other. The rope went through some pulleys on the boat and stretched out from one side to the other.

A horse on one side pulled it across to the other bank. On the return trip a horse on this side pulled it back. The flat bottomed boat was big enough to take the wagon and seven horses and men on one trip.

They headed into the Territories that looked exactly like the country on the other side of the river. The big difference was no town, no farms or ranches that he could see.

Spur had heard about Judge Isaac Parker and his work there at Fort Smith. The judge had been appointed by the President and approved by Congress back in 1875. The Federal court in Fort Smith had been a total shambles from inexperience, graft and neglect.

Judge Parker was 36 years old when appointed. He had already been a city attorney in St. Joseph, Missouri, a worker for President Lincoln's election, a judge in a backwoods district in Missouri, and a two-term representative in the U.S. Congress in Washington. He served on the House Committee on Indian affairs and was known as a friend of the Indian. He was also a devout and hard line Methodist with a strict moral code.

The first eight weeks on the bench at Fort Smith, Judge Parker tried 91 defendants. Of the 18 men charged with murder, 15 were convicted. One of the convicted men was killed trying to escape, eight were given long prison terms and six were condemned to hang.

A large new gallows had been built on the courthouse land that had one long trap that could drop 12 men to their deaths at one time.

On his first hanging, six men were dropped into hell by the master hangman, George Haledon.

More than 5,000 men, women and children jammed the fort compound to see the first of many public hangings that would make Fort Smith and Judge Parker famous.

Congress had authorized Judge Parker to have his U.S. Marshal—also appointed by the President—hire up to 200 U.S. Deputy Marshals to fan out through Indian Territory and bring in any felons they found.

These marshals didn't need a warrant for an arrest. They could bring back anyone they even suspected of a serious crime. They also brought back witnesses to testify at the trial.

The marshals received no salary. They were paid $2 for each felon brought back alive, but received nothing for a corpse unless there was a reward for the man dead or alive. Usually there was no such reward.

Spur had been interested in the wagon that accompanied them. It was a mobile office, containing a jail for prisoners, a kitchen, arsenal and dormitory.

Healthy prisoners were marched alongside the wagon at gunpoint. Wounded ones were allowed to ride inside, chained to the wagon.

Spur heard that the marshals went in groups to protect themselves from gangs of outlaws in the Territories. It was Indian Territory and reserved for the Indian tribes that had been moved there. However, as many as 20,000 non-Indians were in and out of the area from time to time, hiding, farming, hunting, and suspicious of the U.S. Deputy Marshals whether they were law violators or not.

Spur rode up front with Marshal West. They had been on the trail for over four hours when the marshal pointed to smoke about a mile ahead.

"That's One-Eyed Louie's place. He married an Indian and is living there legally. He's also the first stop for outlaws coming into the Territories in this section. A kind of rough and ready country inn."

"Will he talk?"

"Oh, yeah. Louie is so close to the court that he has to play like he's in both camps. He's on whoever's side is occupying his place at the time. You'll see."

When they stopped in front of a log structure that looked as if it had grown year by year, a large man with a patch over one eye hurried out of the front door.

"Deputy West. I'm honored you come to my poor inn."

"Need to talk to you, Louie."

"Come in, come in. We can talk over a shot of whiskey. The good stuff from the back room. Right this way, Deputy West."

"Bringing along a friend, Louie. This is Untied States Secret Service Agent Spur McCoy. He's from Washington D.C. and he wants to ask you some questions."

"Me?" Louie said. He was a bear of a man, with full beard, wild hair and wearing the tops to long underwear and a pair of much patched and washed jeans. "What do I know? Come, come, more than welcome."

Soiled Dove

The rest of the marshals dismounted and sat around waiting.

The inside of the inn was as rustic as the outside. Mortar of some kind had been used to plug up the holes between the logs cutting down on the wind whipping through.

A rough plank bar sat on barrels at one side. Behind this section, dirty blankets covered the walls to cut down more of the cold winter winds.

Louie set up shot glasses on the bar and filled them from a bottle of whiskey without any label on it. Spur sipped it and put it back on the bar.

"Louie, I'm hunting three men and a women on horses. You see any group like that who rode in here during the past four or five days?"

"Don't see many women out here. I remember a whore who decided to do some business on her own. She made a circuit of camps and inns and houses. Did right fine for a time. Then one old boy lassoed her, tied her to the bed and nobody ever saw her again. Lots of folks heard her screaming to get away. Figure she finally found a man who would take good care of her."

"Bound to happen. But what about a woman and three men last four or five days? They been here, or past here?"

"Can't rightly say."

"You best say, Louie, or I'll thumb out that other eye of yours and you'll be blind for the rest of your damned life." Marshal West said it and Louie took a step back.

"Well now, didn't know it was so all fired important."

"Important enough for a twenty-dollar reward for the man who helps me catch them," Spur said.

"Well now," Louie said, a gleam building in his dark eye.

A gun butt slammed down on the makeshift bar. Marshal West turned the weapon around and angled it directly at Louie. "That's legitimate, correct, honest information we want out of you, Louie. No wild chases up into the hills. No fifty mile rides for no more good than hide and hair. You know anything straight, you say so. Otherwise you pour us another shot and we'll be out of here."

Louie thought for a minute, pulled at his beard and picked at his nose. Then he sighed.

"Aw, hell, Marshal. I was just fun'in you. Never seen no four past here. Business been damn slow lately." He refilled the marshal's glass, looked at Spur's full one and shrugged.

"Good, Louie. My job's to see that your business stays slow. Thanks for the shots, we'll be going." The marshal downed the rot-out-your-gut whiskey and headed for the door. He still had his six gun in his hand. Spur followed him.

When the seven men mounted, Marshal West looked at a big man with a full beard and twin six-guns in his belt.

"So, John?" he said.

"Nobody left the back door, not like that other time when we was chasing that Boney guy."

"No movement at all back there, right?" West pressed.

"Damn right, nothing."

"Wait for half an hour just past the bend out here and see if he sends anybody on a ride. If nothing after that time, catch up with us."

They pulled back on the road and followed the slow progress of the heavy wagon along the muddy and narrow track through the open spaces and the small hills and deep brush and hardwood forest.

Five miles up the track, Marshal West held up his hand and the whole procession stopped.

"Smoke over yonder," he said. They saw smoke coming up through some trees that almost dispersed it but not quite.

"Never been anybody over there before," one of the men behind him said.

"Best we take a look," West said. "Could be nothing, then could be a still or such. Importing or making whiskey in the Territories is against the law."

They left the wagon and rode toward the smoke keeping to the wooded sections of the small hills. When they were a quarter-of-a-mile away, they tied their horses and moved ahead on foot. Three of the men had rifles, the rest their hand guns. Spur went along.

West bellied down a hundred-yards from the smoke source and Spur slid in beside him. They looked through some scrabble brush at a small clearing and a new cabin made of poles, not real logs. None of them were more than six-inches thick and there were cracks between them two-inches wide in lots of places.

Smoke came out of a hole in the roof. Around

the outside of the cabin was a pole fence with a six-foot wide gate. The structure itself was about 12-feet square, with a second story built toward the back of it.

"Firing slots up in that second story," the marshall said.

"Noticed that. Two in the first floor as well. One hip shot horse at the far side, but I don't see no humans."

"Couldn't be Indians. They wouldn't do that much work on a place just so they could pick up and move. Got to be whites."

"Outlaws?" Spur asked.

The marshall nodded. "More than likely." He was quiet for a moment. "See that line of brush ahead? We can move up through that and get to twenty-five yards of the place. Find yourself a good thick tree to hide behind. I'll call out when we get up there. The others are moving in around the place close as the cover will allow."

Ten minutes later both men were in place. Spur found a tree that looked like a sycamore and bellied down behind it. Marshal West looked at him and nodded, then turned to the cabin.

"Yo, you in the log cabin. We're friendly, just want to say howdy. Anybody home?"

A rifle shot sounded from inside the small fort and the round cut through the brush six-feet over Spur's head and ten-feet to the side.

"Not a neighborly thing to do," West called. "We ain't aiming you no harm. Just stopped by to say howdy."

Another rifle shot came, this one closer to where they lay.

"Most friendly folks ride up and call out with their hands in plain sight," the voice inside said.

"Not sure of who you are. This cabin is new. Warn't here three months ago."

"True. Who you be?"

"U.S. Deputy Marshal out of Fort Smith. You got any reason to be hiding?"

"Not a bit," the voice said and a man in stiff pants, a long sleeved shirt and a sweater vest came out a side door. He carried a rifle but it pointed at the ground.

"Lay the rifle down, friend, and we'll come out," West said.

Just then a shot went off behind the cabin, then two more and a man cried out in pain.

"Don't move or you're dead," West barked. The man with the rifle turned to look behind him, then slowly put the rifle on the ground.

"You got no trouble with me, Marshal. I ain't wanted nowhere. Come see for yourself."

As he talked, one of the marshals who had been behind the cabin came forward, prodding a young man ahead of him. The man showed a wound to his left shoulder.

"Caught us one trying to run away," one of the marshals said. "Then he fired at me. Reckon we can charge him with attempted murder."

Both men were herded out of the fence into the clearing and Spur and the marshals went up and checked on them.

"Don't recognize either of them from wanted

posters," Marshal West said. "You two got names?"

One was Wilbur Halverson, the younger one Buff Halverson.

The marshals all shook their heads.

"Tell you what we're going to do, Wilbur. Since we don't have no paper on you two, we'll let you go. All you have to do is pay a five dollar fine for assault with a deadly weapon and we'll forget about the whole thing. Oh, we'll file a paper on you with the court so everyone will know about you two."

"Can't fine us, Marshal. We didn't do nothing wrong."

"Wilbur, just living over here in the Territories is wrong lessen' you're Indian. Don't look to me like you're much Indian with that blond hair."

"Didn't do nothing wrong," Wilbur maintained.

"Good enough. Take your choice. Five dollars now, or a ride for the next three weeks in our chariot out there on bread and water and then facing up to Judge Parker."

Wilbur glowered, then dug into his pocket. He came up with a half eagle five dollar gold piece and tossed it to Marshal West.

"Didn't do nothing wrong," Wilbur said.

"At least you're still free."

Wilbur nodded, hooked his thumbs in his belt and waited. "What about my shot boy?"

West looked at the man who still bled from the shoulder.

"Hell, Wilbur, you can patch him up. You've had worse. Couple of weeks he'll be out selling liquor to the Indians. Y'all be careful now."

West signalled and the five other Marshals pulled back and headed for their horses.

Spur and West rode back to the main track and the wagon.

"That happen often?" Spur asked. "Fining people."

"Now and again. Judge Parker said we can do it when we have a mind to. Good way to keep some of these misfits in line." West grinned. "Then too, since we don't get no salary, helps us deputies to make enough to keep body and soul together. Nobody gets rich being a U.S. Deputy Marshal in Indian Territory."

Not rich, Spur decided, but they could make enough on a good day to salt some cash away. With the average lawman making about two dollars a day, it wouldn't take many fines for the deputy marshals to do better than that.

Marshal West turned and whistled and John, the marshal with the full beard, rode up beside West.

"Coming up on Half Breed Oliver. Ride ahead and check him out. If there's more than two horses in the pen, come back and tell us quick."

The marshal rode off with a grin.

"Half Breed Oliver?" Spur asked.

"Yep. He's been living over here in the Territories for so long, he wouldn't know what the other side of the border looked like no more. Has a still somewhere that we ain't had the time to find. That'd get him five years no problem. Outside of that he does a little farming in the valley, runs some cattle and does some trading with the Cherokee."

"Sounds like he's working hard at making a living."

"He is. Better'n most you meet in the Territory. Half black, half Cherokee. Polite, soft spoken. Got a sweet little black wife and six or seven drops running around. Still, I'll put his ass in Judge Parker's courtroom if'n I can find his still."

A half hour later, the bearded marshall, John, came riding back, the grin wider now.

"Swear old Half Breed's having a damned party. Six extra horses in his corral. Been there a time. Horse turds all over the place."

"Hear any yelling, loud talk?"

"Nope, quiet, like they is sleeping or drunk or maybe playing poker."

"We'll go in as usual. You and James in back, rest of us out front. We can get to within thirty-feet of this place in the brush."

They dismounted as before and worked up on the little clearing. It had a clothes line, a log cabin well chinked and a stone fireplace out the top. Flowers grew around the front step. A lean-to held some hay next to the pole corral. Eight horses milled around there.

To the side, Spur saw a vegetable garden with tomatoes ripe and he saw pole beans ready to pick.

They worked up to the closest place to the front door and Marshal West's big voice boomed out.

"Half Breed Oliver. Marshal West. We're back. Might as well come out peaceful and not get the children hurt. Bring your friends, too."

A dead silence greeted his demands. He said it again and Oliver came out the front door, his hands in the air. Right behind him came another man with hat pulled low and his six-gun's muzzle pushed hard against Oliver's head. He had a saddlebag over one shoulder.

"Back off, Marshal, or your man here is dead meat. Y'all hear me?"

"Hear you, dumb bastard. You hurt Oliver or his family and you're the dead meat. You want that? We got ten marshals out here, all with seven shot Spencer repeating rifles. You go up against 70 shots with your five? Not smart."

"I'm getting a horse and riding away with Oliver, or he's a dead man."

"You giving up the others inside?"

"Hell, they all skunk-drunk in there. Passed out and fucked out. You can have them. I get away and Oliver here don't get hurt. Deal?"

"Let me check the inside. You the bank robbery guys from across the river?"

"Yeah. Told the dumb bastards not to stop so close to the damn border."

"You taking the money?" Spur asked.

"Hell, we only got a thousand dollars. I'm taking what's left, yeah. Deal?"

West stood up and walked into the open. "You give me the rest of them without a fight, it's a deal. Let me look inside."

The robber pulled Oliver to the side of the door and Marshal West hurried through the opening.

He came back a minute later and waved at the gunman.

"Get the hell out of here."

The outlaw walked Oliver to the corral, let go of him a minute to step through the poles. The second the robber's six-gun swung away from Oliver, a rifle barked and the. 52 caliber slug plowed into the man's head. It hit just over his left eye and tore the top of his head off.

Spur ran for the front door with two other marshals. Inside they found four men passed out on the floor. Oliver's naked wife lay on a bed built against the wall. She had been spread eagled and tied down.

Oliver rushed in the door and covered his wife with a blanket, then he cut the cords tying her down.

Marshals handcuffed the men on the floor and slapped them trying to awaken them. They threw cold water in their faces, then waited.

Spur looked at Marshal West. "What about the deal you made with that dead man out there? You said he could go free."

"I let him go. One of the other marshals shot him, not me. Hell, we don't make deals with these owlhoots."

He shook his head looking at the men on the floor. Two of them lay in their own vomit. "Damn, we're stuck here until we can get them sobered up enough to walk," West said. "Then we'll handcuff them together and tie the first one to the back of the wagon. If these bastards can't walk, we'll drag them. I don't hold with rape."

Soiled Dove

Marshal John came in with the saddlebag the dead outlaw had carried over his shoulder.

"Money inside," John said.

Marshal West emptied it on a table. Inside had been loose bills and one bound stack of tens. West counted it as they waited. Oliver vanished into a back room with his softly crying wife. Spur didn't see any of the children.

"Two thousand, three hundred and forty seven dollars," West said. The marshals all stood around watching. West counted out seven stacks of $100 each.

"Our commission," West said. He handed $100 to each of the men and pocketed one stack, then handed the last pile to Spur. "Your share," West said.

Spur took it without comment. That way the marshals were covered. He couldn't turn them in without implicating himself as well. These men deserved the money. The bank would get most of it back, more than sixteen hundred dollars. They would be happy.

Oliver came in a few minutes later.

"Kids?" West asked.

"Got away into the woods when we seen them coming. Bess and me couldn't go. My lady gonna be hurting for a while."

West seemed to be thinking. He nodded. "We'll charge them all with rape, as well as the robbery. Since we're so close, we'll take them back to the fort. When their trial comes up, I'll send a man to bring you and your wife to the fort to testify. No sense you coming back now, you being so close."

"Appreciate it, Marshal West," Oliver said. He combed fingers through his black hair. "Damn them. I'd live somewhere else, but black folks don't rightly cotton to us. The Indians say we're not some of them. No place else. Damn them. Guess we'll move deeper into the Territory. Way over on the far side and find a little valley where we can raise some cattle and chickens and maybe a little grain. Yeah, that would be nice. Keep away from these damn outlaws."

The men on the floor were starting to stir. They were dragged outside and buckets of water dumped on them. In half an hour they were awake and sober enough to walk.

Spur took Oliver inside and without a word passed the $100 to the man and turned to leave. Oliver grabbed his arm.

"Suh," he said. Tears welled in his eyes and splashed over. "We . . . we thank you, suh. You not a marshal. Bess and me and the kids thank you. Now we can move. I ain't seen a hundred dollars cash money ever in my thirty-five years of living. We thanks you."

Spur shook Oliver's hand and walked outside.

Just before darkness they took the ferry back across the river and turned their prisoners into the jail under the big courthouse at Fort Smith.

As they put their horses away, Marshal West touched Spur's shoulder.

"Know you're a Federal officer and all, and you might not agree with our commission out there today. Don't happen often. Three times now in more'n five years service. Don't hurt nobody much, but means a lot to the men."

"No problem," Spur said. "I took my hundred, too."

West laughed softly. "Sure you did. I didn't see you, but I'd bet a year's ration of whiskey that you don't have that hundred on you right now. My bet is that Oliver suddenly came into some cash money so he can move west."

"Could be, Marshal West. Could be. Leastwise you know I won't be turning you in or saying a word about what happened out there."

Marshal West watched Spur closely. Then he grinned. "No, I reckon you won't. Sorry we didn't find your friends. We'll watch for them. My guess, they didn't go into the Territory." Marshal West touched the brim of his hat in a soft salute and walked away.

Spur agreed. If they hadn't touched either of the two settlers on the main trial, they probably hadn't entered the Territory. Now he was ready for a big supper and then maybe some sleep unless Lillian, the hotel maid, remembered to come see him. She just might. Spur grinned.

He'd change his room without telling the room clerk. He remembered the threat on his life. It had happened to him a lot and he found ways to deal with it. Tomorrow he'd worry more about that.

Spur reconsidered. Maybe he wouldn't change rooms until after Lillian found him. Yeah, that would be good. Spur grinned thinking about the night ahead.

Chapter Five

After a big supper, Spur McCoy went back to room 212 in the Wentworth Hotel and tried to relax. He couldn't stop thinking about the case. There were too many threads to it, all right, they were more like heavy ropes pulling every which way.

He had to follow down every lead, every chance that a man or woman might have something to do with the train robbery. He was finding out that this was a lot more than simply a smash and grab crime.

Spur waited until ten o'clock. It looked as if Lillian wasn't coming tonight. He slipped across the hall into another room that was unoccupied, locked the door and put the straight backed chair back under the doorknob. Anyone breaking in would have to crush the chair. More than enough noise to wake him.

Spur awoke the next morning alive and hungry. He had heard no noise or attack during the night. Good, maybe the letter threat was just a crank. He'd be watchful, as always.

After a quick breakfast, Spur went to the post office in the Mallory General Store and asked for the Postal Inspector. Bret Hardy was finishing his work in the office. He looked worn and tired out.

"McCoy. Figured it would be you. You're the last bit of trouble I need to convince me I should turn in my resignation. What now?"

"Just a little information. I need to know the name of the person those bearer bonds were being sent to."

"McCoy, you know I can't give you that information."

"Oh, but I'm sure you can. This is a Federal criminal case. I can wire my boss, who will talk to the Secretary of the Treasury, who will call your boss—"

Hardy held up one hand. "Enough. He'd probably tell me to do it. The man who launched a complaint about non-delivery of registered mail is Gregory Johnson Lowell. He's something of a legend around here. Rich man who came out of the shipping business down in Little Rock. Made his fortune and moved here to retire about ten years ago. Built a big mansion up the slope a ways and has been a fountain of good works and hard cash for public works and civic pride ever since."

Hardy frowned. He rubbed one hand over his

face and Spur caught the weariness there. "You don't think he's a suspect or anything like that?"

"Right now everyone, including you, is a suspect, Mr. Hardy, until I get a handle on this case. I want to talk to this man and see what impression of him I come away with. It could be productive, and it might not be. That's what I get paid for."

"I wish you good luck. I'm getting a lot of angry telegrams from the department. They want this robbery solved quickly."

"So do I. Oh, is registered mail also insured?"

"Can be. This one wasn't. No postal clerk would insure it for its worth, $100,000 is what the man claims."

"Guess it's about time I go see this gentleman."

"Good luck. From my contact with him he's as rough as a new shelled corn cob."

"I'll be on my guard."

Fifteen minutes later, Spur stopped in front of a three story mansion he figured must have 30 or more rooms. It was painted white with a soft brown trim with windows all over the place. Around the front, was a ten-foot-wide covered porch. He strode up the walk of paving stones to the porch filled with pots of blooming flowers. Polished and varnished double doors with glass panels blocked his entry into the house. He twisted a bell knob on the outside of the wall that sent a ringing note through the inside of the house.

Almost at once the door opened and a man in full butler livery stared down his thin nose at Spur. The man was as black as midnight in a coal mine, stood an inch taller than Spur and looked as if he could wrestle an alligator and a grizzly bear at the same time.

"Yes, sir?" the butler asked.

"Spur McCoy. I'd like to see Mr. Gregory Lowell, on United States government business."

"Oh, step this way, sir. Would you please wait here so I can see if he is receiving?"

"Tell him it's about his lost bearer bonds."

The big black man didn't react, he turned and walked out of the entryway which was as big as most people's living room. The walls had original oil paintings, most three-by-four feet or larger. Spur had seen the style before but didn't know the artist.

Red upholstered couches stood in front of two of the walls. The third had a window that opened on a garden.

Before Spur had seen enough of the garden, the butler returned.

"Right this way, Mr. McCoy."

They went down a long hall with a soft carpet underfoot. Every ten-feet another oil painting brightened the passage. They passed several doors, then the butler opened another and stepped back.

Spur entered the room and saw that it was a library, with hundreds of leather bound volumes on wall shelves behind glass doors. The center-piece was a flat desk of free form design made from remarkably beautiful quarter cut oak burls that had been glued together in an eye stopping pattern.

One window slightly to the right and in back of

the desk was shaded with floor to ceiling drapes of some rich brocade. Behind the desk sat a man in his seventies. He had a full head of starkly white hair, a sturdy white moustache and mutton chop sideburns of the same texture and color.

He stood and held out his hand across the polished surface.

"Mr. McCoy, United States Secret Service. Yes, I heard you were in town. My name is Gregory Lowell. Please, sit down."

Spur shook the offered soft hand, then looked at the roundbacked early Quaker chair and hesitated. It was an antique from a hundred years ago or more and must be worth more than the average working man's wages for a year.

"Early Quaker?" Spur asked.

Lowell lifted his brows in surprise. "Close. Actually that's a Pennsylvania Dutch pastor's chair from about 1680. However, it is sturdy and in excellent condition."

Spur sat gently and looked up at an inquisitive Gregory Lowell.

"You said something about my missing bonds."

"I have no new information on the loss. Just wanted to chat with you a minute to see if it might help me to solve the puzzle of the robbery of the express car."

The wealthy man's face reflected his disappointment. "Certainly, anything that I can do."

"The bonds were mailed by registered mail in a package from Kansas City, as I understand."

"Yes, that's where my broker is. I wore out the financial men in my native Little Rock. Some misunderstandings. This particular type of invest-ment I would rather have in hand, than in the safe of some brokerage house. I imagine some experts would tell me that's the end product of a bitter and poverty ridden childhood. At any rate, I do like to have my convertible instruments close at hand."

"So you have a safe of your own? Or do you use the local bank?"

Lowell chuckled. "Oh, my, no. I wouldn't use the safe at either of the two banks. Mine, as a matter of fact, is much better than theirs."

"Any special reason your bonds were on that particular train, Mr. Lowell?"

"None whatsoever. I wanted them. I told my broker to send them by registered mail and he did. We've done this dozens of times over the years with no problems. He sent them on the train that those terrible outlaws chose to rob."

"How do you suppose the robbers recognized the value of the bonds? Speaking for myself, I've never owned or even seen a bearer bond. I wouldn't know one from a stock certificate or any other type of a certificate on fancy printed paper."

"Yes, yes. I did do some thinking on that one. My theory is that one of the men had some edu-cation and some familiarity with stocks and bonds. Actually, they are quite simple to tell apart by reading what the fancy lettering says. I can show you if you would like."

Spur waved the idea away. "Thanks, but I don't have time to educate myself on bonds right now. My job is to find them, not to be an expert on them. How many individual certificates are there?"

"Eleven, as I recall. I can check my records if you would like."

"That would be most helpful. I had no idea if they were in amounts of a hundred dollars, or of fifty thousand dollars."

Lowell stood and took a leather bound record book from a shelf on the wall behind his desk and leafed through it, then took a wooden pencil from his desk and ticked them off down a column.

"Yes, eleven bonds in total."

"Good. Now, do you know of anyone other than your broker who knew that you were receiving those bonds, and who knew on which train they would be sent?"

Lowell held the pencil like a saber for a moment, his forehead wrinkled and his eyes hooded under the bushy brows. Slowly he shook his head.

"One or two others in the brokerage house in Kansas City would know they were going to be sent by registered mail. Those in the mail room, perhaps another clerk or another broker. They would have to be retrieved from my file in the basement safe, of course. Perhaps four or five individuals might have known they were being sent."

He shook his head. "But they would have no idea which train they would be sent on. I'm not sure that's possible to find out from the sending end. I don't see how anyone, not even I, could know exactly which train that registered mail would be on."

Spur leaned forward then relaxed and stood. He held out his hand. "All right, that is one element I'm concerned with. Thanks for your cooperation. We're doing our best to track down those bonds for you and to catch the perpetrators." Spur turned and looked at the chair again.

"That's a beautiful piece of furniture. Hand crafted in the old manner. I'd imagine that it will be in excellent condition in another five or six hundred years."

Lowell smiled. "Indeed. Unless someone becomes tired of it and it winds up in a fireplace some chilly evening."

They both smiled and Lowell walked him to the front door. This time he noticed that along the hall there were some spots where paintings had once hung but now were gone. He filed the detail for possible use later.

Outside, he walked down the incline to the rest of the town. The house had a fine view of the surrounding area and the town. The Arkansas River flowed by not too far away. He was surprised by the size of the river and the boat traffic it carried.

Spur remembered the letter threat, and now stopped and watched behind him. He thought he saw a shape slide in back of a buggy parked on the dirt street but he couldn't be sure. He walked on, waited until he figured anyone following him would have to be in an open area behind him, and he whirled around.

A man in range clothes and wearing a gun on his hip turned down a side street away from Spur.

He had been the right distance behind and caught in the open.

Spur walked a little faster now. Someone was following him and didn't want him to know it.

Amy Lowell Hellman sat in the only comfortable chair in the small house's living room and stared at the magazine without seeing it. She was unhappy. Amy had been unhappy for the past five days cooped up in this house in Fort Smith. The kidnapping off the train had been a hoot. She had enjoyed that more than anything she had done in years.

Amy grinned as she remembered the strong one, Knute, picking her up out of her seat on the train, throwing her over his shoulder head down and walking out of the train with her bellowing and pounding on his back with her fists. It had been so grand!

They had horses then and she rode in on Knute's mount. Her thighs got all chafed and she was so hot and excited with her cunnie right on the horse that she wanted to mount Knute right there as he rode. She grinned wondering if it could be done while riding a horse. She'd have to try it sometime.

Doug was supposed to meet her there the first night, but he sent a note saying he had some other business he had to get settled first. What could be more important than her . . . and the twenty thousand dollars they had stolen from the train.

Damn! She'd never seen so much money all in one place in her life. Then they ripped open the registered mail in those two mail sacks and found some more money and those stocks or bonds or whatever they were. Russ had found them and hadn't let them out of his sight ever since. She had no idea how much they were worth but it must be a lot.

Doug had come once the second day, and kissed her a dozen times and played with her tits, and told her to be patient. One more little item he had to take care of.

She felt a little strange. She'd been in this house with the three robbers for five days and hadn't even seen one of them naked. They told her Doug had warned them away from her. Nobody could diddle her or he'd get his balls shot off.

Who was he to order something like that? If she wanted a man, she had him. Doug's shit was coming to an end in a rush. She stood from where she had been sitting and saw Russ first. He was the best looking of the bunch and looked like he was hung like a stud horse. She almost giggled thinking of a stallion she had seen in heat. His whanger had been two-feet long when it got hard. Could that horse make it work on that little mare he mounted! Damn! She'd never seen humping and fucking like that in her life.

She felt herself getting wet just thinking about it. She moved over to where Russ sat staring out the window. She stood in front of him and stretched, making her tits push out hard against the thin cotton blouse she wore. He looked up and grinned.

"Deed I would like to do something about it,

Miss Amy, but I like my balls too much to crack them with you."

Amy moved quickly and sat on his lap and at the same time unbuttoned the blouse. She let it hang there with just the sides of her breasts showing.

"You really going to let Douglas tell you what to do? I'm telling you what to do right now. Both the others are sleeping. Nobody will know but us. Come on, right here on the floor. Fuck me right now."

Russ wet his lips and she bent and kissed him. Her kiss was hard and open mouthed and her tongue got between his lips and washed him out as he gave a soft moan. She found one of his hands and pulled it up and pushed it under her blouse until it closed around one of her breasts.

She could feel his erection rising against her soft ass. She pressed the kiss a minute longer then came away. She watched him a moment, then pulled his face down to her breasts. His mouth covered one and his hand the other. He rubbed and chewed and licked at her breasts. Russ gave one more moan and came off her breasts, knelt on the floor and pulled her down beside him.

"Just once and fast and you don't let on to Doug, O.K.?"

Amy nodded and pulled at the buttons on his pants fly. She had it open in a rush and fished around to find his whanger. Amy yelped in delight when she pulled it out. She swore it was ten-inches long. Not so large around but it would poke a hole all the way to her chest once it hit her cunny.

Amy ripped off her blouse, shook her breasts at him, then pulled down her skirt. A moment later she had her pink bloomers off and sat there with her legs spread apart and her knees lifted, showing him exactly what he had been missing these past nights.

"Now," she said. She pulled him with her as she leaned backwards on the floor. Russ knew what to do, not like some of them young boys she taught sex lessons to now and then. He plunged into her and jammed it in again and again until she thought he'd never stop.

At last he was into her sheath as far as he would go and she felt that wild, strange half-hurting sensation when a whanger went in so far it touched a vital part of her she couldn't even name. Didn't happen often.

She wrapped her legs around his back, but he shook his head. He undid her legs, caught them and lifted them up and up until he could rest them on his shoulders. It bent her almost double and her breasts were in her face.

"Oh lordy but that does feel different," she said. Then she began to sweat and she felt the climax coming.

"Do me hard, hard, harder!" Then she roared and screamed, her body shook and jolted, bouncing and trembling and vibrating like she was in an earthquake.

Russ grinned and held on pumping hard to try to keep up with her. He couldn't. Then she stopped. Didn't move at all. He looked at her and then the whole thing started again and she screeched and bellowed and roared and then shook so hard she couldn't say a word or make a sound.

The third time she started to climax, Russ said to hell with it and kept humping her until he exploded himself and pounded out the last of his jism and relaxed, letting her down flat as he rolled to the side panting like the back side of an ox team going up a steep hill towing a heavy wagon.

Knute stepped around the door from the near bedroom grinning from ear to ear. "So you finally poked her," he said. "I been watching and she's too much a wild cunt for me. I like them to stay in one place more."

Sully had been watching from the kitchen where he'd been making himself a sandwich. The uneaten food remained in his hand as he stared first at Russ, then at the naked woman. He'd never seen a woman stark naked before.

"Damn," he breathed, afraid that she would put her clothes on. "Holy damn in a fruit basket, look at them knockers!" He had whispered the words to himself. He put the sandwich down and stood so he could see her better.

Amy sat up and her flattened breasts swelled and jutted forward to their natural position.

"Damn," Sully said. He pumped his hips five then six times against the wall while still watching her breasts bouncing and jiggling and the swatch of hair between her legs.

He pumped his hips again, let out a soft moan

and then felt the thrill that he could never get enough of as his hips pounded hard again and again. "Oh, damn it to hell, it's all over my pants." Sully rubbed his crotch and kept looking at the woman's breasts. He swore that he'd never seen anything so beautiful before in his whole life.

Amy saw Sully watching around the door molding. She smiled.

"Hey, Sully, come here. You ever seen real live girl tits before? Come on out here and show me your whanger. Bet you got yourself one long dick."

Sully vanished back into the kitchen.

Amy laughed and then turned and looked at Knute. "Not a fucking chance, big Knute. You had your chance on the trail. Fact is, I feel kind of fucked out right now. Not a word of this to Doug if he ever comes back."

"He'll be back," Russ said. "Only thing he took the other time was the bonds, he called them. He got all excited, remember."

Amy pulled on her blouse, then her bloomers while the two men watched.

"He'll be back because we got plans," Amy said. "Damn well better be back, that little fucker."

"You do him?" Russ asked.

"Hell yes, that's how we met. We both woke up in one bed one morning. Both of us so hungover we didn't remember anything that happened the night before."

"Here in town?"

"Nah, in Little Rock. I live there. We were at a party."

She slipped into her skirt and hiked it up, then

sat in a chair and picked up the magazine. This time she got interested in the pictures.

"Not a Goddamn word about this to Doug when he comes, you all hear. You say a word about it and Doug will pistol whip you and won't pay you a single greenback."

Russ put his hand on her breast and rubbed gently. "Amy, I think they get the idea."

She slapped his hand away. "Don't. Only when and if I say so. Otherwise, keep your fucking hands to yourself.

Chapter Six

Spur McCoy walked another block knowing someone was following him. He'd been in this situation dozens of times. Each one evolved differently. What terrain or buildings were there here that he could use? He checked the small businesses on the side street. He could dart into one of them.

Yes, only he didn't dart. He pretended to relax, didn't look behind himself and walked into a saddle shop as if he knew exactly where he was going.

Most of these shops had a rear door. The marvelous smell of the new leather hit him as soon as he stepped inside the shop. When he became rich and famous he was going to have his own saddle shop just to play with. The smell of the fresh tanned cow hide brought back a million memories.

When he entered the door, he stepped to the side behind the solid wall and waited. The outside door swung away from him so he'd have a perfect point of attack on the man following him if he ventured inside.

Spur remembered the man who followed him had on a gray hat, kerchief, a blue shirt, no vest and jeans. Spur waited five minutes and the man didn't come in. At this point, Spur was curious who the jasper was. He waved at the leather man, and sauntered out the door to the boardwalk taking care not to look behind him.

This time the tracker was ahead of him, watching a jeweler repair a watch where he sat in the six-foot high display window. Several others watched as well.

Spur started to walk up to the man but he faded away into the crowd so Spur couldn't touch him. Cat and mouse. Spur enjoyed his role of the cat, the hunter. Spur walked to Main Street and turned down it. Here the street was half filled with buggies, freight wagons, farm wagons, and mounted men going somewhere. Where did they all come from?

Spur idled his way, caught the reflection in a side window of the same man behind him, then walked on. This was not getting him anywhere. He slowed so the man came closer, then Spur did a rear march maneuver, spinning around with his left foot forward and moving directly in the opposite direction.

Soiled Dove

In a moment, Spur was ten-feet from his tracker. The man snarled and drew his six-gun. Before he could fire two women came between the men and the gray hat turned and ran. Spur ran after him.

The man in the gray Stetson darted into a dry goods store with mostly women shoppers. He tipped over a display rack of ladies' dresses to slow Spur, ran down an aisle and out the rear door into the alley.

When Spur came to the door he paused, then threw it open. A shot slammed through the opening where the gunman thought Spur was coming out. Spur ducked and moved into the doorway firing twice at the fleeing man.

Spur ran after him.

For 100 yards it became a footrace, then the attacker held his side and sagged behind a fire barrel at the side of the alley and brought out his revolver.

Spur ran to within 40 feet of the man. It was a long revolver shot. He saw a wooden crate ahead that looked solid enough for a fort. He fired one shot hitting the barrel and at the same time darted the last ten-feet to the wooden box and slid in behind it without taking any return fire.

Spur waited for the man to look around the barrel. He didn't. Spur put another round into the barrel, making a heavy dent in the metal but not penetrating it.

A moment later the man was up and firing at Spur's cover. He ran backwards firing five shots until he was out of range, then he turned and ran again, reloading as he went.

Spur sprinted after him. He snapped one shot with a lot of elevation, but it missed. He kicked open his Colt and pulled out the spent cartridges and filled it with new ones until all six chambers were loaded.

At the end of the alley, the ambusher turned down a side street and Spur took the corner wide to prevent another ambush. The man wasn't there. He ran again flat out down the street that led toward the near edge of town.

Spur growled. He hadn't figured on a long chase when this started. Now he was curious to know who had hired the man. It might be worth finding out.

They ran another 50-yards and the man ahead slowed and walked looking over his shoulder. Spur closed the gap to 20-yards and lifted his six-gun. A woman and two children came out of a house just beyond the runner. The ambusher saw them, dashed up and grabbed the oldest, a boy about 12, and held him in front of his chest. The ambusher's six-gun was pressed against the boy's head.

"Don't come no closer or this kid gets his head blowed off," the gunman called.

Spur had slowed to a walk. He kept on moving until he was 30-feet away. He brought up his Colt and held it steady.

"You just go right ahead and shoot, bush-whacker. Then a second later I'll put six slugs into your worthless carcass and you'll be dead, too. You're bluffing with the boy. I've played poker, too."

The boy's mother stood a dozen feet from the gunman, tears streaming down her face. She held her smaller child and wailed.

The gunman said nothing. He looked at the boy, then at Spur.

"I'm calling your bluff, bad ass. Either shoot and die or let him go and run again, your choice."

The gunman turned the weapon toward Spur and fired. He missed by two-feet, but Spur couldn't return fire. He darted one way, then the other, as the gunman shot again, then a third time. Spur had worked backward until he was almost 50-feet away and out of any reasonable handgun range.

"You've got two tries left, hard case. Want to risk them and then get yourself blown straight into hell?"

The gunman scowled, looked at the boy, then at Spur. He had figured out he didn't have time to reload. If he tried it the kid would slip away. Just then the boy spun around in the man's arm and kicked him twice in the shins. The man in the gray Stetson yowled in pain, let the boy go and turned and bolted.

Spur lifted his Colt and ran after him. Spur admitted he'd never been a winner at sprinting, but long-range running was more to his liking. The gunner ahead settled into a steady trot, looking over his shoulder now and then. Spur put on a spurt, sprinting fast to close the gap. He was 40-feet away before the man ahead noticed. Spur got off two shots before his target sprinted ahead. The second round caught him in the side of the arm, spun him around but he kept running, bellowing with pain.

"Give it up," Spur called. "I don't want to kill you."

The man turned and fired one time, then once more. Spur grinned. Unless the man had loaded six rounds, his fangs had been pulled.

They slowed the pace and Spur caught up again to within 20-feet. They had left the last house and now ran across the open country. A shallow draw began ahead and tapered down into a small valley that could hold a stream and was half wooded.

"One more shot and you're a dead man," Spur barked.

The runner stopped suddenly, turned and pulled the trigger. His weapon didn't fire. He pulled the trigger five more times as Spur walked up to him, his Colt trained on the man's chest.

"Enough," Spur said. "Drop it and keep your hands in sight."

The gunner wilted, let the six-gun fall to the grass and shook his head. "Didn't seem so tough when he told me about the job."

"Killing a man is always harder than it looks, especially for a rotten shot like you. Who hired you?"

The man was half a head shorter than Spur. He slowly took off his gray Stetson and fanned himself. "You know I won't tell you that."

"How would I know something dumb like that? You look halfway smart. You followed me, shot at me, ambushed me. Why should I go to the trouble of walking you back to town? I might just as well shoot you right here and let the buzzards have their afternoon meal."

The man's eyes grew wide. His hands jiggled around at the end of his arms. He stared hard at Spur. "You wouldn't just kill me in cold blood."

"What did you try to do to me, give me fair warning so we could have a shoot-out? Tell me now or I'm going to start shooting."

The man shook his head. Spur lowered the barrel of the .45 and from four-feet away shot him in the thigh. The man slammed backward and rolled over screaming.

Spur walked over and looked down at the man cringing and braying in agony on the ground.

"Who hired you to shoot me?"

"Damn, hurts! You fix me. Stop the damn bleeding. No human being can let another one die like this. Look at my blood coming out!"

"Who hired you to shoot me?"

The gunner looked up at Spur, who moved the aim of the six-gun down until it pointed at the man's right knee.

"Oh, God, no! Not in the knee. Damn I'd never walk again. Maybe I can tell you. If'n you let me go. Let me get patched up by a doctor and then let me get the boat downriver. Yeah, I could stay with my cousin in New Orleans."

"Who hired you?"

The man looked up as Spur cocked the Colt.

"Oh, goddamn! All right. Don't shoot me again. Okay, I'll tell you. Some little guy. Didn't get a name. He was at the saloon and bought me a beer and asked if I wanted to make some extra money."

"How much?"

"Two hundred. That's damn near what I made all last year. He gave me twenty, pointed you out to me this morning and I followed you a bit. You didn't know it till you came out of the big house on the rise."

"You local?"

"No, came in last week on the train. I'm a logger. Heard there was some jobs."

"When do you report to get the rest of your money?"

"Tonight, about eight o'clock, in back of the same saloon. The alley. He don't like to be seen much, he says. Strange little guy, maybe five feet tall, cowboy outfit, no, more like a gambler. Fancy vest and all."

"You think he'll be there?"

"Damn well better. Now can I tie up my bullet holes?"

Spur tore strips off the man's shirt tail and bandaged the man's two wounds. The slug had gone all the way through making an exit hole, cutting down on the repair work needed.

Spur and the gunman walked back to town. Spur led him down back streets and they went in the side door of the Wentworth Hotel. Then it was up the back stairs to the second floor and room 212.

He pushed the man inside and tied his hands behind his back.

"What the hell we doing here?"

"Waiting until time to go and report in to your contact. Little guy, remember?"

"Yeah. I'm hungry."

"Good, shows you have a good strong system and can stand to miss a few meals. You'll eat next in jail if you need to eat anything at all." Spur wondered about the room. Anyone could find out which room he had. He checked the hallway, looked in the room he had slept in before and in one swift move, propelled the killer across the hall into room 215. He locked the door, put a chair under the handle and relaxed on the side of the bed.

"What's your name?" Spur asked.

"Does it matter?"

"Like to know the man's name I'm about to kill. Especially if he's been lying to me."

"Faulkner, Hank Faulkner. Used to live in Ohio."

Spur heard some pounding on a door in the hallway. He opened his door a crack and checked. Lillian hit the door to 212 again, then scowled, turned and walked down the hall to the stairs.

Spur shrugged. Maybe next time. He had his first break on this case and he didn't want to let go of it.

Spur spent the afternoon catching up on his copy of *Brother Jonathan,* a weekly "compend" of Belles Letters and the Fine Arts, Standard Literature and General Intelligence. It had changed a lot since he first saw it years ago. But it did have some good continuing fiction that was fascinating.

By six o'clock, Spur was hungry. He tied Faulkner's feet, checked the tie on his hands, and put a gag in his mouth. Then Spur went down to the hotel dining room and ate dinner. He brought back two sandwiches for his prisoner. He had to be strong enough to make the contact with the conspirator who hired him.

At 7:30 that night, Spur took Faulkner down the back stairway and to the alley behind the Black Bart Saloon. They arrived early and Spur hid behind a large wooden crate, with Faulkner perched on top of it. There was a knot hole he could see out of toward the rear of the saloon.

Spur had tied Faulkner's feet but had left his hands free.

At ten minutes to eight by Spur's big pocket watch, the door to the back of the saloon opened and two men came out. They talked briefly, then one went back inside.

The other one looked around. "Faulkner, you idiot, are you out here?"

"Yes sir, right over this way."

The shadowy figure came closer and stopped. "Idiot, why are you sitting on that box?"

"To keep the rats from biting my ankles. You got the money?"

"Sure, you bring me his ears?"

"In this paper sack. Sorry, it has a few blood stains on it."

The small man in the shadows chuckled. "Just so it's Spur McCoy's blood." The figure came forward six feet more and reached up for the sack.

Spur McCoy stepped around the box and charged, jolting into the man's side and splattering him over the dirt in the alley. He skid two feet before he stopped.

"What?" the small man yelped. Then he was down.

Spur dropped his 185 pounds on the smaller man and pinned him to the ground. He brought his six-gun up and cocked it next to the man's ear, then pushed the muzzle into the same ear.

"Who the hell are you?" Spur asked.

"Just playing a trick on a friend," the man bleated.

"Some trick. Who told you to hire Faulkner there to gun me down?"

"McCoy?"

"In the flesh and mad as hell. You want to keep any teeth or should I knock them all down your throat with the butt of my Colt?"

"Easy, easy. Let me sit up and we can talk."

Spur took a leather boot lace from his pocket and tied the small man's hands behind him, then sat him up. Spur struck a match and held it up to the man's face. He'd never seen him before.

"Who?" Spur asked, moving the Colt's muzzle under the man's chin and pushing it upward until he got a yelp of pain.

"Easy. Easy. First off, nobody tried to kill you. Told damn idiot Faulkner there to scare you. Just scare you."

"That why you told him to bring back my ears? Who do you work for?"

"Nobody. It was just a little scare job. A man said he wanted to scare you. I hire people."

"Who was the man?"

"He never said. Paid me in advance. Never saw his face."

Spur knew a determined man when he met one. Not even a bullet in his thigh would convince this one. He'd done this kind of work dozens of times before and probably been caught at it. He would never give up his employer.

"Fine, get on your feet. Faulkner, you, too. Jump down here."

Spur knotted a four-foot long piece of leather bootlace around each man's neck and prodded them down the alley and back to the sheriff's office. He pushed them inside and was surprised to find Sheriff Booth Grimm manning the desk.

"Short two men tonight," the sheriff said. "What do you have here?"

A half hour later Spur had it sorted out, complaints filed and the two men jailed on attempted murder and conspiracy to murder. The small man's name was Marty Runyon. The sheriff knew him. Got into trouble now and then, but not much of a problem for the sheriff.

Spur sat in the sheriff's office trying to sort through the whole thing again. He'd seen everyone in the case except the two sons-in-law of old man Teasdale.

He looked up their names in the small notebook. Doug Chandler, the wild one, and Nate Emerson, evidently the one who did the work around the ranch.

"Teasdale's sons-in-law ever come to town?" Spur asked.

One of the deputies looked up and grinned.

"Hell yes, one of them, Doug Chandler, is a regular hell bent and out of control raging bull most nights. We've had to cool him off in a cell more than a dozen times in the past year. He gets wild and crazy when he drinks too much, which is most of the time."

Spur looked at his watch. He'd lost half the day chasing that damned tail. It was slightly after 9 p.m., early for the saloon trade.

"Might just do a little Doug fishing tonight," Spur said. "Which saloon is his favorite?"

"The one he hasn't been thrown out of lately. I'd suggest the Rambling Rose Saloon. It's got the best whiskey, and Doug does like his drink."

Spur thanked him and left, watched his back on the street and walked well out beyond the boardwalk when he passed an alley. Never could tell how many assassins had been hired. He worked his way to the Rambling Rose without incident and pushed inside.

It was one of the better drinking parlors in town. No upstairs, no soiled doves, not much gambling, mostly just a place to drink. He bought a mug of draft beer at the bar and found a table near the side.

The barkeep told him Doug Chandler hadn't been in yet tonight.

"He usually makes a stop here on his rounds," the apron said. "He's got red cheeks and a whiskey nose you can't miss. Little guy, not much more than five-four, skinny as a winter starved coyote."

Spur sipped at his brew and watched. He got a deck of cards from a nearby table and laid out a game of seven card solitaire. He lost the first four games. On his second beer he won a game and then another.

A man pushed through the bat wings and let out a screech that brought everyone's glance up.

"Eeeeeeeeeeeehaw . . . Doug is here and I want a beer!"

It was signpost enough. The man was five-four, dressed in town clothes and a gambler's red spangled vest. He carried a pearl-handled six-gun on his hip but it was positioned too low and too far to the rear to be much good in a quick draw. The weapon was all for show. Spur wondered if it was even loaded.

Doug Chandler downed a shot of whiskey in one gulp at the bar and it was obvious that he'd been drinking some before that. He wandered to one of two poker games going and watched for a minute. When the hand ended he pulled up a chair and pushed a roll of greenbacks on the table.

"Make room, I'm sitting in," Doug said.

The other five men looked at the stack of bills and nodded. It was a straight money game. No chips.

Spur moved up and watched. Doug was no good as a poker player. He quickly lost thirty-dollars bidding against a pat hand and growled and pushed back from the table. He motioned to the apron who brought him a bottle of whiskey and a glass, took two dollars from him and went back to the bar.

Doug Chandler seemed to be riding alone. Spur saw no one who came in with him or soon afterwards who paid him any attention. He had two more shot glasses full of whiskey, then pushed the glass and bottle to one side and leaned down on the table on his arms. As he did the glass fell off the table and smashed on the floor. No one paid any attention.

Spur thought of the close coordination it would take to stage the train robbery, to know which train to have the governor's daughter on, and to get the bonds on the same train. If that's what happened. If it did, Doug Chandler didn't look like the man to coordinate the conspiracy.

Why would he want to? Oh, he could use the money, but Spur guessed that the $20,000 in bank cash on board had been a happenstance, a serendipity. No way to explain that. The other three elements could have been coordinated, must have been, but was Chandler the man who did the job? Spur voted that he wasn't and finished his beer.

When Spur left the saloon, Doug Chandler was still sleeping on his arms on top of the small table.

Chapter Seven

Spur left the Rambling Rose Saloon and went back to talk to the sheriff. They kicked around several ideas on the train robbery, and were coming to some of the same conclusions.

"If this whole damn train robbery has something to do with the Teasdale ranch, don't see who would want to mess up a sale like that except the boys," Sheriff Grimm said. "That would mean Doug Chandler, the spoiled, wastrel of a son-in-law. But that's a problem. Never heard tell of that bastard doing anything like work. Setting up a three-way swindle like this would take a lot of planning and leg work."

"Agreed, Sheriff. But who does that leave? Old Man Teasdale, the other son-in-law, Nate Emerson? Neither likely candidates. So we're down to the bonds."

"Bearer bonds," the Sheriff said. "Good as cash. What was Gregory Lowell doing sending that many in registered mail? Seems strange to me. Hell, he could take a trip to Kansas City and bring them back himself, or get a certified bank draft made out to himself if he wanted to sell them."

Spur sipped the county coffee and nodded. "Damn strange, especially since the Postal Inspector I talked to said the bonds were registered, but not insured. No postal insurance, I'd guess."

The sheriff rubbed his jaw. "No postal insurance. What about the Railway Express Company? Did Lowell have any insurance with them? Would they be liable for the goods in their railway express car?"

"I can damn well find out in a rush," Spur said. "Railway Express window should still be open down at the station."

He waved at the sheriff, went outside and walked down to the train depot. The window was open that sold tickets and took in express and freight. The man behind the cage looked at Spur's identification and grunted.

"This about that robbery?"

"It is. Does the Express Agency insure or guarantee delivery of items sent in your care?"

The man behind the window began to sweat. "Far as I know there ain't no insurance on items in the Railway Express car. That's all I can say. I got a telegram from the company and they told me not to say anything at all about the robbery.

They said they'd send a man over from Atlanta, to look at things and answer questions, but I ain't seen nobody yet."

Spur nodded. "But it stands to reason that they must guarantee delivery. If something is entrusted to them—"

"I can't say, really, I just can't say. But it figures. It's logical. The company guarantees delivery. What if the people who owned the goods in the Railway Express car arranged to have it stolen and returned to them. Then they would have the original goods, and would be compensated for their assumed loss by the road or the Railway Express Agency."

Spur grinned. "Yes, now I'm beginning to get a new slant on this whole thing. Thank you. You've been most helpful."

"Like I told you, Mr. McCoy. The company told me not to say a word about this to anyone. I never even talked to you, right Mr. McCoy?"

Spur chuckled. "Now that you mention it, I don't ever remember talking to you. Good night."

On his way back down the dark street, Spur watched lights coming on and going out around the small town. The yellow glow of coal oil lamps showed in a lot of the houses. Here and there lamps and lanterns lit stores staying open late.

The saloons were lighted the best. In those that offered gambling, every poker table had one or two lamps on it, and several hung in an arrangement over the bar. Spur was glad he didn't have to light all of them and keep the wicks trimmed and the chimneys washed every day to rid them of the smoke and the ever present soot.

He was just stepping into a splash of light from the Black Bart Saloon when a man moved toward him and held up his hand.

"Mr. McCoy, I'd like to have a word with you."

Spur's right hand had darted to his six-gun but he didn't draw it when he saw no iron in the other hand. He relaxed and saw a well dressed man come into the full light. He was tall and slender in a suit that was not off the local general store rack. An expensive thick gold chain joined the vest pockets, with a gold fob hanging in the center. The man had on town shoes polished until they gleamed even in the faint light from the saloon.

Spur stopped walking and eyed the man. Seemed safe enough. He nodded. "So talk."

"Mr. McCoy, I'm up here from Little Rock, and I'd like to have a word or two with you about the Governor's missing daughter. Do you have a moment?"

"Sure as the sun shines in the morning," Spur said. "This saloon would be the closest spot."

They went in. Spur brought two bottles of cold beer from the bar to keep and he and the stranger sat down at a table. They sipped the beer and then the man held out his hand.

"I'm Fiorello Alger, Attorney General of Arkansas, and sometimes messenger for Governor Hellman. I understand that you're with the U.S. Secret Service working on the robbery and kidnapping situation."

"That's right. So far I have no clues at all to the whereabouts of the governor's daughter."

"Ah, yes, they have covered their tracks well this time."

Spur looked up. "You mean something like this has happened before?"

"Once, a year ago. I never could bring charges, but I'm almost certain that Amy Lowell had a hand in the attempted extortion by means of her own kidnapping."

"It's been done before. Were payments made?"

"No, we nipped it before it got that far. But this time it's much different. She's out of the capitol, we've heard from the kidnappers. We're negotiating with them about money."

"Since you're here that must mean you had some word from Fort Smith."

"We did, a telegram. It was sent to me at my home, without any office designation. That's probably why the local telegrapher didn't figure out what it was about. I'm sure you've alerted him to bring you a copy of any wires sent to the governor or the state house or other high ranking members of the state cabinet."

"Something like that. Do you have the wire?"

The Attorney General reached in his suit coat inside pocket and brought out the yellow papers. Spur opened it and read it.

"YOUR PRECIOUS GOODS SAFE. 120 POUNDS. COST $250 A POUND. RESPOND AT ONCE. REMEMBER, THESE GOODS PERISHABLE. WIRE MR. WHOLESALE, FORT WORTH, STATION PICK UP."

"Mr. McCoy, that's a thirty-thousand dollar ransom note. I'm here to try to catch Mr. Wholesale. I wired that I was considering the price with my committee and would wire our decision by tomorrow. I hope to catch him at the station when he picks up this second wire."

Spur put down his bottle. "Might not be that easy. He'll have someone else pick up the message. You need to have a signal set up with the telegrapher so you'll know someone is accepting the wire sent to Mr. Wholesaler, even if it's a woman. Then we'll follow the person who picks it up and hope it leads to the kidnapper."

"Hope it works. We have no idea who it is this time, but we strongly suggest that whoever it is, is acting with the cooperation, if not in league with, Amy Hellman. The girl is an anchor that's dragging down her father's good works."

"I'll help you all I can. I'm glad for your information. I've been running with a blindfold on concerning most of this case. I have an idea the whole thing is tied together but so far, no solid proof. There's a strong chance the robbers of the Railway Express car are the same ones who set up the kidnapping. How else could the robbers know to go to the passenger car to kidnap Miss Hellman? They must have known she would be on board. The ranch sale and cash and the bank money on board could have been mere chance.

"I never believe in chance until it's proven. Right now it looks like one big conspiracy. If we can unravel one aspect of it, we should be able to take down the whole thing."

The Attorney General sat back. "Well now. I heard about the robbery, but didn't tie it in that much with Miss Hellman's abduction. Thinking on it, you're right. It has to be connected. It would be simple enough to know which train she was taking out of Kansas City and when it would be at that spot on the tracks. Yes, yes, we do have a real bucketful of rattlesnakes here, don't we?"

Spur held out his identification. "Just a formality, but I'd appreciate it if you could show me some identification. I hope I haven't been talking to the wrong man."

"Not at all. I had already checked you out with Sheriff Grimm. He vouched for you. Only right that I do the same."

He passed over a printed card with his name and office, as well as a letter signed by the governor on official stationery with the state's seal, all notorized by a notary public. Spur handed them back.

"You give the culprit any time when the wire would be there?"

"I told him by noon."

"You have any men with you?"

"One, my best man."

"Good, we can do a three layer shadow. One of us starts following the pickup person, then you follow him and I'll follow you. Each block or so we drop off the lead man and the next one moves up. The subject never sees the same person behind him and doesn't think he's being followed."

"Should work. How are you coming along on the rest of this case?"

"Slowly. Not much to go on yet. Still trying to gather facts. I haven't even met one man who may be involved, although it looks doubtful now. I have mostly loose ends and promising suspects."

"More than I have." The Attorney General finished his beer and put down the bottle. "Let's meet at the far end of the train station at eleven o'clock tomorrow. That way we should be in plenty of time. I see you're armed. I am, too." He stood and so did Spur.

"See you tomorrow at ten," Spur said. They walked out of the saloon together.

Spur kept thinking about the rich man in the big house on the small hill. If he was involved, the robbers would have had plenty of time to deliver the bonds to him. His next step would be to launch a claim with the Railway Express Agency and the Atcheson, Topeka and Santa Fe Railway for the lost bonds in the amount of $100,000. He would probably have to sue to get a sum like that back, even if the railroad did agree that it was in part responsible for the loss through negligence.

Spur headed toward the big house on the hill. Why couldn't things be simple like they used to be? A man robbed a bank. You chased him, tracked him, found him, shot it out with him, and took him or his body back with the stolen money. End of case. Nothing was simple any more.

He found a good place to sit down 50 yards from the Gregory Lowell mansion and waited. There still could be some contact between the rich man and the robbers. At least Spur hoped there would be. He held his chin in his hands and watched another light flare in a second story window of the rich man's mansion. What was going on up there?

Doug Chandler was only a little drunk. He had built up a tremendous tolerance to alcohol over the past three years of working at it almost every day. He left the shadows around the small house on Fourth Street and slipped up to the back door. After checking behind him to be sure no one was watching, he eased the door open and stepped inside.

"You take one more step and I'll blow your guts out," a raspy voice challenged.

"It's me, Doug Chandler. Put your damn gun down and light a match. So dark in here I can't see to spit."

A match flared, then a lamp. The yellow glow of light showed Russ Dolan holding the lamp and a six-gun now pointing down.

"Glad to see you, Mr. Chandler. You gonna let us out of here tomorrow so we can get going down river? The men are getting anxious to spend some of that money they earned."

"Tomorrow, maybe, if all goes well tomorrow. Supposed to get a wire. Hell, somebody's got to stay with Amy or she'll be running naked down the street." Doug looked up. "She's all right, ain't she? You ain't been diddling her or nothing?"

"Hey, you said no fooling around with her. I'm not getting in trouble now that this job is most over. You sure we can get the rest of our money tomorrow?"

"Said so, didn't I? You got anything to eat?

Think I missed supper somewhere."

They went into the kitchen. Amy Hellman sat at the table, one hand inside her blouse rubbing a breast as she read a magazine. She looked up.

"Gawd, he showed up!" She dropped the magazine and ran to Doug, hugging him and kissing him until he pushed her face away.

"Later, woman, later. I'm hungry as a horse."

An hour later, Doug and Amy lay naked side by side in the big bed. He had eaten supper, and poked Amy once making her squeal and roar in pleasure.

Now she asked him about the ransom. "It ain't like you thought up this great idea all by yourself, y'know," Amy said.

"We're working on it. I sent a telegram to Attorney General Alger. You said he had your father's ear. I demanded thirty-thousand dollars for your release. He's supposed to send a reply back to the station tomorrow by noon."

"Dumb," Amy said. "As soon as you pick up the wire, they'll arrest you and it'll be all over."

Doug laughed. "Not by a damn site, I won't pick up the telegram. I'll hire somebody, to hire somebody to pick it up and take it somewhere. By that time anybody trying to follow the person with the telegram will be so confused he won't know which way to hell. No one will even see me. Trust me. I know what I'm doing."

"We still going to New Orleans?"

"Just as soon as I get your ransom and I do some more business with a man in Kansas City."

Amy scowled at him. She pouted. "You said the

thirty-thousand would be enough."

"It will be, but we can use a little help, some insurance that we don't run out of cash money. Extra money is always a fine thing to have around. Trust me, we should have the cash back here from Kansas City by next week."

"I have to stay cooped up in here for another week?"

"I didn't say that. Of course you can't come out to the ranch. Too dangerous to use a hotel. What's the matter with this house?"

"I'm getting tired of eating the strange food the men have been cooking."

"I'll hire a cook who can keep her mouth shut." He rolled toward her and stroked her breasts. "Come on, big tits girl, in a few more days we'll be together all the time. I need just a little more time. No more than a week."

"Why? What's coming from Kansas City?"

"Money, I told you."

"How did you get more money? What about the twenty-thousand in new bills from the train?"

"Did you look at those bank notes? They're brand new, just been printed, Federal notes and each one has a different serial number. They're in exact numbered order. The bank knows which numbered bills were sent on the damn train. They know the serial numbers of all of them. We spend any of that money anywhere near here and the Federal marshals and policemen will be storming in here in a flood."

He bent and kissed both her breasts and Amy melted the rest of the way. Her breathing speeded up and a flush came to her throat as she reached for his crotch.

"Believe me, Amy, sweet thing, I'm working this little scheme absolutely the right way."

"Yeah, fine, okay, just make me feel good again. Right now. You rested enough? Right now, push it into me deep right this second."

Doug lifted over her and teased her a minute, then fell on top of her and reached across to the chair where he had put the bottle. He lifted it and took a pull of the raw whiskey.

"When we get to New Orleans, we're gonna get ourselves some damn fine Tennessee sippin' whiskey. Damn but that will be great. Cost near five dollars a bottle. Not like this cow piss they sell in the Fort Smith saloons."

"Yeah, we'll do that, Doug. Come on now, do me again. You know twice ain't never enough for me."

Spur McCoy sat on the hill outside the Gregory Lowell mansion and waited. He turned away from it once, cupped his hands and struck a match to read his pocket watch. Twenty minutes after eleven.

All of the lights in the house had been blown out except in two rooms. One was on the second floor, and one on the first. The butler might be on the second floor. Reading, or drawing pictures, or whatever butlers did when they weren't buttlering. Spur grinned at the word. He didn't even know if it was a real word. A butler should buttle, like a hunter hunts, and a carver carves.

Spur shook his head. He was getting punchy sitting here doing nothing and hoping he could turn up a lead. What if Lowell had been in on the train robbery and stolen his own bonds, and made the Railway Express Agency or the rail line pay for them? If that were true, then this whole can of wiggly worms got even more complicated.

How much longer was he going to sit here and wait? Spur had no idea. He had hoped something might happen, but the odds were against it. The odds were also against the idea that the rich man had been in on the train robbery to steal his own bearer bonds.

Spur shrugged. Another half hour. He thought about the man he'd jailed, both of them. One knew who hired him to try to gun down Spur McCoy. He was an old hand at the business. Odds were that he wouldn't talk—unless he was offered a sweet deal he couldn't turn down. Maybe a hundred dollars and a ticket on the downriver steamer to avoid a five year prison term. Might work, if the threat to send him to jail for five years was made strong enough. Spur decided to talk with the sheriff about the idea. This ambush hirer was local, he'd know the tough approach that hanging Judge Parker took to all crime.

Spur groaned from sitting on the ground so long, stood and stretched. That was when a buggy clattered along the street below. The rig hesitated at the corner, then turned and the black horse pulled the rig up the slope toward the rich man's house. Spur grinned and walked toward the place, staying out of sight in some moon shadows, and getting close enough so he could see who got out of the carriage. His lonesome vigil might have paid off after all.

Spur came within 30-feet of the mansion and hunkered down behind a small tree. The rig had stopped slightly before it got to the front door. A shadow came out of the buggy and rapped sharply with the metal knocker on the mansion's front door.

Nothing happened. The figure knocked again.

A few moments later a light came bouncing along inside the house, visible through glass panels on both sides of the large front door. Then the light steadied and the door swung outward. The butler stepped forward, light in his hand and held it up so he could see who was calling so late.

Chapter Eight

Spur McCoy watched with intense interest the two figures at the front door of the Lowell mansion, but he couldn't determine if the visitor was a man or a woman. After a few words, the butler pulled the door wide and ushered the person into the house.

Spur pondered this development. The rig remained in place. Evidently, the guest had driven it. He could wait and see where the person went after leaving the mansion. That might be hours, or it might be all night. No, if it were an all night visit, the rig and horse would have been put away in stables behind the house.

Spur waited. By one-thirty no one had come out of the place. He retreated slowly, then walked down the slope to the Wentworth Hotel and fell on his bed in room 212. He thanked his lucky leprechaun that Lillian wasn't lurking there waiting for him. Somehow he didn't think he'd have the strength. He snorted remembering her delicious body. Not true. He'd find the strength. Then he slept.

The next morning, Spur talked with the sheriff. The groups of serial numbers had come through. They were in two blocks of 500 numbers each.

Sheriff Grimm eased into his desk chair and preened his full black moustache, then loosened his belt a notch that tried in vain to hold in his generous belly. He sighed.

"Yep, got the numbers in last night in a wire. Come in late, on my desk this morning. The numbers look like this."

He handed Spur the telegram. The numbers were on separate lines. They were for the 1869 series $20 United States Notes with a picture of Hamilton on the left, a big 20 in the middle and a standing figure of a woman dressed in white on the right.

The numbers were A-2811001 to A-2811500 and A-2811501 to A-2812000.

Spur sat down in a chair beside the table and looked at the sample $20 bill that someone had obtained from the bank. It did not have one of the right serial numbers on it but would serve as a sample to show merchants.

"Spread the word," Spur said. "Even if the robbers hear about it, that might help, too. Then they won't spend any of it in Fort Smith."

Spur copied down the numbers on a piece of paper, folded it and put it in his shirt pocket.

He told Sheriff Grimm about the late night visitor at the Lowell mansion.

Grimm grunted and then grinned. "Damn, he's still at it. Lowell don't go out much, but every Thursday night he has one of Madelyn's girls come up the hill to see him. He pays well even though sometimes there isn't much action." The sheriff shook his head and grinned. "When I'm as old as he is, I hope I'm at least still trying to get it up."

"From what I hear from my uncles, age isn't the big factor, it's the desire," Spur said. "Most men will be humping away well into their seventies."

Sheriff Grimm laughed, a thumping, boisterous, belly roar. "By damn, I sure hope so." He wiped his eyes and took a deep breath. "Now what the hell can we do about those train robbers?"

Spur told him about his talk with the State Attorney General.

"Hear you met him as well, Sheriff. He's got a contact set up for about noon today at the telegraph office. Three of us will handle it, but you should know about it."

"Good. I'll have a man there to help if you need it." He scanned Spur with his soft blue eyes, dabbed at them with a handkerchief to slow down the moisture that came uncalled. "You still think these three or four parts of the robbery are all tied together somehow?"

"Looks that way, but so far it's just smoke and fireflies. No real evidence."

"Maybe your noon meeting will turn up something. I'd like to get this cleaned up before the Governor starts yelling at me again. Even the Attorney General is bad enough. He could blow me right out of office if he wanted to for no good reason. That's a powerful position he holds."

"I've heard. You sent your men out to the banks yet to talk about the serial numbers?"

"Went out first thing this morning. I told them to hit all of the stores that might do twenty-dollars worth of business a day."

"Good. I'm going to talk to the two bankers and make sure they check their twenty-dollar bills at least twice a day. Then I'm having an early dinner and be ready about eleven down at the train station. I'll let you know what happens."

Spur shook hands with the lawman and headed for the first bank down the street.

Promptly at eleven that morning, Spur met the Arkansas state official at the end of the train station. The man with him was introduced as Vern. He was medium height, loose jointed and slender. Spur decided he looked like he could use the six-gun on his hip.

Alger, the Arkansas Attorney General, motioned to the telegraph office at the center of the station. "I talked with the agent there. When anyone picks up the wire for Mr. Wholesaler, he'll give us a signal. He's going to pull down a window blind in the left front window."

"Sounds easy enough. Just so he remembers," Spur said. "He still has the wire waiting for the man?"

"He does. I wrote it out for the clerk this morning. He set it up like a real wire."

"What does it say?"

"Says we've agreed to the $30,000 price for the goods, the ransom. He should designate a time and place for the exchange."

"So if we miss the jasper this time, you're still in good faith contact with him."

"That's the idea."

Spur looked over the situation. "Let's have Vern take the first tail. Vern, you can be reading a newspaper on that bench over there about fifty-feet from the telegraph office. I'll be here by the luggage cart so I can go either way tailing Vern. Mr. Alger, you'll be with me, but give me a thirty-yard lead when I leave, then track me. I'll be about fifty-yards behind Vern.

"When I see that the subject thinks he might have a tail, I'll hurry up and pass Vern. Vern, you hang back and when you see Mr. Alger following me, you pick up the trail behind him. Should work."

Alger nodded. "I agree. Vern, you might as well go to your position. Get a newspaper to read."

Vern nodded and walked away. He soon sat on the bench working at digesting the day's news.

"So, now we wait," Spur said.

It was a quarter-to-twelve when the window shade went down. At the same time a boy about ten came out of the telegraph office with a yellow envelope in his hand. The telegrapher appeared in the door of the office nodding. Vern moved out behind the boy, who hurried out the far end of the station. Spur and Alger trailed along behind.

The route the boy took went down an alley, across the main street and along the far side of it about a half block, then through another alley. He never looked behind once. Spur let Vern keep the lead. Behind a saloon, the boy stopped and waited. Five minutes later a sloppily dressed man came out the back door of the saloon as if so drunk he was ready to collapse.

Once the door closed behind him he straightened, looked around, saw the boy sitting on a barrel and hurried over to him without a slip or stagger. He said something to the boy, took the envelope, handed the boy some coins, and slipped the envelope in his soiled jacket's inside pocket.

He turned and walked quickly back to the saloon's rear door, paused a moment and slumped, letting one arm hang loose as he got back into his role as a falling down drunk. He pulled the door open and staggered through it.

Spur caught the door before it closed and walked in after him. The drunk didn't seem to notice him. Spur bought a beer at the bar as the drunk meandered from table to table trying to cadge a drink. When it was unproductive, he staggered toward the front door and slipped outside.

Spur followed the drunk. The man turned and stared at Spur, said something and laughed, then turned away. Fiorello Alger came out the door behind Spur and touched his shoulder and passed him, shadowing the drunk who recovered remarkably. The man walked fast, then jogged forward.

He turned around and saw Alger moving along behind him and changed his pace to a flat out run leaving the gasping Attorney General far behind.

Spur had crossed the street and run forward to keep slightly ahead of the jogging drunk. When he began to run, Spur kept up with him easily from across the street.

The man playing the drunk saw Alger far behind and cut across the street where Spur busied himself looking in a store window. He brushed past Spur looking across the street, continued up the street past three stores, then entered a door that led to the second floor.

Spur followed him. On the second floor there were two establishments; one was a woman's wear and lingerie store. Spur saw the name of an attorney-at-law on the second door and pushed open the panel. He rushed inside.

He found only an empty office. A door was ajar to the rear. He opened it fully, saw a hallway and at the far end, two men at a window. Spur ran that way only to have the man acting the drunk come forward to meet him fists up and ready.

Spur ran at him, knocked down a swinging right hand, tripped the man and pushed him to the floor as he ran past.

When he got to the window only a few seconds later, a fat man in a brown suit had turned away from the opening and chuckled. "Afraid you're a bit late, friend," the suited man said.

Spur looked out the window and saw a black buggy leaving the alley below them.

"You threw the telegram out the window?" Spur asked.

"I'm a lawyer. I do what my client tells me."

"Who is your client?"

"Mr. McCoy, you know better than that. Lawyer-client relationship. Any and all information we share is secret and protected by law. I can't tell you that."

He motioned down the hall. "Now, if you'll follow me, I'll be glad to treat you to a small brandy to compensate for your long run for nothing. It's quite a good brandy, from France as I remember."

Without a word, Spur turned and went down the hall, out of the office and down to the street. Whoever was behind the kidnapping was not only audacious, he was smart as well. Spur shrugged. Next time they'd be faster.

He found Alger and his man waiting below the lawyer's office. Spur explained it.

"Oh, damn!" Alger said "My own profession rising up and beating me. I don't like that."

"I guess all you can do now is wait for a reply to your offer by telegram," Spur said.

"I'm off on my secondary target. I want to find Doug Chandler and follow him for a couple of days. It could prove interesting."

Spur found Chandler an hour later. He sat in the Black Bart Saloon well into a bottle of whiskey. He wasn't drunk, but mildly slowed. Spur sat with a beer, nursing it for half-an-hour. Nothing happened. Then when Spur was at the bar for a second beer, a man came in.

Spur recognized him as the man from the livery. He talked with Doug, and accepted some bills which he pushed into his pants pocket quickly. He left a moment later.

Doug capped his whiskey bottle and took it to the bar keep, said something and headed for the door.

Outside, he walked directly to a saddled horse in front of the saloon and mounted. Spur looked in vain for a horse he could borrow. There were no saddle horses within a block of him.

He followed the rider, who moved through the street traffic of small farm wagons, big freighters with eight horses, and people crossing the street. Soon Spur lost the rancher. Maybe if he had a horse he could find him again. Spur hurried to the livery and rented a horse already saddled and rode out to the place he had last seen the young rancher.

He rode around five minutes in a circle, then saw Doug Chandler riding fast down a street a block over. Spur trailed along behind and saw that the rancher was heading for the ferry that crossed the river into Indian Territories.

An hour before the livery man went to see Doug Chandler, Russ Dolan paced in the small house he shared with his two robber friends and Amy Hellman. He had stood all he could. He hadn't been paid. They'd done the agreed-on work and now were treated like slaves by Doug Chandler. He even made them stand guard over the $20,000 in new bank notes and the $10,000 in used bills. Strange that Doug hadn't banked the money yet, or just carried it with him. He was probably afraid he'd be robbed on the streets.

Dolan had been considering it for two days now. The new bank notes were like poison, he understood that. They were for spending in Texas or Louisiana, not there in Fort Smith. That made the cash almost worthless to him. But the other bills were soiled and folded and packaged in twenties, tens and fives. They would be easy to spend.

He had figured out two plans. The first would be to pick up the ten-thousand in old money, meander out of the house to go for food at the general store, and just keep on going. He'd stop by at the dock and find out when the next boat left downstream. If it was within an hour or two, he'd buy a ticket, walk on board and hide himself in the best spot he could find.

If the next boat didn't leave for three or four hours, he'd simply buy a horse and saddle at the livery, ride down to the rope ferry and ride across to the other side of the Arkansas River. Then he'd be in Indian Territory. No damn law there but Judge Parker, and Parker wouldn't even know he was alive. Yes! He'd feel a lot better in the Territories anyway.

On that steamer he'd be trapped until he got to Little Rock or on down the way toward the Mississippi.

In the Territories with that ten thousand dollars, he'd be king of the shit pile. Yeah!

Earlier that morning, Doug had humped Amy twice before breakfast and rushed out to some "business" he said he had to do. He hadn't been back. Usually, he stayed away all day. If he did today, that would give Russ a bigger head start.

He'd been in Indian Territory before a time or two. Yeah! Now!

He went to the small dresser in the room where the three men slept and eased it open. Sully lay on the bed with one hand covering his crotch.

"Damn, Sully, you jacking off again? Go into the other bedroom and tell Amy to help you. She'd be glad to pump you off."

Sully scowled at him, sprang off the bed and flounced into the other room.

Russ smiled, opened the top drawer, took out the three bundles of used bills and pushed them inside his shirt. Damn, he had ten-thousand fucking dollars in his shirt! He couldn't afford to take any of his gear with him. Not that he had much. Hell, from now on, he'd buy whatever he needed.

Yeah, he was rich. Right that very moment he was a rich man. He made sure the bundles of bills didn't show from inside his shirt, and walked into the living room. Sully had grabbed a magazine. Knute snored on the couch.

"Sully, we're low on grub. I'm going to the general store and bring back some food. You stay here and keep out of trouble." He watched Sully nod. "You talked to Amy yet? Tell her you need to get your whanger pumped off. Hell, she'll be glad to help you."

Sully threw the magazine at Russ who laughed and stepped out the front door. He walked slow and easy as long as Sully would be able to see him, then he hurried. He went straight to the livery and spent ten minutes picking out a horse he liked, then bargained for the horse and saddle.

At last he paid $45 of the stolen money for the ten-year old roan mare, and ten-dollars for the saddle and tack. He mounted and rode at a walk around the edge of town to the ferry. It had just pulled in and let off a sour looking older woman and two small ragtag kids who had dirty faces and clothes too small for them.

Russ rode the roan on board, paid the fifteen cents for the ride across and dismounted. He tied the roan to a hitching rail midships and stared at the water. The Arkansas River, any river fascinated him. Maybe he should take the boat downstream to the Mississippi and ride one of them fancy riverboats down to New Orleans.

Hell, he could afford it now. He could spend as much money as he wanted to. One rule, he wouldn't gamble. That was the easiest way to lose $10,000 in a rush. No sir, he'd play it close to his vest and spend money when he needed to, but he'd be shrewd about it. Most rich men were shrewd, that was probably how they got rich in the first place.

He waited anxiously, watching the street where the ferry tied up, but after ten minutes no one else came. The boatman waved a flag, and the rope moved as a horse on the other side dragged the flat bottomed ferry across the river working hard to keep the boat from floating downstream.

The rope, stretched tight by the current, moved slowly across the swiftly flowing waters. Russ wondered where all the water came from. Then he remembered the rains that soaked the land there and upstream sometimes for days on end. At least the rain made the countryside green.

On the other side of the river, he mounted his roan and turned upstream. He remembered a little about the country. There was a house or an inn, something upstream aways where he could stop and get some food and supplies before he took off into the wilds. The deeper he got into the Territories, the harder it would be for Judge Parker or Doug Chandler to find him.

Back on the Fort Smith side of the river, Doug Chandler rode up to the ferry slip at a gallop and saw it in the middle of the river coming back to this side. He'd missed the son-of-a-bitch. If he bought a horse and headed cross river, it stood to reason that he'd stolen the money from the dresser drawer.

Doug had made a fast gallop to the house and seen the empty spot in the top dresser drawer. The $20,000 in new bills were still there. Sully told him Russ said he was going after food at the general store.

Russ had stolen the money. Damn him! He'd ridden away fast but got to the ferry much too late.

He could only wait now for the ferry to get back and take him across. That would put him two, maybe three hours behind Russ Dolan. He'd find him in the Territories. Dolan didn't know them the way Doug did. He'd find the bastard somehow.

Spur McCoy watched Doug Chandler as he rode up to the ferry. Evidently, he was going across. Why? Might be productive to follow him. He looked furious about something. Could it have something to do with the missing ranch sales agreement and the ten-thousand dollar payment?

There was no chance that Spur could ride across on the same trip with Chandler. He'd recognize Spur or at least be cautious and curious. The round trip took about 45 minutes for the slow boat. That meant Spur would be that much time behind Chandler once they both were on the far side of the Arkansas River. It would have to do.

Spur dismounted and watched from the shade of a building as Chandler rode onto the ferry after it tied up on this side. Chandler had talked with the Captain and after some exchange of what could have been money, the ferry left at once.

Spur McCoy settled down to wait for the ferry to come back. At least he could see which direction the rancher headed out from the ferry. Chandler wouldn't know he was being followed and would have no reason to try to confuse anyone. Spur guessed that Chandler was chasing someone. Why else was he in such a rush after the livery man gave him some information or a message? The livery man! He could have sold or rented a horse to someone and come and told Doug because he knew Doug would be interested and would pay for the information.

Somewhere far ahead of both Spur and Doug Chandler, Russ Dolan grinned, felt the bundles of absolutely wonderful cash money inside his shirt, and for the first time in days, laughed out loud. He was off on the best part of his life so far, and from here on, with all that cash, it could only get better and better.

After several miles of following the horse trail upstream through the brush and woods along the banks of the river, he saw smoke ahead and remembered. One Eyed Louie's Inn, he called it. A rough conglomeration of a series of small buildings that were made of logs and had been added on to year by year. Louie was a big guy with a black patch over one eye. A rough bastard, as Doug remembered.

It was well after noon by the time Russ approached the place. It looked innocent enough. No rigs or horses tied out front. He wanted to meet as few people as possible.

Louie growled at Russ when he came in the door. Louie wore his usual costume: tops of his long underwear and a dirty pair of pants that cracked when he bent them at the knees. He had a full beard and wild hair. His unwashed face showed several sores that he picked at from time to time.

Russ carried his six-gun in his hand and Louie snorted. "Don't need no fucking gun to get a meal, if'n that's what you want. My old woman's got some rabbit stew cooked up proper and enough bread and wild berry jam to fill up a regiment. You want dinner or not?"

Russ nodded and sat at a makeshift table on a wooden bench. The food was more than he could eat even sopping up the liquid with chunks of fresh baked white bread.

He gave Louie a dollar for the dinner, but the

one-eyed-man kept holding out his hand.

"Two dollars for dinner this side the river. You can afford it or you wouldn't be here."

Russ growled himself this time and handed over another dollar bill. He had taken the ones in change when he bought the horse. Five ones were all the livery man had. He carried the ones in his pocket. He wondered about shooting Louie and taking over his Inn, but changed his mind when he saw how Louie carried a derringer in his waist band. Besides, this place was too well known, too close to Fort Smith. Judge Parker's U.S. Deputy Marshals would be past here every other day heading out to sweep the interior.

He drank another cup of coffee, waved at Louie and rode away from the place glad he still had his whole skin. There was an undercurrent of violence with One-Eyed Louie that he didn't like. He wondered how many solitary travelers had gone into Louie's place and never come out again except in a bloody tarp headed for a shallow grave.

With his belly full and a canteen of fresh water looped over his saddle horn, Russ rode steadily along the track. Here and there he saw where a wagon had been dragged through the trail. If enough of them did that, soon the track would turn into a road of sorts. Twice he saw where small trees had been chopped down almost to ground level to let a wagon get through.

It was nearing dusk when Russ smelled smoke. Just over a small rise he saw the cloud of soft gray lifting from a stand of hardwood trees half-a-mile east.

Russ rode forward. The smoke must come from a cabin or a camp he couldn't see off the main track by a quarter-of-a-mile. Never would know it was there if it wasn't for the smoke. This might work for a few days.

Russ turned in at a lightly traveled trail when the road came within 500-yards of the smoke. He worked through the woods carefully and stopped when he could see the place plainly. A man came out the front door of a rough built log cabin. Russ looked again. The person he watched was a Negro man.

Damned if his luck wasn't holding. What was a nigger doing over here in the Nations unless he was running from the law?

Russ moved up cautiously, then changed his tactics and rode into the clearing a hundred-yards from the Negro man. Now he could see the man at the side of the cabin picking tomatoes.

Russ called to the man who lifted, stared a moment, then came upright with his hand near a six-gun pushed into his belt on his right hip.

The Negro man watched Russ come.

"Afternoon, looks like you been riding a piece. I'm Oliver, most folks call me Half Breed Oliver, which I is. Half Cherokee."

Russ Dolan grinned, then drew his six-gun fast and held it on the half breed before he could even bring his hand up. "Don't move your little finger or you'll be known as the dead Half-Breed Oliver."

Chapter Nine

Russ Dolan held his cocked six-gun on Half Breed Oliver's chest as he eased up to the black man and took the revolver from his belt.

"That's right, nigger man, you just stay calm and that way you keep your black hide alive. Good boy. Now, you march up there to the front door and tell your woman not to do nothing stupid like unlimbering a shotgun. Only make herself into a widow." He pushed Oliver's shoulder and headed him toward the house.

"What you want? We got nothing to steal."

"Hell, I don't need nothing. Got me plenty of cash money. Just want a place to stay the night, maybe two or three days. Need food and shelter out here in this damn wilderness. Forgot how God-awful uncivilized it is out here."

They came to the front door of the log cabin and Oliver looked over his shoulder. "I don't want no trouble. I ain't fighting you. We be glad to put you up a few days, that what you wants."

"Now you're talking like a good darkie, yeah, like a fine darkie slave. Inside, boy."

Russ looked around the inside of the cabin. It was nicely finished with a wooden floor, a ceiling and two inside walls made of sawed lumber. A kitchen stove at the far side looked to have a fire going in it, and a Negro woman in a bright red blouse and brown skirt stood there with a ladle in one hand working over the stove.

"Oliver, I declare, where are those tomatoes?" She said it before she turned around. The ladle trembled in her hand but she didn't drop it.

"Oliver?" she asked.

"This here's a friend stopped by for some supper. Reckon we got plenty, right, Bess?"

"Plenty. Hope you like fried rabbit, split potatoes and gravy, new peas and all the tomatoes you can eat."

Russ grinned and motioned for Oliver to sit at the table that was already laid out.

"Where are your kids?" Russ asked.

"I sent our one boy down to the lower pasture to pick some dewberries," Bess said turning back to the stove. "He'll be back soon. That boy never misses a meal."

Russ sat at the table where he could see both Oliver and Bess. He laid the six-gun beside the plate. There were five settings on the big plank table that had been varnished to a bright golden gloss.

"Bess, that rabbit smells fine, and them spuds must be about done by now," Russ said. "Your kitchen smells like spices and wood smoke and fresh bread like my old Ma used to make. What about the other two drops, Bess?" Russ asked. "Don't play games with me. You got three kids."

"Around somewhere," Bess said with a quick look at Russ. "When they gets hungry, they come in."

She brought a platter filled with golden fried rabbit pieces and a plate of potatoes cut lengthwise and dry fried in a big skillet. The gravy came next with the aroma of giblets and rabbit drippings good enough to make Russ's mouth water. She set on a plate of sliced fresh tomatoes and a dish of fresh green peas. Slices of bread and a crock of butter already were on the table.

They sat and ate. Russ hadn't known how hungry he was. He ate half the rabbit and potatoes. The other two ate little, only picking at their food.

Russ stretched out the meal, having another helping of the rabbit, grabbing the last leg and thigh. He finished his coffee and tapped the cup for more. Bess brought it, a calm, steady expression on her plain face. She poured it out, steaming from the wood fire, fresh boiled and smelling like cinnamon bark and a touch of cedar shavings.

"Looks like your drops done missed their supper," Russ said. He wiped his hands on his pants and stood, taking the revolver with him.

"Now for the entertainment," Russ said. "Big

mama, what was your name again?"

"Bess," she said evenly, but she shot a frantic glance at her husband.

"Bess. Good." Russ cocked the six-gun when Oliver half rose from where he sat at the table. The muzzle swung toward the Negro man. "Not you, old man, I want the woman to stand up. Come on, Bess. Up. That's the way."

Bess pushed back the chair and stood. Her face was rock hard, frozen in a neutral expression.

"Good, Bess. Good. Now I want to see what kind of tits you're hiding under that fancy red blouse of yours. Strip off that top and show me your swingers. Bet they big as watermelons." Russ grinned in anticipation. His eyes gleamed and a drip of saliva came out of his mouth and ran down his chin.

Oliver started to rise again and Russ lifted the weapon so it aimed at Oliver's head.

"Another half-an-inch out of that chair and your head just gonna explode all over this room, boy. You want that?"

Oliver let out a long breath and settled back in the chair. He had swung his legs around for a quick dive at the gunman. He sat but left his legs in the same position, away from the table.

Russ looked back at Bess. Her hands hung at her sides. He drew a knife from his boot in one swift motion, brought it up and caught the neck of her blouse. The sharp knife blade sliced through the cloth and down to the hem without touching her skin. The blouse gaped open revealing the rounded sides of her dark breasts.

"Yeah, good black stuff. Heard about black pussy all my life, but I never had me none. Guess that's gonna be taken care of right now. Ain't it Bess, sweet black pussy girl?"

She stared at the far wall.

"Bess, I ain't gonna hurt you. Just a little poking and some grabbing and sucking. Hell, you been fucked three, four-hundred times. What's one more?"

Russ reached up and pulled the blouse off her shoulders and her arms throwing it on the floor. Her big breasts sagged from their weight and had soft, darker colored nipples. She tried to turn away.

"Don't do that!" Russ barked. "No fucking black pussy gonna turn away from Russ Dolan."

He grabbed one of her breasts with his hand and squeezed it until Bess screeched in pain. Russ grinned and stared at the woman, forgetting for a moment the man in the chair. It was the chance Oliver had waited for.

Oliver came out of his chair like a charging cougar, his hands reaching out like rapiers. In two quick steps he was on the man. His right hand fisted and came down on Oliver's gun wrist like a sledgehammer, slamming the weapon from his fingers. It fell to the floor and the sudden jolt dropped the hammer and the revolver went off. The .44 lead slug smashed into the wall. The sound of the shot in the closed cabin sounded like an artillery piece going off.

Bess pulled her hands up to cover her ears.

Oliver's charge carried him into Russ, blasting

145

him halfway across the room. Russ fell and Oliver smashed down on top of his back pinning him face down on the floor. He grabbed Russ by the hair and slammed his head twice on the plank floor. Russ turned his head enough so it hit on the side. He screamed in pain.

"Stop it, you bastard!" Russ bellowed. He tried to push off the heavier form. He got one hand free and punched Oliver in the face. Oliver never noticed the blow. He caught Russ's ears and used them as handles and smashed Russ's face twice into the floor boards, mashing his nose, bringing gouts of blood and a continuing scream of agony.

Russ heaved with all his strength and bucked Oliver off him. He sat up trying to get the blood out of his eyes. Oliver leaped to his feet and swung one heavy booted foot at the outlaw who had tried to rape his wife.

"Never again!" Oliver shouted over and over again. He kicked Russ in the face with all the furious strength within him. His heavy leather toe caught Russ under the chin and snapped his head back hard. There was a crack and Russ slammed to the rear sprawling on his back on the floor.

Oliver surged forward, dropped with both knees on Russ's chest and heard two ribs crack and dagger downward. Oliver grabbed Russ by his hair and pounded his head into the hard floor boards a dozen times until the back of it was a mass of bloody pulp.

"Enough, Oliver," Bess said softly. "He's already dead."

Oliver sat astride the man and stared at his

head, then remembered the terrible cracking sound when he kicked him. He took a deep breath and stood. He scooped up Bess's ruined blouse and put it around her shoulders.

"Never again, Bess. Never again am I gonna let one man or six rape you like those others did. I'll die first. Mark my words. Never again, Bess."

She put her arms around him and held him like a child. Then she kissed his forehead and he moved away.

He looked at the man who called himself Russ Dolan. "Bess, you go find the kids. Tell them they did good by hiding when a stranger come with a gun. Bring them back for supper. I'll have this trash out of here by then. Run along."

She leaned in and kissed Oliver gently on his lips, her smile a glorious outpouring. Then she hurried out the rear door.

When she came back, twenty-minutes later, it was growing dark. She had the three kids with her and peered into the big room and saw that the body was gone.

The planks had been scrubbed clean. There was another batch of split potatoes in the fry pan. She rustled up more food and let them share the rest of the rabbit.

When Oliver came into the cabin, it had just turned dark. He lit two lamps and had a cup of scalding coffee as he watched the three children, two boys and a younger girl, finish their supper. The oldest was 12, the youngest, eight.

"Hello in the cabin!" a voice boomed from outside.

Oliver lifted the double barrelled shotgun from the pegs near the door and angled it outside as he unlatched the outward swinging door.

"Ahoy outside," Oliver said, letting the shotgun command the area directly in front. "Who's there and what do you want?"

He heard a chuckle. "I'm Chandler. I got no gun on you, so take it easy with that scattergun. I can see it in the light from your lamps. I mean you no harm."

Bess blew out both lamps and Oliver went through the door like a black shadow into the faint smudgy moonlight. He held the shotgun covering the man on the horse ten-feet away.

"Who's Chandler and what do you want?"

"Mind if I step down so we can talk?" the man asked.

"Slide down on this side of your mount, and keep your hands free. I don't like trouble, but I don't back away from it."

"I've heard that about you, Cherokee Oliver. Hear you're a good man. An honest one. Fact is, I'm hunting a man who rode away from me with some of my goods. You seen a lone rider out this way this afternoon? One-Eyed Louie said he came this direction."

"Mr. Chandler, I'm off the trail. Mostly nobody knows I'm here, which is fine by me. I don't bother them and the owlhoots don't bother me. What this outlaw steal off you?"

"Enough to make me unhappy. You see any sign of a tall, slim man? He's riding a chestnut mare from what I hear. Something like that chestnut in your corral."

"Don't recollect seeing nobody today. Been working hard getting some corn planted down in my plowed land in the little valley out here. Cleared the land two year ago."

"Not worried about your farming, Oliver. Was Dolan here, or wasn't he? I'll swear to Judge Parker that's his chestnut mare. Tomorrow we might just find a new grave hereabouts."

Chandler paused. "Would be neighborly of you to invite me in for some coffee. I been on a long ride."

"Fresh out of coffee, Chandler. I told you what I told you. Time for you to ride out." The shotgun kept Chandler covered.

"Look, Dolan was no friend of mine. I don't care if he's dead and fed to your hogs. I just want my goods back that he stole. You don't tell me what happened to Dolan tonight, I'll be back tomorrow with six of Judge Parker's Deputy Marshals and we'll take this little place of yours apart until we find what I'm looking for. I know the judge. He's a fair man, but he's tough. He's especially mean when it comes to murder."

"Mount up, Mr. Chandler. You'll be riding. You try to come back tonight, I'll be waiting somewhere along the trail and I'll shoot and find out who I killed when the sun comes up. Best you be riding and keep riding back to the ferry."

Chandler mounted and kept his hands well away from the six-gun on his hip.

"You haven't seen the last of me, Half Breed Oliver. Dolan won't get away with stealing from me, and neither will you. When I come back tomorrow you have the goods ready and waiting for me, and we won't take it any further."

He swung the horse around and walked it slowly out the unsure trail toward the main track.

Oliver watched him go, then slipped forward with the shotgun, hammers both cocked, until he could hear the squeak of the saddle leather and the steady clopping of the horse's hooves. He followed Chandler silently all the way to the main trail and heard him move upstream. He'd probably go to One-Eyed Louie's to stay overnight. Then he'd be back in the morning.

On his way back to his cabin, Oliver rigged a thin wire across the trail chest-high for a man on a horse. Impossible to see at night, and hard to see in the daytime. He'd take it down at sunup.

Back at the cabin, he went to the lean-to beside the corral and dug out the saddlebags from the chestnut mare. He'd thrown them in the corner and piled hay on top of them when he unsaddled the dead man's mount. There had been a small roll of five-dollar bills in Dolan's pants pocket, and another sheaf of them in his shirt. Oliver had taken the money when he buried the body. Now he picked up the saddlebags and carried them into the cabin and dropped them on the table.

Bess had put the kids to bed in the back room. She stared at the saddlebags and at the two wads of five dollar bills.

"This Dolan, he steal the man's money?"

"Looks like."

Bess was good at doing numbers. She sat down at the table and counted the five dollar Federal notes.

"Twenty-seven of them," she said. That's a hundred and thirty-five dollars. More cash money than we've ever seen in our whole married life."

"Not ours," Oliver said. "Even after what he did and tried to do to you, the money ain't ours."

He upended the saddlebags and shook them out. Two bundles of greenbacks fell out.

"Good Lord!" Bess said. She crossed herself even though she wasn't Catholic. "Good Lord, those are ten and twenty dollar bills. Must be several thousand dollars worth."

Oliver shook his head. "What did we do to bring all of this trouble down on our heads? That's killing kind of money. That Chandler would kill all five of us to get that much money. For that kind of money he'll be back tomorrow morning with six hired gunmen and they'll tear our place apart and cut me up into small pieces. Come daylight, I want you and the kids five miles up that little creek out there all the way to the spring. You watch your back trail. Any riders come your way, you hide your tracks and you fade into the brush."

Oliver shook his head. "Lord above. I don't know what I done to deserve this. I killed a man, but he deserved killing. He would have done my Bess and then shot us both. I know that for gospel. Lordy, wish I'd been born more Cherokee than Negro, then I'd know how to handle this kind of trouble."

Outside Half Breed Oliver's cabin, Spur McCoy

lay in the early evening darkness. He'd moved silently as a Chiricahua Apache through the underbrush until he was within 20-yards of the cabin and in time to hear most of the conversation between Oliver and Doug Chandler.

So a man named Russ Dolan had stolen something from Chandler. He figured Chandler had stopped by here and that now Oliver had whatever the item was that had been stolen. If it was money, a lot of money say from a train robbery, then Chandler would be back in the morning. First he'd need to ride into Fort Smith and get help, hired help in the form of gunmen from some of the local saloons.

He was bluffing about Judge Parker. Spur guessed that Chandler wanted to stay as far away from the hanging judge as possible.

Spur had bought some provisions at One-Eyed Louie's place when he stopped there for supper. Now he chewed on a strip of jerky and some hard biscuits and sipped from his canteen. His horse was more than a quarter-of-a-mile away. He had one blanket with him, but the night was going to be warm. He'd pull back 50-yards and make himself a small cold camp and catch a few hours of sleep.

With dawn he wanted to slip into Oliver's place without getting shot and have a long talk with the man. They had struck up a quick friendship the last time they met. If he was lucky, the Indian half of Oliver would cooperate with Spur.

Doug Chandler would be a problem. Oliver had said he wanted to move, but it took a man some time to get ready. He had livestock and poultry. He might want to wait for some crops or garden to produce. No chance he'd want to move before morning.

Spur pulled back silently, not cracking a twig or letting a branch of the luxuriant hardwood undergrowth swish back. He found a good spot and dug a place for his hips in the soft earth, and lay down on his back. Spur set his mental alarm clock to awaken him at 4:30. It never failed. He looked for the cowboy's clock high in the heavens but couldn't even see the north star through the canopy of hardwood bright green leaves over his head.

Spur shrugged and went to sleep.

Chapter Ten

A sound not natural to the woodsy surroundings awoke Spur McCoy in his brushy camp. It was still dark. He lifted on one elbow and listened again. He heard the sound of an unhappy cow, then the creak of leather. A horseman was moving.

The sounds came from the direction of Half Breed Oliver's place. Spur took his Spencer rifle and moved through the woods the way his Indian friends had schooled him. When he lay down in the fringes of brush at the edge of the clearing at Oliver's place, he knew what was happening.

Three children, the oldest about 12, moved upstream along a small creek. One led an unhappy milk cow. The smallest rode on a horse. Two more horses were led by Oliver's wife. On both horses were sacks filled with something.

Soiled Dove

If Oliver expected trouble he was getting his family out of the way. As Spur watched, he saw the mixed blood man come jogging down the trail from the main road. He wore a filled holster that was tied down to his thigh. A second revolver showed pushed in the right side of his belt. Oliver was ready for trouble.

Spur waited until the family was out of sight in the darkness up the small valley to the rear of the house. A few stragglers of gray mist evaporated with the coming dawn and then the light devoured all that was left of the darkness and it was daylight.

Spur gave the call of a mourning dove and watched Oliver straighten up from where he had been near the cabin. He frowned, shook his head and went back to working on the door.

Spur gave the call again and this time Oliver laughed.

"That's the worst imitation of a mourning dove call I've ever heard. But it got my attention. Damn, I wish I was more Cherokee. Come on out, whoever you are. I won't shoot anybody dumb enough to make that bad a call."

Spur eased up from where he lay and held both arms straight out from his sides as he came out of the brush. He carried the Spencer rifle in one hand by the end of the barrel.

"Well now," Oliver said when he recognized Spur. "The Federal man, Spur McCoy, who is somewhat more than human. How come you up and out here so early?"

Spur walked up to the cabin and took the

Negro-Cherokee's hand when he held it out. The grip was firm, his smile genuine.

"Just happened to be in your neighborhood, figured you was good for a hot cup of coffee."

"Usual, but not today. You saw my family leave?"

"Did."

"I got some troubles."

"I know. I followed Doug Chandler from Fort Smith and heard most of your exchange with him last night. I'd guess that Mr. Dolan is no longer a problem for anyone."

Oliver wiped one dark hand over his face that showed only touches of the Cherokee lineage and shook his head. "I can't afford to say yea or nay, about that. What I do know is that your Mr. Chandler gonna be back here about noon with enough shooters to make me look like a walking dead man."

"They'll have two of us to take out," Spur said lifting the Spencer.

Oliver looked up quickly. "You'd do that?" He rubbed his face with his hand again. "No questions? No wonder about Russ Dolan? No asking what it was Dolan must have stolen?"

"No questions. You want to fort up here, or pull back to a defensive position with rifles to take them by surprise?"

Oliver grinned. "You musta been in the big war. Talkin' like a soldier."

"Did my part. They might torch you."

Oliver nodded. "Me and Bess worked most of the night taking things out and stashing them in the woods. Gonna move anyway. Figure I can get the rest of what I want to save hidden before they get here."

Spur slung the Spencer over his shoulder. "Let's get at it. Give us more time to fort up. Save out a pair of shovels. We might want to move some dirt and dig a hole."

Oliver grinned and scratched his head. "You always . . ." He stopped. "I mean are you always so . . ." He stopped again and chuckled. "Yep, I reckon you are. Never met me no white man like you before, Spur McCoy." He held out his hand. Spur shook it and they walked in the front door of the cabin.

Three hours later, Spur and Oliver put down their shovels and looked at their handiwork. They were on a sharp rise behind the cabin and slightly away from the main trail. They had cut some brush and taken down one four-inch tree with an axe. Now they had a perfect field of fire at the trail coming to the cabin, along both sides of the structure and half of the space across the front.

They had dug into the soft soil behind a pair of rocks that extended two-feet out of the ground. One firing slot was between the rocks, and another on the far side of the largest boulder. They stood on their knees and were at the right level to fire on the area below.

For protection to their rear they had rolled in a number of foot-thick rocks and stacked them up forming a two-foot barricade. With the two-foot deep hole, they had four-feet of protection all the way around.

157

"About noon?" Spur asked.

"Depends if he rode back to town last night, or stayed at One-Eyed Louie's place. About a two-hour ride to the ferry from here."

By eleven o'clock, they were in their fort. They had emptied the cabin of everything that would move and that Oliver wanted to save. Oliver had moved his farm wagon a quarter-of-a-mile up the creek before Spur got there.

They had jerky and two loaves of fresh bread and two canteens of water, as well as a big slab of ham. They could hold out all day if Chandler wanted to force the issue.

"He might not even put up a fight," Spur said.

"Maybe. My guess, we won't be shooting at him to advertise that we're here. He'll go a little crazy, might burn down the place. But I don't mind that. I'd just as soon not have to shoot down anybody he brings along."

Spur nodded. "Killing a man is nothing to take lightly. Sometimes it has to be done. Best is to try to forget about it. If it was a case of him or you dying, it's an easier task."

Oliver nodded. He looked at Spur for a long minute, then rubbed his face and glanced away. He started to say something, then stopped.

By eleven-thirty they could see four horsemen coming up the trail from the main road toward the cabin.

"Chandler could probably find only four men who were sober at that time of morning in the saloons," Spur said. He motioned to Oliver's single shot Winchester. "I'll let you take the first shot.

You might decide you don't want them to burn down your cabin after all. You built it a log at a time, I'd imagine."

Oliver nodded. "Deed I did. Bess helped some."

Soon the riders below came out of the trees into the clearing and Spur heard a man's voice call. He and Oliver were a little over a hundred-yards from the cabin.

"Oliver, you can come out now, with the money. You know what I want. I can get as nasty as I have to. I'm not leaving without what's rightfully mine."

The two men hunkered down and waited. Directly overhead were branches from trees that grew at each side. Smoke from their rounds would blow toward them and into the branches making it almost impossible from below to locate the source of the rifle fire by spotting the smoke.

A six-gun cracked below and a window shattered. It was the one in front and Spur saw Oliver wince.

Chandler motioned with his revolver and a man dismounted and ran to the cabin door. He jerked it open and ducked behind the wall. Nothing happened. The man peered around the edge of the door, then rushed inside.

He came back a minute or two later.

"Nobody here. Place has been stripped clean. Looks like they done moved out."

"Overnight they moved?" Chandler asked not believing it. "We didn't see any wagon tracks. Moving out would have loaded a farm wagon heavy. No deep tracks anywhere." Chandler shook his head.

"Oliver didn't move, he's trying to fool us. I'd bet if we start to burn down his cabin here, he'll surface in a rush."

Chandler sat his horse thinking. He waved at one of the other riders.

"Go up that little valley and look for wagon tracks and fresh horse sign. They're here somewhere.

"Hugh, get some brush and put it up against the doorway there. Let's torch this place. He won't like that."

Oliver watched with growing anger. "Hoped they'd think we had moved out and that they'd ride away. Ain't gonna be that easy."

He levered the round into the chamber and angled his Winchester over the rock aimed at the man below gathering fire wood and brush.

The slap of the big caliber rifle going off sent a shock wave of sound down the valley. The bullet preceded it, bored through the brush gatherer's left thigh and punched him six-feet away from the cabin door.

Oliver pulled the Winchester back out of sight and watched below. Chandler dove off his horse and ran behind the side of the cabin and out of sight.

The other rider kicked his horse in the same direction and was soon lost to view. The wounded man screamed at them, then began crawling and hopping on one foot to get out of the line of fire.

On the rise, the two men waited. Below at the cabin, the three remained hidden from sight.

After five minutes, a voice bellowed from below.

"Oliver, you have the advantage. Take an army to dig you out from up there. We're leaving, but we'll be back. If you haven't decided to move out of here, you better. You'll be watching over your shoulder every day for the rest of your life wondering when I'll show up to gun you down."

Spur lifted his rifle and put four rounds into the ground in front of where the horses grazed. They spooked, running wildly into the brush and away from the spraying of dirt and rocks. One man ran after them.

Spur didn't fire. Another man angled from the last bit of protection from the cabin and ran into the brush. Only one remained, and Spur figured he was Doug Chandler. He was shorter than the other two.

The third one then ran for the woods, almost got there when he stumbled and fell. He turned and looked at the slope before he surged to his feet and vanished into the brush.

Spur had reloaded the tube that held the rounds and pushed it back into the Spencer's stock so he had eight rounds again.

"I'll circle down and toward the trail and make sure that they get moving that way, then send them on their journey with some .52 caliber reminders."

"I don't think you have to do that," Oliver said grinning. "They sounded convinced."

"True, but I'd just like to do it as a public service. I'll be back. You want to load up your wagon now that your belongings are all out of the cabin?"

"Might. I need to talk to you first. Got myself a small problem."

"I'll be back in an hour or so."

When Spur got back from his herding job on the Doug Chandler gang, he found a wagon in front of the cabin already half loaded. A team of horses was hitched to the front and Bess and the kids brought boxes and gunny sacks of goods down to the wagon from the hill and out of the brush.

Oliver had moved the kitchen range to the door of the cabin. He waved and Spur gave him a hand. Together they carried the small four plate cook-stove to the wagon and settled it into a place that had been saved for it.

Oliver pointed Spur into some shade and they sat down.

"Like I said, Mr. McCoy, I got myself one small problem."

Oliver reached inside his shirt and brought out two bundles wrapped with brown paper and tied with string. He tossed them to Spur. The Secret Service agent pulled back the brown paper on the corner of one package and then the other.

They were used U.S. banknotes. Spur looked up. "About ten-thousand dollars worth here?" Spur asked.

Oliver rubbed his dark face with one hand and nodded.

"Somehow I'm not surprised. You knew what Chandler was hunting, but you didn't say a word about it. Would you have let me walk away from here with all that stolen money?"

"Can't say. I didn't have to decide, did I? So what are you going to do with it?"

"My Cherokee half says take the damned money and get as far back in the Territory as possible. Damn strange, isn't it? If I took the money and ran inside, I wouldn't have anyplace to spend it. I'd be no better off than if I don't take it.

"Then my Negro side jumps up and I remember my ma who was born and raised a slave, and she would say: 'Son, ain't your money. Ain't no business of yours. Get rid of it fast as your black hands can do the job.'"

Spur drew designs on the bare earth in front of him with a stick. He rubbed the design out and scratched the figure $10,000 in the dirt.

"That's a lot of cash money, Oliver. Your kids and your wife wouldn't have to worry about going hungry, ever again. You could move into some small town and let the kids go to school and buy your Bess some pretty clothes and make out like you were a gentleman. You'd have enough money to last you the rest of your life."

Oliver took a deep breath and stared out over the green valley. "Yeah, I thought about that. Thought about going back to Georgia and buying the little farm my Pa used to slave on. Thought about finding the Cherokee Nation and trying to help my Pa's people. Thought about a hundred different things that I could do.

"Trouble was, I couldn't do none of them. You gave me that hundred dollars last week. More money than I ever seen before. It'll do us all good in a few months. I kin spend it a little at a time,

get Bess that dress, better clothes for the youn-
guns, maybe find a school somewhere.

"Hell, I don't *need no damn ten-thousand dollars.*"

Spur turned the bundles of money over. "Right,
Oliver, it's a lot of money. Average working man
in a town makes about thirty-five dollars a month.
That's four hundred and twenty dollars for a
whole year's work. Ten thousand dollars would be
almost 24 years of that man's work."

"That's stolen money, Mr. McCoy. I can't have
no part of it."

"It's not only stolen, it's been twice stolen,
maybe three times, depending how you count. Actually, it belongs to some gent in Kansas City who
tried to buy a big ranch north of Fort Smith."

"He'll be wanting it back."

Spur put a line through the drawing of the
$10,000 in the dust. "So you're telling me you
don't want to keep the money."

Oliver watched his wife and kids loading house-
hold things into the wagon. Bess packed in everything neatly to conserve space.

"Yes sir, that's what I'm saying."

Spur grinned. "Good." He unwrapped one bundle of bills and began counting out the fives and
tens until he had a stack of $1,000. He straight-
ened them until they lay neat and straight in one
pile. Then he wrapped the rest of the bundle up
and tied it with string as it had been.

"When valuables get lost, Oliver, there usually
is a reward for finding them. In most cases, a ten-
percent gift is considered to be fair. That means

that for finding this stolen ten-thousand dollars, you get a reward of one-thousand dollars. It's not dirty money, it's not something that's tainted or evil or bad. It's a thousand dollars in good United States Notes, legal tender for all bills public or private."

Oliver shivered. He looked at the stack of money but didn't say a word or move.

"Bess?" Spur called. The Negro woman looked up, nodded when she saw Spur motion her to come over and walked to where he and her husband sat.

"Bess, Oliver here just did a good deed for some gentleman in Kansas City. He recovered the man's lost ten-thousand dollars. A reward of ten-percent is granted to you and Oliver for this wonderful action. I want to put this thousand dollars in your care, since Oliver seems a little stunned right now to take charge of it."

The black woman stared at Spur a moment, her face slack and serious.

"No tricks, Bess. No conditions attached. Nobody will know what you did or that you have the money. It's yours to do with whatever you want to do."

Bess's face cracked and a big grin exploded over it. Then she shrilled a high yell of delight. She picked up the bills with total awe, and held them to her bosom. Then she screeched again in absolute joy.

She sat down beside Oliver, reached in and kissed his cheek.

Bess looked at Spur. "We thank you, Mr. Mc-

Coy. You're a good man. Oliver is a good man. The two of you make one mighty strong team. Oliver and me will take good care of this money. More than we ever hoped to have in our whole lives. We'll put it to good use, believe me. Now, back to work. If'n we want to get this wagon loaded and out of here before dark, we gots to get our asses in motion. Don't want to be around nowhere when that Mr. Chandler come back with more of his guns."

The six of them worked the rest of the afternoon without stopping for more than cold water and jerky to chew on. By four o'clock they had the last of the goods on the wagon, including a chicken coop on the top of the load holding a dozen hens and fifteen young ones. In another few weeks they would be ready to make fryers.

Oliver took off his hat and slashed at the sweat on his forehead. "Does it," he said. "No crops to speak of. Gonna be lots more tomatoes, but the next people who claim the cabin can use them. Lost two chickens, but they'll make out."

Two milk cows on rope tethers stood waiting behind the wagon. Bess climbed on the seat on top of a wooden crate and picked up the reins.

Oliver rode the chestnut mare. He patted the deep red animal with three white stockings.

"No sense letting her go to waste out here in the Territories," Oliver said. The kids walked beside the wagon as it moved out the trail.

Spur stayed with them until they hit the main track that angled generally west and upstream on the Arkansas. The way here was wider, as if more wagons had used it.

"There's a better road leading north and west about fifteen-miles upstream," Oliver said. "Leads into the least settled part of the Territories by the whites, but it's got a passel of Indians in there. I figure I can get along with them. Lot of them know I'm half Cherokee by now."

Oliver rode close to Spur and held out his hand. "Appreciate what you done for me. Oh, about Dolan. He held us all under his gun first night he came and we fed him. Then he went for Bess. I swore I'd never let another man touch her, after what happened a few days ago. I caught Dolan off guard and tackled him and smashed his head on the floor. He paid for his sins, whatever they were.

"Ain't proud of that savage few minutes. I swore never again for Bess and he was about to do her and I went kind of crazy."

Spur pumped the man's hand again. "None of my business, Oliver. I don't have any authority over here. I think it all worked out about right. I'll see that the rest of this money gets back to its rightful owner. You watch your step and keep that cash hidden away where nobody would think to look for it. I hear there's a passel of outlaws in this country."

Oliver nodded. He tapped the six-gun at his hip and another one stuck in his belt. "That's why I carry both of these and they're loaded with six rounds each."

Spur waved and headed downstream toward

the ferry. He should be there just before dark and the last run across the river. He wanted to turn in the $9,000 to Sheriff Grimm before it went through any more hands.

Chapter Eleven

On his ride back to the ferry, Spur McCoy reviewed the case. He had recovered the ranch payment money. It would go to Teasdale or to the prospective buyer. He had no idea what the status of the sale of the ranch might be. He'd have to check with Teasdale who was a sharp old boy.

Spur had nothing on the bearer bonds, the $100,000 worth, the largest single element in this train robbery. That could have been the motivation for it and the rest of the stacks of money just serendipity.

The $20,000 in new bank bills hadn't started to surface anywhere. Which would show that the robbers weren't totally stupid.

The kidnapped daughter of the governor hadn't turned up yet, dead or alive, but some progress in finding her had been made. Maybe if it progressed to a money-for-girl exchange, they'd do better. Whoever set that one up was clever and lucky.

He caught the last ferry, paid his dime for the horse and a nickel for himself, and soon was across the river and riding down Main Street to the sheriff's office.

It was a little after eight o'clock. The sheriff was there doing some paperwork.

"You still working?" Spur asked.

"No, I'm playing slap and tickle with a big titted whore."

"Good, don't like to disturb a man having fun at his hobby."

Spur dropped the two packets of bills on Sheriff Grimm's desk.

"I'm bought, who do you want me to kill?" the sheriff asked, riffling through the bills. "How much here?"

"Not sure, somewhere around nine thousand. It's probably the cash from the Teasdale farm sale, but I can't be sure."

"Teasdale. That's what bothers me. The old man is straight as a Cherokee arrow."

"Take your word for it. That don't account for his son-in-law, Doug Chandler."

"Chandler. Trust him about as far as I can spit with my mouth stitched shut."

"He was the one trying to get this money. Claimed a man called Russ Dolan stole it from him. Unfortunately, Mr. Dolan is now three-feet under the sod somewhere. A citizen turned in this money after we persuaded Mr. Chandler to re-treat."

"With hot lead?"

"Good guess. Let's count this and then you can give me a receipt. I want you to hold the cash until we find out who is the legal owner."

They called in a deputy and the three of them counted the money twice. The total was $8,965.

"Whoever stole it didn't have time to spend much of it," Sheriff Grimm said. Spur didn't say anything about the 10-percent he had given to Half Breed Oliver. That was government business done in the Territories and out of the sheriff's jurisdiction.

"So, if Chandler was involved in the ranch sale money, which was in that Railway Express car, is he in on the rest of the robbery and kidnapping and bond theft?" Sheriff Grimm asked.

Spur held up his hands. "I wish I knew. At least we have a suspect we can watch. I need to take another ride out to the Teasdale ranch and talk to the old man. Let him know what's going on, and get the name of the man who he supposedly sold his ranch to. We probably should notify him about the money. I'll tell Teasdale, as well."

The money went in the big safe in the sheriff's office. Spur pushed the receipt for the money into his wallet and hurried out the door. He was starved and hoped the restaurants were still open.

One was.

After he ate, he wandered up the slope where he could see the Lowell mansion. The same two lights were on that he had seen before. No carriage or buggy waited out front. He walked back to his hotel. He could use a good sleep in a soft bed.

As he came through the lobby, he saw Lillian reading a magazine. She smiled when she saw him, winked, put down the reading matter and went up the stairs as he asked for his key at the desk. There were no messages. When he walked up the steps to the second floor, he found Lillian waiting beside his room 212 door. He smiled.

"About time you came back. Where you been the last couple of days? I kept trying to see you but you were never in."

"Busy."

"I bet. Some redhead probably with tiny tits and a shriveled up cunnie."

"Hey, right, Lillian, you must know her pretty well." He unlocked the room and they went in. Nobody else was in the hall.

He locked the door, turned the key halfway around so it couldn't be pushed out from the outside and set a chair back under the doorknob to double lock it.

Spur turned and watched her. What a lovely young woman. Breasts high and full, a pretty face that right then had a curious grin.

"Now, Lillian, should we discuss the international situation, or concentrate more on the troubles of the republican party in getting its message out to the voting public?"

Lillian giggled and started unbuttoning her blouse.

"You are funny, and a tease. Why don't you tell

me what you've been doing all this time." She smiled. "Do that as I undress you. Then we'll find something even more interesting to do."

Spur sat on the bed and let her undress him. He was tired, but not that tired. She left his short underwear for last and pulled them down with delightful ministrations. When his erection jolted out of the cloth she squealed and pounced on it, battling with it until she won. She gave it a quick kiss and pushed Spur down flat on the bed.

Lillian gave a little cry and began a slow, gyrating strip tease that showed off her charms to the ultimate. Her blouse dropped off her arms and to the floor. She lifted her chemise to show the bottom swell of her breasts then dropped it. She danced in front of him grinding her hips and shaking her shoulders and at last her chemise whipped up and off showing her big breasts and all of their fancy swinging and bouncing that brought a cheer from Spur.

She hung over him, dropping one breast to his face. He licked the nipple, then kissed it and opened his mouth as she lowered her orb into it. Spur chewed for a minute or two, biting the rock hard nipple that had sprung tall.

She moaned and fell on top of him, grinding her hips against his erection.

Then she lifted up, ripped her skirt and bloomers off in one swift motion and lay on him again.

"Me on top the first time," she pleaded. She lifted off his hips, pulled his erection to the right position and lowered herself thrusting him deeply within her ready sheath.

"Oh, damn!" she crooned. "Oh, yes! This is the place, this is the way, just good old fashioned fucking, a man and a girl getting it done the right fucking way!"

She moved then, gently forward and back as the lubrication began working. She sighed, then lifted and began to ride him like a young stallion on his first mare in heat.

"Yes, yes, yes," she crooned. She tried to kiss his lips but she couldn't stretch up high enough. Her movements went faster and faster and her breath came in gulps and gasps. Then she shuddered and stopped moving. Her whole body trembled and then vibrated and jolted as the spasms of release tore through her. She moaned again and climaxed another time as she shook and bounced over him. Her eyes were closed and she wore an expression of ultimate pleasure.

She rested a moment, then a third climax ripped her apart and she squealed and moaned and panted until he thought she would be used up and shrivel into nothing.

Slowly her hips began to move again. She opened her eyes and her hips worked up and down on him. His hips thrust upward in response and soon they set up a cooperative movement and he felt his own desire mounting.

He made it last as long as possible. Pounding hard, then taking a rest when the pressure began to build too high. When it eased off he began again and at last rolled her over without coming out and slammed his hips against hers, driving her upward on the bed each time until he could stand it no longer. He vaporized, blasting into her in the ultimate primal act and then collapsing on top of her driving her slender body deep into the mattress.

She lay there exhausted herself. Her hands touched his back, then dropped at her sides.

Ten minutes later they both sat up on the side of the bed. His hands found her breasts and played with them.

"That was beautiful. You know how to make a woman do the best she's ever done."

"You were fantastic. You know just what to do for me."

They grinned at each other, then she rubbed his chest. "Hey, talk around town is that you're some kind of a detective, a Federal detective. Is that right?"

"Something like that."

"I don't understand. What is there to do here in town for a man like you?"

"A detective detects."

"Oh," she said not understanding.

He laughed. "Lillian, I'm here working on the train robbery case. It's no secret. I'm trying to find the men who did it."

"Have you found them?"

"No. Not yet, but I will."

"Maybe I can help you. I hear a lot working around the hotel."

"Good. Who did the robbery?"

Lillian grinned. "Silly, I don't know. I meant maybe I could see who comes and goes, things like that."

Dirk Fletcher

"Maybe."

"You let me know who you want me to watch, or whatever. I'd like to help."

"Good. The best way you can help right now is on your hands and knees and let those two marvelous tits hang down in my face. I love your floppers."

"They love you. Just don't bite so hard you make them bleed. Hey, you haven't spanked me yet either. I love to get spanked until my little fanny is red. Makes me just hotter than all day in hell."

"I'll remember that."

She went on her hands and knees and he lay back moving under her. "Most beautiful sight in the world," he said.

"Shut up and start chewing," she said.

Later, he pushed her down on her stomach and affectionately spanked her round little bottom until it glowed pink. He was ready to stop when she begged him for more spanks. She soon climaxed, rolled over top of him, humped her hips against him until she whimpered and then relaxed so much he thought she had passed out.

After the third go-round that night she sat up and began to dress. "I have to go. Can't stay all night. Love to, but I got to go. I'll try to see you tomorrow night. You be here?"

"If I can be. Remember, I'm trying to get some work done, too."

She nodded, shrugged into her clothing and went to the door.

"It's late, maybe I should walk you to where you're going," Spur said. "Almost midnight. You

176

could get robbed or roughed up out there."

He pulled on his pants quickly, then his boots and shirt.

She worried about it a moment, then shook her head. "No, that's thoughtful of you, but I'll be fine. I have a derringer in my reticule. Nobody will bother me."

He finished dressing and opened the door for her. "If you're sure, I'll let you go."

She reached up and kissed his lips gently, then hurried out the door.

Spur strapped on his gunbelt, made sure she was down the hall, then he followed her. He was curious where she had to go so suddenly. It was as if she had just remembered some date she had.

He saw her from the top of the stairs go out the hotel's front door and hurried after her. She never looked behind. He followed her down a block, then she turned right into the residential section and went two more blocks and over two. She walked directly to the back door of a small white house on Third Avenue and went in without knocking.

Spur took down the number of the house, 426 Third Avenue, and walked back to the hotel. He took a look at the big dipper and saw it showed just about midnight. He wondered where she had to go in such a rush. He'd find out tomorrow, check out that house, or find out who lived there.

While he was out, Spur decided to take a look at the mansion. He walked six blocks in that direction and saw that the same two lights burned in the three story structure. Maybe they were left on all night to discourage burglars. Maybe he stayed up late counting his money. Spur stared at the lamp light for another minute, then turned around and hurried back to the hotel. With a little luck, he could still get a few hours of sleep.

The next morning over breakfast, Spur evaluated the case. The only real lead he had was Doug Chandler. Somehow, the man had obtained the money from the aborted ranch sale. To do that he would have to be in on the train robbery.

The big question remained. Was he also involved in the rest of the thefts and the kidnapping in the same robbery?

Spur went to see the local banker. He chose the largest firm, the First National Bank of Fort Smith, and talked with the man he had spoken to before, the president, Frank Baum.

"Yes, yes, we have an account here for Mr. Lowell. We used to do a lot more business with him than we do now."

"Why would he keep bearer bonds in his own house instead of a more secure area, such as your bank?"

Baum snorted. "Why? The old skinflint would think we were snooping into his goods, just to find out how much he's worth."

Baum looked around in the open area near his desk in the bank. There were no private offices. "I didn't tell you this, but I'd say that Mr. Lowell is not as flush with money as he used to be. At one time he carried fifteen to twenty-thousand dollars in a checking account with us. Now his balance is . . ." He looked around again. "Balance is in the low three figures, under five-hundred dollars. Heard about the bearer bonds he had stolen. Somehow it don't seem reasonable to me."

"Why not, Mr. Baum?"

"If you had a hundred-thousand dollars in cash in Kansas City and not a lot to do, wouldn't you take the train up there and bring it back in person? Why trust the mail or the railroad with that kind of fortune?"

"I see what you mean. A tremendous temptation for anyone who knew what was in that big envelope."

"Temptation isn't the word for it, Mr. McCoy. I'll work thirty years and never see that kind of money."

"Yes, I see what you mean. Mr. Baum, are there any other indications that Mr. Lowell might be running out of cash or at least getting somewhat low?"

"Yes sir, I'd say a couple. We don't have a stock broker here in town. Now a man like Mr. Lowell has lots of money in stocks and bonds, and now and then he'll buy and sell. I'm the closest thing to a broker in town. I buy for a few locals and sell now and then.

"Mr. Lowell used to have some business for me that way every week or so. Haven't seen a sign of him around here for six months now."

"Anything else?"

"I think so. Lowell has a party now and then in his big house. Before his wife died, it was most every week. Now he plays poker Saturday nights instead, at his place, of course. My wife and I went to a soiree up there couple of weeks ago.

"Didn't have the fancy liquors set out, the buffet was limited, not like it used to be. Conservative, almost frugal. Then on the way down that long hall, we noticed the oil paintings. He used to have more than a dozen expensive pictures there. He told me he paid over twenty-thousand-dollars for some of them. I noticed the blank spaces on the wall. Some of the most expensive paintings are gone now."

Spur nodded. "I noticed that when I was up to see him. So there did used to be paintings all along there."

"Indeed. Well, far be it from me to hit a man when he's going down, but I'd say that Mr. Lowell is starting to pinch his thousands."

"Mr. Baum, what do you know about insurance on the Railway Express goods?"

"Isn't any regular insurance. But I know for a fact that most anything that gets lost out of an express car is covered by the company. Yes, I'd say that the hundred-thousand in bonds would be covered, if the broker in Kansas City swears the bonds were sent, and Lowell can show the ripped open envelope that the post office delivered to him that was empty."

Spur reached out and shook the banker's hand. "Thanks, Mr. Baum. If I need to bank any money, I'll certainly bring it here. Oh, any results on those stolen twenty dollar bills?"

"Not hide nor hair of them, Mr. McCoy. We don't get a lot of twenties, but you can be sure we check every one. If we take one in it's our loss, right?"

"I'm afraid it would be, Mr. Baum. Stolen goods."

They shook hands again and Spur walked back to the boards outside the bank. So, the rich man might not be quite so rich after all. Still, a hundred-thousand in bearer bonds was a tidy sum.

If there actually were a hundred-thousand in that envelope. There might have been some cardboard and sheets of plain paper. Maybe one bond on the outside. The more Spur thought about it, the more improbable it became. That would take collusion by the brokerage house in Kansas City by at least two, maybe three persons. The cash split and the chances that someone would talk would be too much.

He decided he'd go under the assumption that the bonds were actually shipped, and stolen by Mr. Lowell or someone in his employ, perhaps the late unlamented Russ Dolan and two friends. If that were true, there had been plenty of time for Dolan and friends to turn over the bonds to Mr. Lowell.

What if they didn't? That brought up a whole new set of ground rules and suspects. He'd have to work on that one.

Spur set off down the boardwalk toward the sheriff's office. He hadn't talked to the Attorney General for a day-and-a-half. He wondered about any developments on the kidnapping.

He found the Attorney General and Sheriff Grimm talking in the sheriff's cubicle. They waved him in and the sheriff shut the door.

"We're making some progress on the kidnappers," Fiorello Alger said, a broad grin breaking across his face. "He wired for us to set a time and place. I had the wire sent back here. Had to threaten the local telegrapher that if he told the man anything about my being in town, I'd throw his ass in jail for twenty years.

"So, you set a date?"

"Tomorrow morning at dawn on the train heading for Fayetteville. It leaves here at six-oh-four and stops at the Casper summit for water. We're to leave the money at the summit and Amy will be released 50-yards down the tracks at the same time. Any false moves and Amy will be shot dead."

"I don't like it," Spur said.

"Neither do I," Alger agreed.

"Too many things can go wrong," Spur said.

"Out of my jurisdiction, just over the county line," Sheriff Grimm said. "Can't help you."

"You could," the Attorney General said. "If you won't, I'm empowered to press into state service five of your deputies. You might as well volunteer them."

"Hell, I only got six deputies. Two on night duty."

"I'll take four. I want three at the pickup site and one down the tracks. We'll go out on an engine or a powered hand car tonight and get there long before the kidnappers will."

"Too many men," Spur said. "You take three deputies down the tracks and leave the pickup spot to me. You take the cash to the spot on the tracks he told you, then get back on the train and pull it out. The girl should show up down the line. He won't move on the money until the train is out of sight."

"I don't like this even more."

"It'll work. One man can hide better than four. I've done this kind of job several times before."

The Attorney General sighed, looked at the Sheriff who nodded. "Oh, damnit to hell, all right, we'll try it."

"When is the next train out?" Spur asked.

"One heads north about eight tonight," the sheriff said.

"Good, I'll be on it. I'll leave the pickup of the lady up to Mr. Alger. I want the kidnapper. He's got to be tied in with the rest of the train robbery and I want to know all the details. That's why I want to go for him alone. I need him alive."

Chapter Twelve

Spur McCoy looked up at the sun. It wasn't quite noon yet, he had most of the day before he caught the train out tonight. There would be time to ride out and talk to Mr. Teasdale. He'd check with the sheriff first, then go and quiz the old rancher about the sale and the recovered money.

He stood on the boardwalk pondering the situation a moment. In the whole robbery scheme he had only one suspect but he had no solid evidence against Doug Chandler. Somehow he was tied into it, but at this point Spur had no information exactly how.

His only other possible suspect was the rich man, Gregory Lowell, who just might have tried to steal his own bearer bonds to double his money. Not much to show for a week's work.

The damned kidnapping! He had no idea how it tied in. Maybe if he could nail the man who picked up the money that would answer a lot of questions. He frowned. He hadn't thought to ask Alger if they actually were going to deliver the money, or would it be a dummy package with money on the outside? If it was not the real cash, and Spur didn't nail the guy fast, that could lead to big problems. He started to go back inside to ask Alger about it, but decided against it. They were going through with the delivery, whether real or fake it didn't matter a lot to Spur. His job was to catch the pickup man, quickly.

He wasn't enthusiastic about spending another night in the woods. He was going soft. Time was he'd spend three weeks outside on the trail, and fight during the day. He sighed. He wasn't 25 years old anymore, that was for sure.

Spur picked up a rental horse and gear at the Anderson Livery barn and an hour-and-a-half later, rode into the Triangle T ranch owned by the Teasdales.

A ranch hand met him, took his horse and tied it to the side of the corral. Spur walked up to the house. He knocked on the kitchen door and the cook came, waved him inside.

"Reckon you want to see Mr. Teasdale. He ain't feeling so chipper today. He's in the front screen porch. You find it?"

Spur said he could and headed toward the front of the house. It was well furnished, better than most of the town houses. A lot of thought, time and money had gone into the decorating and furniture. He pushed through to the screened-in porch on the front of the big house and found Dylan Teasdale sitting in a leaned back chair with his feet on a stool. A robe lay over his legs even though it was pushing eighty outside.

"Mr. Teasdale?"

The man looked around and Spur was surprised how much he had failed since he had seen him only a week before. His hair had not been combed over his balding skull. His face seemed even paler now. He looked many pounds lighter than he had been.

Teasdale squinted at Spur, then nodded. "Yeah, the government man seeing about my goods. You find that bill of sale yet and my ten-thousand dollars?"

"That's what I want to talk to you about, Mr. Teasedale. You told me before that the sale had been agreed upon and the final sales contract was coming in the mail, along with the ten-thousand dollar down payment. Is that right?"

"Indeed it is."

"So until you get that sales contract and accept it, the ranch is still yours. No sale has been completed. Would that be correct?"

"I guess. I'm no lawyer, but I got one in town."

"Could I ask you who the person is who agreed to buy your ranch?"

"Yeah. William James. Lives in Kansas City. Gonna hire a manager to run the spread for him."

"When was he supposed to come and take control of the ranch?"

"Damned if I know. He said he'd put it in the

letter them bastards stole off the train." Teasdale frowned, rubbed his face and looked up quickly. "So you telling me there ain't no sale for sure yet. Not as long as I didn't accept the contract and signed it and took his money."

"Looks to be about the size of it. You hadn't signed the contract yet, had you, Mr. Teasdale?"

"Nope. I wanted the ten-thousand first."

"Mr. Teasdale, we have recovered most of the ten-thousand dollars. Almost nine thousand of it. We believe it to be the money from the registered package, but we're not certain. We're keeping it in the sheriff's safe until this case is settled. I suggest you contact this Will James and have him come to Fort Smith so we can talk to him."

"Yep. Send him a letter tomorrow."

A young man ran onto the screen porch from inside the house. He wore range clothes and a wide brimmed hat that had seen a lot of rain, sun and wear. He looked to be about 25, slight, his face sweating and his eyes sparking.

"Oh, Father Teasdale, there you are. Didn't know you had company."

"Not company. Business. Nate Emerson, this is Spur McCoy from the Federal government. Working on that train robbery. Mr. McCoy, this is my son-in-law, Nate."

They shook hands. The young man's message just couldn't wait. It bubbled out of him.

"Wanted to tell you that old Nel had her foal. Prettiest little thing you ever saw. No problems. Little guy is standing now after an hour and nursing. Prettiest sight this side of Omaha."

Teasdale nodded. The touch of a smile started on his face, then retreated. "Hell, Nate. We may make you into a rancher yet."

"I tell you I'm trying, Father Teasdale. Oh, them yearlings. We got them moved to a new range. Looks like should be enough grass to last them the rest of the summer."

"Good, now get back out there and tend to Nell. She'll want some water and some oats. Stay with her a couple more hours."

"Yes sir," Nate said and hurried out.

Spur waved at the door Nate had gone through. "Looks like a fine young man."

"Yeah, could be a good rancher. If I have time enough with him. My daughter Louisa May's husband. Not much chance the other one will amount to anything. I expect to hear any day he's dead or in jail. Just a no good little bastard."

"I met him in town once."

"Then you know. Now I'm tired. My damn heart just won't do what I want it to. Doc says I'm to stay sitting down or laying down and give it a rest. Hell, I'm only 56. should have twenty years yet."

"One thing you don't need to worry about is the ranch. Far as I can see, it isn't sold. If you still want to sell, you can take that up with Mr. James when he comes to town." Spur turned his hat around in his hands.

"What I'm trying to figure out, Mr. Teasdale, is if the ranch sale and that ten-thousand has anything to do with the train robbery. Was somebody deliberately trying to snarl up the ranch sale? What do you think?"

"Could be. If anybody wanted that, it would be Doug Chandler. Much as I hate to say it." The man thought a minute then nodded. "Yeah, I'd say he is a good suspect. I told him that I'd worked out a deal with James. Even told him the day when the registered mail package was coming to town so he could get it at the post office. James really wants the ranch. He said he'd bring the contract down himself, but he had some important meetings that day, so he mailed it. Registered."

Spur nodded. "Well, I don't want to tire you out any more than I have. Good seeing you again, Mr. Teasdale. I'll let you know what we find out about the contract and the money."

Teasdale held up his hand as Spur headed for the door. "Just a minute, McCoy. You look like a good judge of horses and men. You saw the boy, Nate Emerson. What do you think?"

Spur smiled and took two steps back toward the invalid. "Mr. Teasdale, the young man looked to me like he loves horses. Every rancher should love his mounts. I'd say that's about as good a starting place as you can have with a young man. Now, teach him all you know about ranching and I'd say you have a winner."

"What about Chandler?"

Spur took a deep breath and looked away. "Your business, Mr. Teasdale. I'd figure you have a will. You could make some kind of a division of the ranch and only a little cash money to Chandler. But, like I say, that's your business."

Teasdale waved at Spur and he went out and found his horse.

He was part way up the 20 miles to the railroad summit, but he reversed his field and rode back to town. There was plenty of time, and he'd rather ride the train 20 miles than ride it on his horse. He snorted. That was a sure sign he wasn't a kid anymore.

Spur made it to the station a half-hour before the train arrived at 8 p.m. on its way north. He sent a progress report telegram to General Halleck in Washington hoping it would keep his Secret Service boss happy.

The conductor said the water tower at the summit was just past the 22 mile marker. Spur would be sure when they got there. If he went to sleep, the conductor would awaken him. Spur looked at the written instructions the kidnappers had wired to the state Attorney General:

"BRING PAYMENT FOR MERCHANDISE IN LEATHER CASE. LEAVE FIFTY YARDS SOUTH OF WATER TOWER IN CLEARED SPACE TWENTY YARDS FROM TRACKS. AFTER DEPOSITING PAYMENT, RETURN TO THE TRAIN AT ONCE. NO DELAYS PERMITTED. YOUR MERCHANDISE WILL BE BROUGHT TO TRAIN AT FIRST PASSENGER CAR NEAR WATER TOWER. NO MISTAKES."

Spur read the copy of the telegram and pushed it back in his pocket. Fifty-yards south of the water tank. Easy enough. Twenty-yards from the tracks. Was there already a cleared spot there, or would the kidnappers make one? How were they getting Amy Hellman from Fort Smith, if that's indeed where she still was, to the water tower?

Had they gone up on a morning train and got off there? Maybe a buggy road ran nearby from Fort Smith up to the small towns between there and Fayetteville. Maybe.

Spur gave up and relaxed. Soon the train slowed and outside he could see the red lanterns of the trainmen as the long string of cars slowed to a stop near the shadows of a water tower.

Spur slipped off with his small carpetbag and walked up to the tower. He watched the men lower the spout into the engine and fill it up with water to replace that used on the long haul up the hill. He left the tower and paced off 50-yards down the tracks, and looked across the right of way. Even in the faint moonlight, he could tell there was no kind of clearing there. It was a brushy patch that would take a lot of work to cut down small shrubs and trees to make a clearing even ten-feet wide.

Spur faded away from the tracks into the brush. A few minutes later he heard the train start up and roll up the last few feet of the grade, then start the downhill run to Fayetteville. He found a faint animal trail and used it to get a quarter-of-a-mile into the trees and brush. He found a spot under a large tree that was shielded by brush and spread out his blanket. He'd have a nap and then listen to the night sounds.

He hoped he'd hear someone chopping brush, but he figured he wouldn't. The train had taken almost an hour to climb the 22 miles to the summit. The one in the morning would probably go at the same speed which meant the State Attorney General and the money should arrive at the Casper summit about seven o'clock. It would be full light by then.

It didn't give the kidnappers much time to make a clearing. Or were the instructions meant to be confusing? Once the man with the money stepped off the train and headed south, it would be easy for the kidnappers to appear out of the brush, grab the money, knock down the messenger and vanish back into the brush that grew up to the right-of-way along much of the area south of the water tank.

He stopped evaluating the situation and listened. A night bird of some sort called for its mate. Far off he heard an answering call. He heard a coyote give his mournful wail. It started a whole chorus of coyotes until he thought he was at a concert in the Back Bay Boston Park.

Nowhere did he hear anything but the natural night woods sounds. He sniffed and now that the train smoke had blown away, he could not detect any smell of wood smoke. That could mean the kidnappers weren't in the area, or they didn't have a fire, or that he was upwind of any such wood smoke.

Spur settled down on his blanket. It was another warm night. He set his mental alarm clock for five a.m. and closed his eyes. He would be asleep almost at once and be surprised when he awoke in the morning.

Soiled Dove

There were no signs of dawn when he awoke. He figured it was four o'clock, but didn't bother to check his pocket watch. That would mean striking a match and might give his position away. He rolled up his blanket and put it in the carpetbag. He checked his six-gun and added a sixth cartridge to the cylinder, then eased the hammer down on the live round.

He chewed on some jerky and a biscuit he had brought from the hotel kitchen, and moved down the trail toward the tracks. Spur stopped and listened. A squirrel chattered somewhere in a tree. He could hear some small feet scampering through the brush, maybe a rabbit out for an early morning feeding on tender shoots of grass.

He moved slowly so he wouldn't make any noise. It took nearly a half hour to walk to where he could see the shining rails in the moonlight. He was well south of the water tower and moved north to about where he had been the night before.

Spur lay in the grass and leaf mulch listening. He was close enough now so any preparations should be within earshot. Nothing moved, no sounds came except natural ones. He moved another ten-yards toward the tower.

Faint streaks of light penetrated the blackness. The streaks became swaths and then a general brightening until in one instant, it was dawn. The tracks gleamed below him. He was on a rise about 30-feet above the tracks. He could see nothing out of place around the water tower.

When would the morning train arrive? Furiously, he tried to remember where the passenger cars had been. Yes, up front, near the engine and wood car, just in back of the Railway Express car. Passenger cars always were before freight cars. So the money man would be getting off three or four cars back from the tower.

It was full light now and Spur burrowed deeper behind some grass and weeds so he couldn't be seen. He was disappointed. He had fully expected to see some activity here by the kidnappers, unless they came up on the same train that the money man did. That would solve a big problem of transportation for them. He scowled hoping it wasn't so.

He was sure that Alger wouldn't think to search the passenger cars on the way up to the water tower. Amy Hellman could be in a disguise with a long dark wig, a big hat and dark glasses. Damnit! That could be it.

But once they got off the train to pick up the money, what would they do then?

The slight sound in the background had been nudging at his consciousness and now it came full blown. A horse blew somewhere in back of the water tower.

Yes! Someone would meet them here with horses and they would ride away with the money. Spur changed directions, pulled back and worked north toward the rise behind the water tank. A spring up there somewhere must supply water to the tank so there would be a trail of sorts.

He worked forward silently, using his Indian training, never breaking a stick, never putting his foot down until he knew it was safe.

It took him a half-hour to move the 60-yards to where he guessed the horses must be. He came to a small opening and there, with heads down, were two horses nibbling on the summer grass. Spur froze behind a tree and peered around it at ground level. He was still well concealed.

A man cleared his throat and Spur saw a puff of blue smoke behind and to the right of the horses. One man sat there smoking. He had his eyes closed, Spur guessed, taking it easy until the train came when someone he expected would come racing up the trail with a leather bag filled with money.

Spur plotted his course. He had to work around the clearing, a small natural mountain meadow, and come up on the man with total surprise from behind. He hoped he had enough time. He checked his pocket Waltham. It showed five minutes after six.

The train had just left Fort Smith heading north. He hoped that it wasn't early.

Twenty minutes later, Spur had worked to within ten-feet of the dozing cowboy. The man wore a cowboy hat, boots, range clothes and a red bandanna at his throat, handy if a mask were needed.

Spur rested a minute, then crawled ahead.

When Spur was six-feet from the man, the cowboy yawned, growled and swore, then stood up. He had a six-gun on his hip and a rifle near at hand.

Spur stood and charged the man, hitting him

with his shoulder in the middle of his back just as the man evidently heard Spur and tried to turn. They both went down with Spur sprawled on top of the cowboy. Spur wrapped his arm around the man's throat and pulled hard.

"Easy, friend, or I'll strangle you," Spur growled. "You want to be just caught or wind up dead?"

The man below Spur went limp in answering. Spur eased up on the stranglehold, pulled the man's arms behind him and tied them with a piece of leather boot lacing from his pocket. He stood, rolled the man over and stared at him. He'd never seen him before in his life.

"What are you doing here?" Spur asked.

"I'm hunting deer. Trail over there they always come down."

"Where's your rifle?" Spur asked.

"Right behind you."

"And why do you have two horses?"

"One to haul the deer out on. I live ten miles from here. I ain't about to drag a gutted buck ten miles."

Spur heard the train whistle down the tracks. Spur laughed at the man's explanation and tied his feet with another piece of leather boot lace.

"Now, tell me why you're really here. Who are you meeting here when the train stops for water?"

"Nobody, damnit. I'm deer hunting."

"Sure you are, and I'm Abe Lincoln brought back to life."

Spur could hear the train engine laboring up the incline. He took the man's kerchief and tied it around his neck and across his open mouth in a safe gag. He could still make some sounds, but not yell.

"You have any kind of a signal?" Spur asked. The man on the ground shook his head. "I bet."

Spur looked at the horses. They were safe enough. He walked down the faint trail along a pipe that carried water to the storage tank.

He figured he was still 50-yards from the tracks when he heard the train grind to a halt at the water tower below. He was maybe 50-feet higher than the tracks. That's when he remembered that the telegram said to leave the money 50-yards south of the water tower.

How was the kidnapper going to pick up the money and come up here to the horses? Easy. Run through the brush. That way he'd keep any chase away from the spot where the horses were.

Spur ran down the trail another 30-yards, staying out of sight of the train and stopped behind some thick brush. He could see the trainmen lowering the water spout and turning on the flow.

He looked down the tracks, saw the second and last passenger car and the conductor who stepped down checking his watch. What had happened south of here?

Spur waited. He heard some commotion to the south, then one shot fired and the faint sounds of someone running through the brush. The sounds came closer, then stopped. Spur frowned, then heard a mourning dove's call. Hoo, hoo, hoooooo.

That was the signal. Spur tried to do the call and knew he had fumbled it terribly. The running sounds came again but seemed to be going away from him, then circled above him. The horses!

Spur pulled his six-gun and ran flat out up the partly overgrown trail. He had another 40-feet to go when he heard saddle leather creak and then the sound of horse shoes hitting the ground and fading. He stormed into the small clearing and found one horse munching away and the man lying on the ground trying to laugh.

Spur untied the man and marched him down to the train leading the horse behind him.

Fiorello Alger and the conductor stood beside the engine arguing. They both looked up when they saw Spur and his prisoner.

"Lost him," Spur said. "This one rode in with a horse for him and he went around me and got away. No chance I can track him in these damn hills. You get the girl?"

Alger scowled and hit the engine with his hand.

"Yeah, we got her. She'd been riding in the first passenger car and none of us thought to check it. She said she was held at knife point all the time, but she couldn't identify the man who held her.

"I put the money at the spot and somebody picked it up. I got off one shot but I was too far away. I should have had a pair of sharpshooters with rifles trained on the spot."

"So he got the money, and you have the daughter," Spur said. "Worked out just the way you wanted it to. Let's get this horse in one of those empty stock cars and we'll ride into Fayetteville and then back on the next train south. Gives me plenty of time to use my best torture methods on this prisoner. Come to think of it, I better do that in a stock car as well. I hate getting blood over all those nice upholstered seats."

Chapter Thirteen

The horse was put on board the train and it headed on north. Spur had relented and the prisoner was put in the end of the passenger car. The ticket holding riders were asked to move to the front of the coach.

Spur pushed the man who said his name was Sully into the seat and loomed over him.

"Who hired you to bring the horse to this spot?"

"No one, I was out hunting. I always get a deer this time of year and my favorite mount spooks if I try to carry the dead animal on it back to my cabin."

"What's your name again?"

"Sully. Sully Whisper."

"You rode up here from Fort Smith, right?"

"No. I live in the woods about five miles back.

Hunt and fish, do odd jobs now and again for pocket money. Name's Sully."

"Where did you get the two-hundred dollars in your pocket? That's more than half-a-year's wages for an honest man."

"I got lucky at a poker game in Chester, up the tracks."

Spur looked at the conductor who was watching. "We stop at this Chester place?"

"Flag stop. Won't stop unless they put out the flag."

"Signal the conductor to stop, flag or no flag. We'll get off there and wait for a southbound."

Attorney General Alger had been at the other end of the car talking quietly with Amy Hellman. She had assured them right away that she was fine, no harm had come to her and that her kidnappers treated her kindly. She whispered to Alger that she hadn't been raped or molested. He gave a sigh of relief. Alger came back, a grim frown on his face.

"I don't like it," he said. "Something just doesn't seem right with what she says and the way she says it, but I can't pin her down on anything wrong. She said they had held her in a house in Fort Smith and went north this morning on the same train we did. She had on a dark wig, dark glasses and a big floppy hat so no one could recognize her.

"The kidnappers were on the train, too, or at least one of them. She claims he had a knife touching her side all the time so she couldn't scream or try to get away from him."

Spur lifted his brows and nodded. "Yeah, seems like a good story, knowing her wild ways. But I wonder."

"So do I," Alger said. "But wondering and proving she was part of the conspiracy are two different matters."

Spur went back to Sully.

"Clever how you tied down those guns in the train robbery."

Sully grinned, then shook his head. "Don't know nothing about no train robbery. I do a little farming. Mostly some fruit trees and vegetables and corn for the winter."

"And you won two-hundred dollars playing poker."

"That's right."

The train whistled, then a minute later stopped at the Chester store. There were two other buildings there, one of them a house. Alger went to help Miss Hellman off the train, and Spur nudged Sully to his feet.

Two trainmen put down the makeshift ramp for the horse to get off the cattle car and then the train pulled out.

They all went into the store and found a chair for Miss Hellman. Spur took Sully outside and grinned.

"Now, little man. You and I are all alone, no witnesses, it's just your word against mine. Can I help it if you fell down the steps at the Chester store here and got all bloodied?"

Sully backed against the side of the store and held up his tied hands in front of his face. "You can't hit me, you're a lawman. You can't do that. I'm tied up and helpless. I'll scream like bloody murder."

"Well now, 'can't' is an interesting word. We'll see if I'm able to hit you or not, won't we?" He waited a minute. "Want to change your strange story about hunting deer?"

Sully shook his head, his glance moving from side to side as if looking for an escape route.

"Then why does that horse you have carry an AL brand? That's the brand on my horse, too best in town. Both are from the Anderson Livery down in Fort Smith."

Sully scowled a minute, then grinned. "Yeah, right. Bought her from Anderson last time I was down there to play some poker about three months ago. I got robbed by that horse trader. That mount ain't all that good."

Spur stared at the man for a moment, then shrugged. "Hell, maybe you are telling the truth. Seems like one damn big coincidence. Oh, you have a bill of sale for that horse, I'd bet."

"Yeah, back in my cabin. This mean I can get my horse and try to find that guy who stole my other mount?"

"Nope. We're going to hold you as a witness to the theft of your horse. Shouldn't take more than a few minutes for you to give a statement to the sheriff down at Fort Smith."

"But. . . ."

Spur looked at him. "I could throw you in jail for a few days, see if you change your story."

Sully did a quick change of attitude. "No, that's

fine. I'll give a report to the sheriff."

Spur untied the man's hands. They would have a two hour wait before a work train came through and they could ride in the caboose.

Nothing happened before the work train arrived. Spur watched closely but he saw no one else come out of the woods and board the train. He wondered where the kidnapper was with the $30,000 he had been paid. He could be riding back toward Fort Smith. Or he even could have boarded the northbound that they got off of in Chester. Damn!

Spur took the untied man inside the store so he could talk with Amy. She didn't even look at Sully. She sat nibbling on a homemade cookie and sipping a glass of lemonade.

"Miss Hellman. I know you've been talking to State Attorney General Alger, but would you mind if I asked you some questions?"

"Not at all. You are?"

"Spur McCoy, United States Secret Service. Federal case because of the mail theft. I understand these two outlaws captured you off the southbound train. Is that right?"

"Oh, yes. I screamed and beat at them, but one just threw me over his shoulder like a sack of grain and carried me out of the train. Then he put me on his horse and we rode away."

"Where did they hold you during the kidnapping?"

"Oh, we rode back to a house in Fort Smith and they kept me blindfolded so I couldn't identify them. Then they wore bandanna masks when they were in my room. They tied me up until I promised not to try to escape or scream or break the window. But they didn't mistreat me."

"Can you give us a general description of the three men?" Spur asked.

"Well, yes. One was tall and thin, I think he had a moustache. One was shorter and younger and the third one was large and a little heavy, stocky. He's the one who carried me out of the train."

"Could you identify any of them if we caught them?"

"Oh, my. I don't know. I never thought about it."

"What about the man who brought you on the train? He didn't have a mask and you weren't blindfolded."

She smiled. "Of course not, but they put dark glasses on me, like the kind blind folks wear. Well, I couldn't see a thing and he had to lead me to my seat and all. No, I couldn't identify that man either."

"I'm sorry. This man here, Sully, have you ever seen him before? Was he at the house? Maybe he was the younger and smaller of the three."

Miss Hellman turned and stared at Sully, then she shrugged. "No, he couldn't have been one of them. Even without the mask, he isn't the same as the men at the house. This one looks pleasant, almost nice. No, he wasn't one of the three."

The disappointment showed through Spur's expression. He shrugged. "Well, we tried. Will you be going back to Little Rock with the Attorney General?"

"We were talking about that. Yes, we'll be taking the first boat for Little Rock after we get to Fort Smith. I like the boat, it's so peaceful floating down the river that way. He'll wire my parents that I'm rescued as soon as we get to Fort Smith."

"Good. At least we have one aspect of this robbery problem cleared up. Now there are only three left to worry about."

An hour later, back in Fort Smith, Spur escorted Sully to the sheriff, who took a statement from him about the stolen horse, then Spur and Sully walked to the street.

"The sheriff will let you know if he finds your horse, Sully. I guess that's all we need from you right now. If you can remember what the man looked like who got away with your mount, you be sure to tell the sheriff."

Sully looked a little surprised, then his eyes glinted. "Yeah, figured you'd let me go since I told you I didn't have nothing to do with that kidnapping you been talking about, and I wasn't in on no damn train robbery either. So I can go now?"

"Looks like it. Just don't get in trouble, Sully. I for sure will remember your face forevermore."

Sully turned and walked away.

Spur let him get half a block down, then screened himself by a bevy of women and followed the man. He went first to a hotel, the Claremont, and registered. He didn't even look at the room, but left by the side door and went into the first saloon he came to. Spur watched from near the door as Sully took two mugs of beer to a back table, gave one to one of the soiled doves from upstairs, and sat and drank with her. A short time later, they hurried up the steps to the cribs above.

Spur went outside and kicked at the boardwalk. He was sure that Sully would make a straight run for the man he was working for as soon as he got his freedom. Instead he acted like an innocent man, getting a hotel room, then a whore. His story just didn't hold up. The coincidence was too great. But there was no way to prove it, except by catching the man who picked up the ransom. He could have waited for a northbound train and be halfway to Kansas City by now. Spur wished to hell he knew where that man was who picked up the money. Since Doug was involved in the ranch money, could he also be a part of the kidnapping as well?

Doug Chandler lay in the weeds of the alley behind the house he had rented in Fort Smith and watched the back door for twenty minutes. He saw no activity. There was little chance that the Federal man or the sheriff knew about his hideaway here, but he wasn't in the mood to take any chances. After his close escape of the trap at the summit, he was going to be doubly careful.

Knute should be inside guarding his $20,000 in new bills. He felt the bulge in his jacket pocket. Damn! Another $30,000. This was the way he liked to do business. Now he had the option of picking up Amy in Little Rock or taking the ransom money and the twenty-thousand in new bills and riding the train north to Chicago or even New York. He didn't need her. He'd think about it. She was one luscious chunk of fucking woman.

He lifted from the alley and walked to the back door and went inside, his right hand on his six-gun butt ready to lift it at the slightest cause.

No problem. Knute lounged in the kitchen working on a sandwich he had made. His six-gun was up covering the door when Doug came through. They both grinned and put the hardware away.

"Any trouble?"

Knute took a bite and shook his head. "Nothing happened. Nobody came to the door. Not a damn thing."

"The money still safe?"

"Oh, damn right. I looked at it. Never seen that much before, damn that's nice. But you say the bank people know them little numbers on the bills. How'd they know that?"

"Never mind how, they do. I'll pay you in used bills. That's what it's time for right now. Pay day. Get your gear together and I'll count out your money. You earned it. Five-hundred dollars for you, just as we agreed."

Knute looked surprised. "You really gonna pay me that much? Damn. I figured you was just talking and I'd get maybe fifty. Damn, all five-hundred. I ain't never had that kind of money. What do I do with it? What if somebody robs me?"

Doug grinned. "Hey, right now I'm packing around thirty-thousand dollars and nobody knows it. Put half of your money in your boot, tie it to your ankle. Put some in a shirt pocket. I'll give you mostly twenties so it won't be so bulky.

Just don't flash it around and nobody will try to rob you. Now get moving. I want you on the afternoon boat down the river."

Knute hesitated. "What . . . what you gonna do? Anything I can help you on? Like working with you, Doug."

"Nothing I'll need any help with, Knute. Actually, I'm gonna find Amy in Little Rock and get a cabin on a river boat and just fuck up a storm all the way to New Orleans. So you see, I won't be needing your help."

Knute guffawed. "Oh, yeah, no help needed there. I'll get my gear."

Ten minutes later Knute was out the door after stashing his $500 in four places in his bag and his clothes. He still looked self-conscious about it.

Doug sat at the kitchen table sipping from a bottle of whiskey. He'd been too dry too long. He took another pull and sat there trying to figure out what to do next. He had damn near $50,000, should he try for more? Why not? the old coot wouldn't need it. Hell, he'd be dead before he spent all the cash he had on hand as it was. Yeah, help spread the wealth a little bit. That was the idea.

He tipped the bottle again and then heard a knock at the front door. Who would knock? Who knew he was here? He pulled his six-gun and hurried to the front door. Just before he got there the knob turned and the door swung inward a few inches.

"Doug, are you here? Doug Chandler, I need to talk to you. This is Nate. We've got some big problems out at the ranch."

*   *   *

Knute had left the house five minutes before Nate Emerson arrived. He walked toward the river, found the small landing where the steamer stopped and saw a boat there taking on passengers.

"Going downriver?" he asked someone in line to board.

"Better be, or I'm in all sorts of trouble," the passenger said.

At the head of the gangplank, the purser stood taking tickets and cash.

"How much to Little Rock?" Knute asked. He held some bills in one hand and his carpetbag in the other.

"Two dollars," the purser said. Knute gave him two singles and walked on board.

He'd never ridden this boat before. There were three cabins for the rich folks, a few chairs and an inside room with benches and chairs where you could stay dry when it rained. He stood at the rail watching the men get the boat ready to leave.

A few minutes after they left the dock, someone edged against the rail beside him. He glanced down and saw Amy Hellman. She didn't look at him but spoke softly.

"Knute, did Doug get away all right? Did he come back to the house here?"

Knute looked back at the shore, pretending to ignore her. "Yeah, he did. Gonna meet you in Little Rock."

"Good. Don't let on that you know me. Be bad for both of us."

Soiled Dove

He kept looking at the shoreline and the girl pointed downstream and walked away from him. He sighed with relief.

Amy Hellman smiled as she pranced to the cabin. It was on the main deck and had a porthole which could be covered. She went in and locked the door behind her. It was small and crowded with a single bunk along the wall, one chair and a small dresser.

Attorney General Alger sat in the chair reading some papers from his leather case. He looked up and nodded. "I see you got us away from the dock. That sort of thing doesn't interest me anymore, especially when I have work stacked up I should be doing."

She sat on the bed and pouted a moment, then she unbuttoned her white blouse and let it swing open just a little to prove she wore nothing under it.

"Mr. Alger, I thought since we have over sixteen hours on the river that we might have ourselves a good time."

He didn't look up until the last two words. When he saw her blouse open and the come-on smile, his mouth gaped wide and he showed a shocked, surprised expression. But he didn't look away from the swell at the inner edges of her breasts.

"What do you say, Mr. Alger? It isn't like anyone is going to suspect anything. You're here on business."

Alger dropped the papers he was reading and stared. She flipped back one side of the blouse showing her large breast with full pink areola circling it and a hot red nipple.

Amy grinned at his expression. "Come over here and sit beside me, Mr. Alger, I really think we should get better acquainted since we're traveling together."

"Oh my god," Alger breathed.

He put down the leather case of papers and moved to the bed and sat beside her. She pushed back the other half of her blouse and let it fall to the bed behind her.

"Mr. Alger. I'd like you to meet my titties. They're excited about getting to know you. Pet them a little to show them that you like them."

"Oh god!" Alger said. His eyes were wide, his breathing quickened and he moved his legs to let his growing erection find space in the cramped quarters in his suddenly tight pants. His hand reached for her breasts and then he was fondling them with both hands, rubbing them, tweaking her nipples.

A moment later he bent and kissed her orbs and she leaned her head back in delight, crooning to him, encouraging him.

He sucked one breast into his mouth and chewed gently on her firm flesh, then he bit her nipple and she lifted her head and nodded.

"Now, I think you've got the right idea." She reached for his crotch and he pushed her hand away. The next time she reached he made no move and she unbuttoned his fly and worked her hand inside his trousers.

"Oh, my, what a dandy!" she crooned. She fished his stiff penis out of his pants and kissed the purple tip. His hips bucked twice and she moved away.

"Now we don't want you to do anything too quickly, do we, Fiorello? Is it all right if I call you by your first name?"

She didn't wait for an answer. Instead she loosened his belt, knelt beside his legs and pulled down his pants. He lifted up and she tugged them from under him then down and off his legs.

His penis tented out his underwear. She giggled, patted the stiff pole holding them out, then pulled down his underwear until his erection sprang free and clear.

"Oh, yes, now we're getting to the good part. What a dandy. So strong and sturdy. I just want to kiss him." She pulled his underwear off his legs, then knelt between his parted knees and kissed his penis.

Fiorello Alger moaned as her lips slid around the arrow tip of him and sucked him into her mouth.

"Oh, god!" Fiorello hissed.

She bobbed back and forth on his lance and his hips bucked. Then he jolted into a climax pumping six, then eight times into her mouth.

Amy swallowed again, and pulled back from him as he finished.

"There, now, that was easy, wasn't it? We'll give you ten minutes to recover, then see what you can do with your big rod jammed up my tight, juicy cunnie. Why don't you finish undressing me just to keep your interest up. Let's get rid of your jacket and tie and shirt as well. I covered up the port hole before we left the dock so we have some real privacy. Come on, Fiorello, you're going to have to help me."

He did. Before they made their first stop the Attorney General was on his hands and knees on the bed over the woman, her knees parted and lifted and he pounded into her with all of his might. She squeezed him on every stroke with her inner muscles and the Arkansas state official climaxed the second time within fifteen minutes of the first one.

He dropped on top of her, crushing his chest against her flattened breasts.

"Damn, I don't believe this is happening," he said looking down at her from so close she was fuzzily out of focus.

"It's happening, Fiorello and it's going to go on happening until you can't get your wand to stand straight up. Don't you like it?"

"Like it? Yes, I love it. I just never expected that a wonderful looking girl like you with a marvelous body would let me anywhere near you, let alone fuck you till I drop."

She laughed. "Why not? I love to fuck. Besides, now when I want you to do something for me, I know that you will. I wouldn't want to have to tell Daddy that you took advantage of me five times on the boat back from Fort Smith."

"Oh, God! You wouldn't do that?"

"Not as long as you cooperate with me, help me when I get in trouble with Daddy. First, you'll guarantee to him that I had nothing to do with my kidnapping."

"Well, of course, it was obvious from what you

said. . . . " He frowned and stared at her.

"Oh damn it. You were in on it, weren't you? You know who it was on that train, you know who brought the payoff money. You lied like a fucking trooper."

Amy grinned. "Damn, Fiorello, I think you're catching on. How else could I get thirty-thousand dollars out of my skinflint dad? He's made enough in graft from the state to more than pay for it. You won't say a word about this to Daddy or my Mother. You will convince him I had nothing to do with it. If he asks, you'll say yes, you think I've recovered enough to go on a shopping trip to New Orleans."

"You wouldn't."

"Of course I will. You don't think I can spend all that money in Little Rock and not attract attention?" She reached down and began to bring him back to the ready.

"Fiorello, have you ever fucked standing up? Bet you haven't. Yes, it can be done. Come on, get it hard and I'll show you how. This is only number three. You better be able to get it up at least three more times or I'll be highly disappointed in you."

Chapter Fourteen

Doug Chandler looked at his brother-in-law, Nate Emerson, and lowered his six-gun.

"Thought you were a robber or something. Now what the hell you talking about? I ain't got no time for none of your little problems with cattle getting stolen or some horse that's stuck in a swamp somewhere."

"Isn't that kind of trouble. Father Teasdale is sick, real sick. He can't move his right side and he can't talk. I come for Doc Irving. He said I should bring you along. Sometimes these kind of attacks are fatal."

Doug grinned. "I'll be damned. Then let's go. Let me pick up a couple of things in a carpetbag and we'll get riding out of here. Doc taking his buggy?"

"Yes, he's already started out there."

"You go on, I'll get my horse out of the livery and catch up with the two of you."

Nate nodded and hurried out the door. Doug chuckled. Yeah, now if the old man was to kick the bucket about now it would be perfect. Then Doug himself would own half the ranch. That was real money. Place and the cattle must be worth at least $500,000. Yes. He put the new bills from the train heist in the bag, and the $29,500 he had left from the ransom and threw in some clothes. Then he walked out the door and headed for the livery. In less than two hours he would know how bad the old man really was.

Later at the ranch, Doc Irving examined Dylan Teasdale. He was conscious. His eyes looked at one of them and then the other as if he wanted to say something, but he couldn't speak.

"Dylan has had a stroke," Doc Irving said. "His left side is paralyzed and he can't talk. In cases like this, the paralysis often goes away quite rapidly and the ability to speak often returns. Not a lot we can do for him right now but to keep him warm and comfortable."

Teasdale's right hand clutched at the doctor's arm. Doc Irving looked at him and the hand made writing motions.

"Yes, get a pad of paper and a pencil. Dylan wants to write something. This way he can still communicate with us."

Emily Chandler brought a pad and pencil. She was a big woman, heavy, with long black hair and a weathered, unattractive face.

Teasdale took the pencil and Emily held the pad and he wrote slowly but plainly.

Hurt, damn hurt!

Doc Irving nodded. "I know, Dylan. I'm giving you some laudanum that will ease the pain. You have another nap now and you'll feel better when you wake up."

The man on the bed looked pale and thin. Louisa May came into the room, saw the others leaving and went with them. She was a pretty woman, younger than her sister, and now concern shaded her face. She went to her husband Nate.

"What did the doctor say?"

"What we figured. He had a stroke. Can't tell how bad it will be or when the paralysis might go away. Just have to wait."

In the living room near the big stone fireplace, the two men sipped at whiskey cut with branch water. The two women whispered where they sat on the couch.

"Looks bad," Doug said.

Nate nodded. "He's better now than when I found him on the floor in his bedroom early this morning. Figured he tried to get up to come get some help and fell. Seems better now. His mind looks to be in good shape, he just can't talk."

"Stroke, isn't that when something gets scrambled in the brain?"

"Blood vessels break, something like that. But strokes come in all kinds and sizes. Little ones just go away in a few days, I've heard. Bigger ones can take longer. Real big ones will kill the strongest man."

"He's gone downhill fast," Doug said. "Six months ago he was wanting to fight me. Damn, look at him now."

"Gonna happen to all of us sooner or later."

Doug shook his head. "Not to me. I don't plan on living a long life and having to suffer that way. Better to go out in your prime with a six-gun or a knife in your hand. Looking at that old man, a quick end in a shootout seems a lot better."

"He isn't dying. My mother had three strokes and she's still alive. Strokes don't always kill a person."

"But they can, usual do from what I've heard," Doug said. "Maybe not the first one."

"No way to talk, Doug Chandler. Let's show a little respect."

"Hell, I'm being practical. Can you run the damn ranch? What happens if he does die? Somebody's got to take over. Sure as hell ain't gonna be me. I'm no cow turd kicker. You don't know the business yet. Hire a manager? What the hell we do if the old man dies?"

Emily moved over and stood beside Doug. When she heard the last few words he said, she bent and began beating his chest with her fists.

"He isn't going to die. He isn't. I won't let him die. A lot of help you've been around here, Doug. Where you been for the last week and a half? You been with that little whore in town again, ain't you?"

He caught her hands and held them, then pushed her away.

"Shut up, Emily, shut up!" He drew his hand back.

"Or else you'll beat up on me again, like you did two weeks ago? Big strong man."

Emily pulled back and began crying. Louisa May caught her around the shoulders and held her as the two women walked out of the room.

"You're a real bastard, you know that, Doug," Nate spat.

Doug grinned and then laughed. "Hell, Nate. I remember you're the guy who said you tried out Louisa May's pussy up in the haymow one Sunday afternoon before you married her. She wasn't much good at fucking but then her old man did have a half-million dollar ranch. You said that, remember?"

"I've learned a few things since then, Doug. I'd say that you haven't learned a damn thing in five years."

"Shit, has it been that long? How have I been able to stand it? Maybe I won't stand it much longer. If the old man dies, I own half this damn ranch. You remember that, it's a fifty-fifty split in the will."

Doug stood and walked back into the living room. "Just remember that I don't have to live here or with that cow of a woman and her two brats to own half of the Triangle T. Hell, I can live in Little Rock or New Orleans or New York City, and I still own half the ranch."

"You're worse than a bastard, Chandler. I don't

know why I even came to tell you about Father Teasdale."

"How long before he'll be better, if he gets better?" Doug asked.

"I don't know. We'll talk with Doc Irving."

The doctor came from the upstairs bedroom then and walked up to the boys. "I can't get your hopes up. I've seen cases like this before, and the stroke seems to be quite strong. It's been at least twelve hours now, and there should be the start of some improvement. I want you to watch Dylan closely, and keep a record of any changes, good or bad. If he gets back some of his speech, that will be a good sign."

"How long before he might show some change?" Doug asked.

"This isn't something the body can hurry," the doctor said. "It could be in a day or two, or it might take two weeks."

"I can't stay around the ranch that long," Doug said. "I have some important business."

Doc Irving looked at him hard for a moment, then shrugged. "Up to you. This man is seriously ill. There's a chance he'll be this way for some time. There's a chance that he'll improve and be able to walk and talk again. But there's also a chance that at any time he could have another stroke. They almost always are more serious the second or third time and those can be fatal.

"I'll leave you a supply of laudanum. One teaspoon every twelve hours, or more often if he complains of serious pain. Now, I have to get back to the Billbrays. They have a baby due in the next few hours. I've done all I can for you folks."

The doctor took his black bag and moved to the door. The two men went with him to the back door, then let the screen door close and looked at each other.

When the doctor stepped into his buggy, Nate began. "Never have liked you much, Doug. But on this one we need to stand together to help the girls. That man is their father. I know how I felt when my dad was so sick."

Doug scowled in disbelief. "This used to be just business with you, Nate. A good way to get some real money, to settle down. We saw things almost exactly alike."

"We don't anymore. I love that old man in there like he was my father. I won't let you do anything more to hurt him." Nate stood away from Doug and his hand was near the six-gun on his hip.

"Hey, you're wearing iron. You never used to want to own one, let alone learn how to shoot."

"I learned. I can use it. One more warning. You so much as slap Emily again and I'll hunt you down and shoot you where you stand. Is that damn well plain?"

Doug laughed. "So you're dicking both the sisters now. Probably in the same bed at the same time. Hell, I couldn't care less. Help yourself. Use Emily all you want. You just see that you raise any pups that she drops. As for me, I'm getting out of here first thing in the morning. I'll stay the night."

Doug grinned. "Now that does bring up an interesting idea. You're so all fired hot for Emily—"

"Shut up, you son-of-a-bitch. I've never touched that woman." Nate's face flushed red, his eyes bulged and he took a step toward Doug. "You filthy bastard. I should run you off the place right now. If you sleep here tonight, you better sleep in the barn with the other animals."

"Not a chance. I'll make up with Emily in five minutes and have her bloomers off in ten. You watch if you want to. You might learn something."

Nate turned and stormed out of the house.

Doug grinned. He always had Nate's number. He wasn't about to use his six-gun, he was too yellow bellied. Doug shrugged and went back up the steps to look at the old man.

Nate's wife, Louisa May, sat by his bed, a cool cloth on his brow. He wrote something on the pad and gave it to Louisa May. She was the beauty of the family. Small and cuddly, soft blonde hair like her mother's had been, a beautiful face and a sweet little body that Doug had dreamed about having for years. Maybe he would the day before he left the county and headed out for good. Yeah, just maybe.

She looked up and saw him and an automatic frown came over her pretty face. "Father doesn't want to see you, Doug. I think you better go. It's not too late to ride into town. That's what Father told me to tell you."

Doug grinned, ignoring her remarks. "I got to thinking, Louisa May sweetheart. I never have seen you naked. Damn but I'd like that. We could get all hot and sweaty and make wild crazy love.

223

How about right now? I'm sure your pa wouldn't do anything about it."

Louisa May reached in her reticule and pulled out a small two-shot derringer.

Doug chuckled. "You want me to think you know how to use that, let alone hit me at six-feet? Not a chance." He moved toward her and her face turned white. When he was only three-feet away, she fired.

The little gun going off in the closed room echoed like a stick of dynamite. The round dug into Doug's left shoulder and pushed him back a step. He brayed in pain. The round went in but it didn't come out. Damn .22, he guessed.

"Christ, woman, you shot me." It was more a surprise than an accusation.

Louisa May looked calm. She nodded. "Indeed I did, Mr. Chandler. It wasn't as hard as I thought it might be. I shot a rattlesnake a week ago. This makes two. Get out of this room, get out of this house and off this ranch, or I'll aim for your forehead the next time. It's small, but that little piece of lead can kill you. Now go."

Blood dripped from his arm. The pain built and built and he swore at her.

Before he could move, Nate stormed into the room. He checked the old man on the bed first, then stood beside Louisa May who still held the derringer aimed at Doug.

"I shot him," Louisa May said.

Nate nodded. "Too bad you didn't kill him. Get out of here, Doug. Right now." Nate drew his six-gun in a journeyman fashion and Doug was surprised.

"You even learned to draw? Damn, you might be worth killing yet."

"Out!" Nate spat.

Doug had never seen that deadly look in his eye before, or heard that determination in his voice. Doug knew when to fold his hand. He backed up to the door, holding his bleeding shoulder tightly with his right hand.

"I'll be back. I still own half of this ranch. I'll be back with a lawyer and we'll see who shoots who then." He stood at the door shaking his head. "Bastards. All four of you. I thought I could wait out the old man. Almost did. Damn you all to hell! I'll be back for my half of the ranch one of these years. You'll never know when I'm coming. You'll be looking over your shoulder every day from now on."

He turned then and walked down the hall and the stairs. He stopped in the kitchen and barked at the cook to tear up some dish cloths and tie up his bleeding arm. Then he rode.

He had to get to town and have Doc Irving dig the slug out of his arm. Then he had one more small errand to take care of. It was a $25,000 errand. Doug smiled just planning it. He didn't know why he didn't do this before. He was thinking small then. Now he was thinking big. He checked his carpetbag. It was still tied behind his saddle and hadn't been opened. No reason it should be. He gritted his teeth against the pain now throbbing in his shoulder and rode faster. He had to get to town in a hurry and didn't care if he killed the horse to do it.

It still took Doug almost two hours to get back to town. By then it was dark and he rode to Doc Irving's house and office and knocked on the door. His wife came and looked out. She was small and so fat she was almost round.

"Sorry, the doctor isn't seeing any more patients tonight," she said gently with a smile. "You come back tomorrow about eight and he'll see you."

"Martha, is that a patient?"

"Yeah, Dr. Irving. Doug Chandler. I need a bullet dug out of me. Sorry to bother you."

Ten minutes later Doug had bitten a piece of cedar in three pieces as the doctor probed for the small .22 bullet. It had scraped an arm bone and would hurt like crazy, the medic said.

"Least it didn't break the bone. I've got it wrapped up good, but we'll have to watch for infection. You come back in two days and let me change the dressing and take a look at it."

Doug said he would and gave the doctor a five-dollar bill. The medic looked up in surprise.

"For your house call and the digging," Doug said. "I always pay my bills."

Doug left the office and headed for the saloon down the street. He changed his mind when he passed the Diner's Delight cafe. He had a big supper, then got a bottle of whiskey at a saloon to deaden the pain of his wound. Back at the little house, he drank a water glass full of the whiskey and didn't feel a thing. The pain was still there.

Soiled Dove

The anger in Louisa May's eyes was still burning in his memory.

He'd burned down some bridges tonight out at the ranch. Damn sure. What the hell now? Amy Hellman would be good to help him forget his troubles. Damn, the way she could wiggle that little ass of hers! He shook his head. Business first. It wasn't too late.

He hoped the old man didn't have one of his whores there. He checked his six-gun and pushed it back in leather. Doug took the bottle with him as he walked the four blocks over and then up the hill to the mansion where Gregory Lowell lived. The lights were on, and there wasn't a buggy out in front. Good, the rich man's whore wasn't there. He didn't want any witnesses. He checked the door when he arrived but it was locked. He pounded the knocker on the brass plate and waited.

The butler opened the door a crack, saw who he was and let him in.

"Where's the rich man?"

"He's in the library, sir, right this way."

"I know the way. I don't want you to come."

The tall black man who looked like he could snap a man's back with his bare hands nodded. "I understand, sir." He stood there as Doug walked through the lighted house to the library.

He found Gregory Lowell behind his desk working on an account book. Lowell looked up when he heard the door open. The oil lamp blinded him from seeing who it was until Doug was almost at the desk.

"Ah, Chandler. I thought you might be on your way elsewhere by now. I understand your collection of your ransom went smoothly."

"True," Doug said. "Another few dollars. I figure that your claim will go through on schedule. Is it launched already?"

"Of course. I wired my broker two days after the robbery as soon as the post office found my empty envelope. It should be coming through within the month, they said."

"Bully for you, Lowell. I've changed my mind. You paid me two-hundred dollars to set up the robbery and bring back the bonds to you. I should have charged you more."

Lowell smiled, took a six-gun from a drawer and placed it on the desk top near his right hand. "I know how men can change their minds, Mr. Chandler. However, a deal is a deal. You agreed to make an extra two-hundred dollars for a robbery you were already going to do. Let's leave it at that and stay on generally wary, but friendly terms."

"Can't do that. I'm about to leave town and I need another $50,000. I'd figure some of those bonds will cover it. Then they really will be stolen and you'll still come out $50,000 ahead. Seems like a good deal to me."

Lowell stood shaking his head. "No, Mr. Chandler. That's absolutely out of the question. The matter is closed. I'm going to have to ask you to leave. I'm working on some important and private matters here. Let's not have any trouble over a most profitable operation for both of us. You must have taken in almost fifty-thousand yourself."

"Did that, Lowell. Don't figure you deserve to make no hundred-thousand when I only made fifty. I want half of those bonds you're working with there."

Doug had never seen a stock certificate or a bearer bond of any kind, until he got them from the mail sacks his three men brought back. He'd studied them carefully. At last decided to turn them over to Lowell who knew what to do with them. He should have kept them all and told Lowell they hadn't been in the registered mail. Now the bonds lay on the rich man's desk.

"Half of them, Lowell. I'm not in the mood to argue. I could take them all, but I know your position here. It's the best deal you're going to get."

"Impossible. That's my money, my bonds, not yours." Lowell's face had gone murky, as if most of the blood drained from it. His hand shook as he touched his cheek. He looked down at the six-gun.

"Don't even try it, Lowell. If you're dead none of them bonds are going to help you. Play it smart and hand me half of them, right now."

To emphasize his point, Doug drew the Colt from its holster in a fast motion and trained it on Lowell.

"Oh, my," Lowell said. He took a long breath, then another one and put his hand on the desk as he started to sway. He caught himself. "A little dizzy," he said. Then in a move Doug didn't think the man could make, he grabbed the six-gun, cocked it and got off a shot as Doug brought up his own revolver from where he had let the muzzle tilt toward the floor.

Lowell's shot boomed into the room followed closely by a second thundering explosion of Doug's Colt. The noise rumbled in the room bouncing from wall to wall.

Doug felt Lowell's bullet slam past him and hit the wall behind. His own round drilled into Lowell's chest and jolted him backward over the chair and slammed him against the bookcase wall. He sagged a moment, then slid to the floor. Doug figured he was dead by the way he fell.

Doug darted forward, grabbed the bonds, folded them and pushed them inside his shirt. He buttoned the shirt and turned toward the library door as he heard footsteps running that way. Doug knelt behind the desk eyeing the library's door. A moment later the butler came racing up holding a sawed off shotgun in his hands. He saw no one, then Doug lifted over the desk, brought up the revolver and fired.

Just as he did, the butler pulled the trigger on the scatter gun. The buckshot shattered a dozen glass doors covering the bookcases behind the desk, cut grooves across the top of the cherry wood desk, and turned the library into a smoke-filled room of death.

Doug had ducked in time after his shot, and now peered over the desk again figuring it was a double barrelled weapon. He saw the big black butler leaning against the inside wall. His hands were empty. One pressed against his chest, the other scratched to grab hold of the wall.

He looked at Doug, then slowly slid down the door jamb and rolled over on the floor on his back. His lifeless eyes stared upward at the library's ceiling.

Doug stood, made one last look at the top of the desk, found another bearer bond worth ten-thousand dollars and pushed it inside his shirt as well.

Then he ran out of the house by the back door into the blessed blackness of the night and hurried along the streets to his small rented house. There were few lights on in the houses he passed. None was close enough to have anyone inside who could have heard the shots.

He had to get ready to leave. How? He still had his horse. He worked on it quickly as he packed a few clothes and some personal things in his carpetbag. He took out the bonds, flattened them and put them between sheets of the local newspaper and lay it all in the bottom of his bag. Then he piled in everything else including the bundles of new and used currency.

By the time he had his bag packed and his six-gun reloaded, he knew what he would do. No sense in taking a chance on someone spotting him getting on the downriver boat here in Fort Smith.

The steamer made its first stop downstream from Fort Smith at B16 Bend. There was a small settlement there. He'd ride his horse the five miles, sell the horse and get on the steamer there. Then a quick trip down to Little Rock and he'd be away free and clear.

Doug grinned as he mounted the horse and began to ride slowly out of town. There was no hurry. The first boat didn't leave Fort Smith until nearly ten tomorrow morning, and it would be near eleven before it left B16 Bend. Yes. That would be the way to go.

As he rode down the south river road, he kept thinking about what he had tied on the back of his saddle. Almost $50,000 in cash money, and another $100,000 in cashable bearer bonds. Doug grinned. He'd never have to do another day's work in his life. Yes, yes. He'd also have Amy Hellman and her delightful body and inventive ways of making love to keep him happy.

Chapter Fifteen

The next morning, Spur McCoy was talking with the sheriff when a woman came screaming into the office. When the sheriff got her calmed down, she explained that she went in each morning to clean house and do some cooking for Mr. Lowell. When she went up there this morning, she found Lowell and his butler both shot dead.

Five minutes later, Spur and the sheriff looked over the murder scene.

"Someone in front of the desk shot both men," Spur said. "Could have shot Mr. Lowell first, then the butler came running in with his shotgun and the killer took him out with one shot just before or just after the shotgun fired once."

"One round in each man," Sheriff Grimm said. "The gunman knew how to kill a man."

Spur looked at the desk. It held an account book opened to a page marked "Bearer Bonds Now Owned."

He saw quickly that this was the same list of bearer bonds that Lowell had shown him before. Sticking out from under one corner of the ledger was an intricately printed edge of paper. Spur moved the account book and found a bearer bond.

"Look at this," Spur said. "A one-thousand dollar certificate. It's from the city of Atlanta. That's one of the bonds that Lowell listed as being stolen from the registered mail."

"So, if he has them back, that proves that he was in on the robbery," Sheriff Grimm said. "Stole his own damn bonds. That way he'd make an even hundred-thousand when the Railway Express paid off on his claim."

"But where are the rest of them, the other ninety-nine thousand worth?" Spur asked. "Maybe that's what got Lowell shot. The man shot him for the bonds."

"Could be. If Chandler was involved with the kidnapping, do you think he was a part of the bond robbery as well?"

Spur grunted as he checked the bond again. It was real. "Starting to sound like he was behind the whole thing. Now, all we have to do is find him."

"I'll send two deputies out to the ranch, and we'll check his usual haunts here in town. I hear he's rented a house somewhere but I don't know which one. I'll also wire the Railway Express not to pay off on those bonds until our investigation is complete."

"You know Lillian, a part time chambermaid at the Wentworth Hotel?"

"Heard of her. She's a part time soiled dove I hear as well, but never been in any trouble I know of. She doesn't have any kind of a record with us."

"She have much to do with Chandler? She told me that she knew him."

"Yeah, now that you mention it. Hear they were seen around town together a lot for a while. Nothing recent."

"Saw her go into a house the other night that didn't seem like it was hers. Think I'll go down there and check. I've got no other leads on Doug Chandler."

Two men came to take away the bodies and Spur left letting the sheriff seal up the house and take care of the rest of it. He walked four blocks, had to go back a block and take another try at it. Then on the second run he found the house where Lillian had slipped away to that night several days ago. He knocked but no one answered. The front door wasn't locked.

Inside he found no one and it looked like the place had been abandoned. There was some trash, a little food, some furniture, but no sign that anyone was coming back. No clothes, no bags, no personal gear.

He searched the place carefully. Under one cushion on the worn couch he found a new $20 bill. It had one of the serial numbers from the missing $20,000 bank money. So the bank money had been in this house. A start.

On the living room table, he found the local newspaper with an advertisement for trips down the Arkansas River on the riverboat. It was circled with a pencil. He tore out the ad and put it in his shirt pocket. It would be a quick way to leave town if you didn't use the railroad.

In the bedroom, he saw the unmade bed and under one blanket lay a pair of pink bloomers. He wondered if they were Lillian's. A magazine lay on the floor. He picked it up and was about to toss it on the bed when he saw some pencilled numbers on the cover. They were: 20 . . . 30 . . . 100 . . . 150,000. He stared at the figures for a minute and then connected them.

There was $20,000 in bank notes, $30,000 from the kidnapping and $100,000 in bearer bonds at Lowell's place. That made a total of $150,000. The numbers matched exactly the amount of money that Chandler could have now if he had stolen the bonds. The killer could have made those notes before or after going up to kill Lowell and taking the money. Was it Doug Chandler?

Lillian might know. He went to the hotel and found the manager. The little man said that Lillian wasn't working today. He had her address if it was important. Spur showed him his identification and said it was police business. The manager nodded and gave Spur her address. It was just a block off the main street.

A man came out of the door as Spur started to knock.

The man was drunk and he laughed. "Hell, don't

have to knock, just walk in," the man said. He grinned and swaggered down the walk.

Spur went inside and saw Lillian come out of a door across the room. She wore a short, see-through gown that barely covered her crotch. The front of it hung open. The raised her brows in surprise when she saw him.

"McCoy. You didn't have to come here. I do house calls." She laughed and crooked her finger. "Right this way, I happen to be free at the moment. How did you find me?"

"I asked the hotel manager. He didn't want to tell me, but he did."

"The bastard. I give him a free one every Tuesday for him doing me some favors. I won't be fucking him for free any more. You must be here for pleasure. Come on in my bedroom. It's right down here."

They went down a short hall to a door she opened for him and he walked into her bedroom. It was done all in pink ruffles and flounces, even pink wallpaper and carpet, a woman's room if he'd ever seen one. She closed the door.

Lillian slipped off the thin robe and stood there naked and delightful. She was a little heavy around the hips but had a delicious young body with breasts surging and bouncing and big and beautiful.

"You want to talk, I can see it. We can do that anytime. Should we fuck first or afterwards?"

He picked her up and carried her to the bed and eased her down on her back. Her knees came up and spread. He sat down beside her.

237

"How well did you know Doug Chandler?"

"Oh, hell. I knew it was gonna be about him. I knew him, but I didn't know him well. I mean, he was my regular poke for a while there, once every night for two months. Then he doesn't come around for a while."

"That's all he was, just a customer?"

"Yeah, so what?"

"I think there was more to it than that."

"Why?"

"One night after we made love you said you had to get home. Only you didn't come here. You went to a house where Doug and some other people lived here in town. Why did you go there?"

"You followed me?"

"You're a rotten liar. I knew you weren't going home."

"Yeah, well, I try. Let's get it done first."

She brought his hands up to her breasts and he left them there. She undid his pants and pulled them down around his ankles, then his shorts and pulled him over on top of her.

"See, junior down there is all hard and ready. Do me hard and fast, then we'll talk."

He pushed his hand down to her crotch and found her hard node and strummed it six times.

"Shit, you know what that does to me? Makes me go wild. Most men don't even think to do that. Just want to get their rocks off. Oh, damn but that feels good."

"Why did you go to that house that night?"

"Went there lots. Business, just business."

"You were whoring the men in the house?"

"No, some other business."

He strummed her node again four times and she almost climaxed, but not quite.

"Do that again, Spur. Please rub me more down there. Feels so wonderful."

"So why did you go to the house?"

"To see a man. Now do me, finish me off or I'll die for sure."

He rubbed her once. "So who did you see at the house?"

"A man . . . oh, shit, all right. I went to see Doug Chandler."

"Doug. Why?"

He strummed her again and she shivered but didn't quite go over the edge into her climax.

"Damn you! I went to tell him everything you told me. He made me spy on you. Said he'd give me two-hundred dollars if I found out what you were doing in town and what you knew."

"From the very first, from that first night?"

"Hell, yes. You think I was bowled over by your charms or good looks or something?"

"It was an idea. Why did Doug want to know what I did?"

"Because he engineered the damn train robbery. He hired the men, set them up, got them the rifles. Yes, he set up the kidnapping with the woman, the dumb blonde with the stretched out pussy."

"What about the bearer bonds?"

"Don't know nothing about them. Know he did go up the hill to see the rich guy after it got dark a couple of times. Took something with him, a big envelope."

"Now, we're getting somewhere. Know what Doug is doing right now?"

She shook her head, held his finger and strummed her clit again and again until she shuddered and roared into a wailing, shouting climax that left her limp and panting.

"Damn you, McCoy. Damn you for leaving me hanging that way for so long."

"So, where is he now?"

"Doug? Probably with that washed out blonde slut."

"She went downriver with the Attorney General late yesterday. Must be in Little Rock by now."

"Yeah, I heard. They pulled it off, the fake kidnapping. Give them that. But Doug knows where Miss Pussy lives in Little Rock. Doug will be going downriver, too. He's hooked on that little whore's cunnie. Can't figure out why. I'm twice as good at fucking as she is."

"You weren't worth thirty-thousand dollars in cash money," Spur said. He caressed her breasts and she started to get hot again. "So Doug Chandler is probably running downstream, at least to Little Rock where he'll hook up with her again."

"Best I can do for you. Now get your big whanger inside me and just poke the hell out of me. I'm getting a'itch down there and you got to put it out."

"You know who the men were who robbed the train?"

"Sure. Guy named Russ Dolan, tall skinny guy."

"He's dead and buried. Who else?"

She looked at him. "Dead? You do it?" She watched him. When he didn't reply she went on. "Knute Safire, something like that, was another one. Big ugly guy who must have an enormous whanger. He got paid off and went down river, I'd guess. The other one was Sully. Smallest and youngest of the three. Don't know where he is."

"I do. Time to go find Sully and have a few words with him." Spur sat up and pulled up his shorts and pants and began to button up his fly.

"Hey, you ain't done me yet. You won't get your money's worth this way."

"I never pay for fucking, pretty lady. That's my first and unbreakable rule."

She sighed. "How you expect a working girl to make a living?" Lillian pouted for a moment. "Oh, hell, go ahead, break off a piece and do me good. I mean real, damn, hard and fast good."

Spur grinned. He shouldn't waste the time, but he was only human. He pushed his pants down and went between her creamy white thighs and found the right place.

She humped to meet him and before he wanted to, nature took over and planted his seeds deep inside her willing soil. She locked her arms around him and wouldn't let him move for five minutes.

"Sometimes this is when I feel the best," she whispered. "I just got fucked good and proper and I'm all warm and happy and want to stay this way forever."

She sighed. "Hell, I know that I can't. So you

get out of here and go find Sully and then get Doug, but try not to kill him. He ain't such a bad guy, as fuckers go."

She lay there watching him as he pulled up his short underwear and his pants. Her legs opened wantonly and she ginned. "One more quick one?"

"Later, maybe later. As you say, I have some business to do."

Spur left the house and hurried down to the sheriff's office. The man was back. Two clerks were busy working on details of the double murder. Spur filled in Sheriff Grimm on what Lillian had told him.

"Nothing we can hold her for or charge her with, but it gives us an eye witness that places Doug Chandler at the heart of the train robbery, the kidnapping and the fake bond theft. If it comes to that, we can get her to testify with no problem."

"So we need Chandler."

"And we need Sully, who we let go yesterday. Is he still in town?"

"I'd guess," Sheriff Grimm said. "He feels safe after getting away with the deception yesterday."

"He have a favorite saloon and whorehouse?"

"Don't know. Use two deputies and go into every dive in town until you find the little bastard."

Two hours later, one of the deputies hurried up to Spur when he came out of a saloon.

"Located him, Mr. McCoy. He's down at Flossie's Parlour. It's the best in town. They offer drinks and food along with the girls. Expensive."

"Personal experience?" Spur asked.

The deputy laughed. "Gosh no, Mr. McCoy. I'm a happily married man."

"Good. Let's go rout him out."

"I don't know, Mr. McCoy." The deputy looked away. "I mean, I never been in one of those places before. Not even on duty. My wife would roast me good."

Spur grinned. "You point me at the place and I'll go in. I don't have a wife to roast me. Where is this place?"

They walked down the main street for a block, then halfway down the side street they came to a well cared for building of two stories with a fancy door but no front windows. Over the door was a small sign, discreetly painted by a professional hand. The sign read:

Flossie's Parlour house, Food and Drinks.

"Not your usual kind of an eating place, Mr. McCoy. I . . . I could watch out back in case he tries to get out that way."

Spur nodded, his grin a yard across. "Good, you go around back and wait. If somebody comes racing out trying to get his suspenders on or buttoning up his fly, you grab him."

The deputy took off around the side of the building heading for the alley in back. Spur never did get the man's name. He eyed the fancy whorehouse door. This whole case was getting messy. Three men dead now to go along with the robbery. Time to wrap it up.

He opened the door and stepped inside. An elegantly dressed woman with her brown hair attractively piled high on top of her head came forward at once. She smiled sweetly and for a moment Spur figured this was a legitimate eatery. Then he heard some wild, raucous laughter from somewhere upstairs and he got back on track.

"Good morning, sir. How may I help you? Are you interested in some lunch? We have a fine pheasant under glass today with an extremely dry wine and a cucumber and dandelion salad that some of my customers say they would die for."

"Sorry, not this time. I need to see the manager, and quickly."

Her friendly face lost its appeal. She frowned and stared at him a minute, then nodded and led him to a door at the side of the entryway. Behind them he heard a piano playing some classical music softly. Beethoven, he thought, and the clink of glasses and silverware. It was a restaurant after all, with all the trimmings, especially the naked girls upstairs.

The door opened and Spur saw an older woman with a large mole on her right cheek. She wore a fancy dress that had seen better days, and her henna red hair had a will of its own refusing to lie down or stay under several silver combs.

"This gentleman says he wants to see you," the hostess said and stepped back.

"I'm looking for Sully, law business. Best if you just tell me what number room he's in so I don't have to kick in all the doors upstairs. You understand."

"You're not the sheriff," she said.

Spur pulled out his identification card and badge and showed them to her. He gave her time to read them.

She nodded. "Don't hanker to have no trouble with the United States Government. Donna, look at your schedule and give the gentleman Sully's room number. You go up and pave the way so we don't have any trouble, and don't make a scene."

"Yes, ma'am."

The girl in the tight dress, Donna, led him back to a small standup desk at the side of the entry that hotel dining rooms often use. She looked at a printed form that had pencil marks on it, and then motioned.

"This way, Mr. McCoy."

"I didn't tell you my name."

"Everyone in town knows who you are and what you're doing here. Too bad you haven't caught the train robbers yet." She smirked, hardly able to contain her enjoyment.

"One of the robbers is dead, another running down the river, and the third one is right down here in room twelve."

"You read well upside down, Mr. McCoy. Let me go in first."

Spur didn't answer her. When they came to room 12 down the long hallway, he pushed Donna gently aside and tried the knob. It was locked. He stepped back and kicked his boot hard into the panel right beside the knob. The latch snapped and the door pivoted open.

A woman screamed.

A naked man lying on top of the woman looked

over his shoulder and furiously tried to get free of his penetration of the woman. She pushed him off her and over the far side of the bed.

Spur drew his six-gun and the woman screamed again. Donna looked in the room and retreated.

"Sully, get your pants on slow and easy. I don't want to see a hideout or that .45 on the bedpost move an inch. Otherwise, I'll shoot you right in your family jewels. You think how much that's gonna hurt and what it'll do to your love life."

"I ain't Sully. I'm Joe Taber."

"Sully, I brought you back from Chester yesterday, remember? I had you at the sheriff's office. I let you go, remember?"

Spur sighed and looked at the naked girl sitting on the bed, making no attempt to cover herself. She shrugged.

"Hell, yes. I'm Sully. Why you want me now?"

"Train robbery. Should put you away for ten years."

"How you gonna prove that?"

"A witness who'll testify that you bragged about the robbery, described it. How you lived in a rented house here in town with the other two robbers and with Amy Hellman, the supposed kidnap victim. How you worked for Doug Chandler all the time."

"Oh hell," Sully said. He bent and pulled on his boots, then slipped into his new shirt and looked at his six-gun.

"Better leave that for me, Sully," Spur said. He motioned for the girl to hand him the gunbelt. She did, but swung it at him hard, then she surged across the bed and jumped on him. Her legs wrapped around his hips and her breasts hit him in the face. She whaled away with both her fists at his face and head until he clawed her hands down and then unwound one leg and threw her on the bed.

While he did this, Sully surged out the door and charged down the hall.

By the time Spur got untangled from the naked whore and he looked into the hall, Sully was out of sight. He grabbed his hat that had fallen off in the soiled dove wrestling, and slammed it on his head and ran after Sully.

Two female heads poked out doors and watched him sprint by. One man came out in his underwear.

"What the fuck is going on out here?" he asked.

Spur brushed past him and ran to the stairs. He saw another stairway going down the back and he used it, jolting down three steps at a time. He had his Colt out of leather and ready for action.

At the bottom of the stairs was a closed wooden door. He twisted the knob and burst through to the outside. Six-feet ahead of him, Spur saw the deputy sheriff sitting in the dirt of the alley, looking around, dazed and confused, trying to find his hat.

Spur grabbed him and lifted him to his feet. "Deputy, Sully just came out that door. Where did he go?"

The deputy shook his head trying to clear it. He rubbed his forehead and wiped his hand across his face. "Oh, hell, he surprised me. Ran me down, took my six-gun and lit off down the alley, the short way. Don't know where the hell he is now."

Spur muttered about incompetent deputies and ran down the alley the way the deputy pointed. The chances that he could find the man now were slim, but he had to make the effort. He charged down to the end of the alley and looked both ways.

Chapter Sixteen

Two strokes of luck saved Spur McCoy that morning. The first was that Sully was not a fast runner. His legs were thick and heavy and he had always hated running. The second bit of good fortune for Spur was that Sully turned the wrong way.

If he had angled to the right, he would have been in the middle of the small town with dozens of people around that he could blend in with or simply slip into a store and disappear.

He chose to go the other way, heading out of the two block long downtown area. Ahead were a few shops and houses, and a block later only the gently rolling and summer green Arkansas countryside.

At the street, Spur looked both ways and spotted Sully pulling on his yellow shirt as he ran 50-yards ahead. He was in the middle of the dirt street and striding toward the last house before the rest of the town ended.

Spur held his six-gun in his right hand so it wouldn't flap on his thigh and raced after Sully. He wasn't about to let a key player like Sully get away again. He saw the man hesitate in front of the last house, then he ran up to the door, pushed it open and vanished inside.

Spur came up to the house warily. It made for a perfect ambush. As he hesitated 50-feet away, he heard a door slam and ran down to where he could see the back of the place. Sully had a rifle now and went charging across the open field in back of the house heading for some trees and brush maybe a quarter-of-a-mile away.

Spur swore out loud. This reminded him too much of the ambusher he had flushed out into the country a few days ago. He'd been easier to capture. This one had a rifle and a six-gun he took from the deputy sheriff. Maybe only five shots for that one since he had no gunbelt with rounds in loops. The rifle could be a seven shot, or he could have a pocketful of rounds.

An entirely different baseball game. Spur heard hoofbeats and saw a man riding across the country 200-yards away and heading for town. Spur fired once in the air and the man looked up. Spur waved his arms, then held up his hand for the rider to stop.

The cowboy pulled his horse up, then walked it toward Spur. When they came close enough to talk, Spur called out.

"I'm a United States lawman chasing a killer. I need to borrow your horse. You have a rifle in the boot?"

The cowboy shook his head. "No rifle, but you're welcome to borrow Skinflint, here. He's a good stallion. Just don't get him shot. I'll be at the Wentworth Hotel when you get back."

"Obliged," Spur said as the cowboy stepped down. "My name is Spur McCoy, U.S. Secret Service."

"Allister Quantrain," the cowboy said.

Spur mounted the dun stallion and kicked him gently as he rode toward the brush. He could see Sully easing into the small woodsy area and getting out of sight.

Spur rode at a gallop for a quarter-of-a-mile and edged into the woods, then began to move slowly forward. He was glad that Sully hadn't used the rifle on him as he rode toward the woods. That could mean he was short on rounds.

Sully knew he was unmasked, knew there was evidence against him. Now he'd be desperate, do anything necessary to escape. Spur stopped the horse and listened.

A leaf fell from a big maple tree and drifted down in front of Spur. It made no noise when it hit the mulch. Far off he heard a songbird staking out its territory. Now and again he heard the splash of water from the creek nearby. Nothing else.

He rode forward at a gallop for 100-yards, then stopped and listened again. This time he could hear someone crashing brush ahead of him. He couldn't tell how far off the man was.

Spur cut out of the brush and rode in the open country beside it for 100-yards, then stepped the light brown horse into the foliage and listened. He heard branches crack as someone moved toward him. Spur slid down from the horse and slipped a dozen yards toward the noise, then stepped behind the largest tree he could see and waited.

He had a good view from the far side of the thick trunk. It didn't cover him completely, but would make him a hard target. Spur waited. The sounds from ahead continued to come closer. Then they stopped.

Now Sully was listening.

After two or three minutes the sounds began again and they seemed to be coming directly toward Spur.

He had learned patience the hard way, tracking down Apaches, and Chiricahua Apaches at that. The pattern repeated itself, noise then silence, then more movement.

Spur checked around the tree and watched. He picked up movement in the brush ahead not 20-feet away. He looked down at his Colt. It wasn't cocked. No chance he could cock the hammer now to be ready to fire in a split second. He had to wait.

The figure moved, and now Spur could see that it was Sully. He had lost his hat. He held a six-gun in his right hand and worked slowly through the brush trying to be quiet.

Spur eased behind the tree now making sure

that it concealed all of him. All he had to do was wait.

Spur saw something coming toward him from the side, low and quiet. He turned his head to see it better. A snake, a big one, four-feet long. It moved slowly through the grass and weeds, across the woodsy mulch floor. It sensed a foreign odor and stopped, its forked tongue darting out again and again testing the air. Its beady black eyes stared at Spur's boots where he stood behind the tree. Standing was the only way he could completely conceal himself.

It was three-feet away now. The snake did a right turn and headed toward Sully. Spur saw that the robber was now less than ten-feet from the tree. Spur edged back out of sight. The big black snake moved forward toward Sully who had evidently stopped again to listen for any pursuit.

Spur edged his head around the tree to watch the snake. He saw that the snake had a round head, not a triangular one. He figured there weren't any rattlesnakes in Arkansas, but he wasn't sure. This one probably wasn't a deadly variety. A black snake, maybe a gopher snake, without fangs, just a half round of not very sharp teeth.

The snake and Sully came closer together. Sully was on his hands and knees now to go under some thick brush instead of crashing through it. He turned from his backward look and stared ahead just as the snake lifted its head a foot off the ground to investigate yet another strange smell. The snake's tongue darted out in question.

Sully screamed, then brought up his six-gun

and fired four times at the snake. The last round hit the snake in the head and slammed it to the side dead on impact.

"Oh God but I hate snakes!" Sully bellowed. He came to his feet and charged straight ahead, past the dead snake and toward Spur's tree. Spur waited and just as Sully came even with him, he brought the butt of his Colt down hard on the robber's head.

Sully looked and saw Spur just before he passed out. He slumped to the ground and groaned as he went limp in unconsciousness.

By the time Sully came to, Spur had his hands tied behind his back. Sully swore and tried to sit up. Spur helped him.

"That harmless gopher snake a friend of yours?" Spur asked.

"Harmless? I saw the way he stuck out his forked tongue at me. About ready to strike."

"He would have beaten me to it by about five seconds," Spur said. "His bite wouldn't do as much damage as one of my .45 rounds."

"You got ahead of me. How did you get ahead of me?"

"I had a horse. Didn't you see me get it from that cowboy?"

"No, I was too busy running for my life. I ain't going back with you. Kill me right here. I won't sit in jail and then prison for ten years."

Spur had been thinking about that. He needed something to offer the kid.

"What if I can get you a deal where you'll spend a year in jail and then get out?"

"Yeah, big chance with Judge Parker."

"Things can be arranged. You didn't kill anyone. You didn't rob a train, you just fired a few shots and rode with the robbers. You didn't blast open the Railway Express car door. Did you?"

"Hell, no. I carried the damn mail sacks while the other two guys got the girl."

"So, all you have to do is testify to the court exactly what Russ Dolan and Knute Safire did, and how it was set up, and paid for by Doug Chandler. It's Chandler we want most."

"A bargain. Can you swing it with Hanging Judge Parker?"

"I think so. Otherwise we don't have much of a case. The girl Lillian isn't what you'd call a reliable witness, especially in this town."

"Hell, I'll try it. Best chance I've had."

Spur shook his head. "Nope. The best chance you had was when I cut you loose that day. You should have taken the train to the end of the tracks out in New Mexico somewhere."

Sully scowled and nodded. "You damn right about that."

A half hour later, Sully had been locked away safely in the Fort Smith jail and the sheriff had a clerk writing up the charges against him. Sheriff Grimm grinned.

"Now I feel a little better, McCoy. You done us a lot of good hereabouts. You said we had another name, Knute something?"

"Knute Safire, Lillian said he went downriver on the boat. We might have a shot at finding him. Is the telegraph in to the capitol yet?"

"Been in a year now. I'll get wires off to every station down the line to the border at the Mississippi. Hard telling how far that young man might run. You say he was about thirty?"

"Around there. How is Judge Parker for making deals with one prisoner to get a conviction on another one?"

"He ain't high on it. Told me once he figured a man should pay his price owed to the law. Sometimes if that's the only way he can get two convictions, he'll at least think about it. You planning on using Sully there to testify against Doug Chandler?"

"Hoping to. Course, first we got to nail Chandler and bring him back to your lock up."

"So, you'll be heading downriver?"

"When does the next boat leave?"

"About two o'clock. You can make it. Oh, on Chandler. Me and the boys talked to everybody we could find who was home up around the Lowell mansion this morning. We found two women who saw somebody come out of the Lowell place last night. Not sure they could identify him, but he wasn't too tall and seemed to be a little on the heavy side."

"It was also pitch black out last night with lots of clouds over the moon. You know what a defense lawyer would do to those witnesses on the stand?"

"Kill them. So give it a try with Parker. We've got nothing to lose."

Ten minutes before the river boat pulled away from the dock at Fort Smith, Spur McCoy stepped on board and paid his passage. He had a 160 mile ride ahead of him. The little river steamer going downstream on the Arkansas River would average about ten miles an hour. With the stops at more than a dozen places along the river, it would take them until eight in the morning to make it to the capitol. Still a lot faster than riding a horse.

Spur asked about one of the cabins and found it available. It was ten dollars more. He paid it, went inside and locked the door. He dropped on the bunk and closed his eyes. He could use a good night's sleep. Twice someone knocked on the door, but he ignored the soft invitations and drifted off to sleep.

When he awoke it was dark. There was no light in his cabin. He struck a match, looked at the time on his Waltham. Nearly eight in the evening. He'd slept six hours. He found the lamp, lit it and saw how it was anchored down to the dresser. It wouldn't slide off if the little boat tipped upside down.

A knock came on the door, three gentle raps. Spur frowned and unlocked it and edged it open a crack on a safety chain.

"McCoy, it's me, Lillian. I saw you getting on the boat and I wanted to come with you. You ever fucked on a boat before? Me, I ain't never. Let me in and we can have at it just every which way until morning."

Spur growled. He didn't like surprises. Now if he'd thought of it first, it would be different.

"I'm working, I need my sleep. Go away."

"You've been sleeping six hours, McCoy. You're

as horny as an old stallion. Come on, open up."

Spur took the chain off the door and unlocked it. As he did, a heavy boot blasted against the door, rammed it open and flung Spur backwards into the cabin. A big, dark form surged inside and dropped on Spur. It had been years since he'd felt such a hard, heavy body slam into him that way. Like the wrestlers at the county fair.

He fought to get the man off him. Spur found one of the man's fingers and he bent it backward until the man screamed in pain. Spur pushed harder until he heard the digit break, then he slammed his elbow into the big man's head and rolled him away enough to stand.

Spur grabbed for his six-gun on the side of the bunk, but the giant shuffled that way making the grab out of the question.

"Who the hell are you?" Spur wheezed.

The man ignored the question. Spur could see him better now. He was big and solid and had a huge head covered with long hair and a full beard. He looked more like a lion than a man.

The man pulled a six-inch blade from his belt. Spur bent and retrieved a five-inch heavy knife from his boot. The room wasn't big enough for much maneuvering. Somebody could get cut up bad.

Spur shuffled to the left, darted out the cabin door into the companionway and rushed toward the aft deck where there was a ten-foot space for better movement. The heavy man came after him, ignoring Spur's available six-gun. Big and not smart, Spur decided.

Soiled Dove

A few men sat on the deck watching the summer sky. One look at Spur and the man behind him, and the deck sitters cleared away but remained for the show.

Spur held his knife like a stick, with the point forward so he could stab with it, but also slash up, down or sideways. The big bearded man came on deck grinning.

"Who hired you, yellow belly?" Spur snarled.

The man lunged forward. Spur danced back, careful not to stumble on any of the gear on board. He feinted one way, darted the other and sliced with his blade. It drew a quarter-inch deep slash across the other man's left arm. His knife remained in his right fist.

Spur berated himself for not carrying a belly gun. He had one from time to time, but he'd lost it when his carpetbag came up missing in Denver the last time. He hadn't replaced it. This would be an ideal time to have one.

He watched the man move again. He wasn't much of a classic knife fighter. Spur guessed the giant would sacrifice one cut on his arm so he could bull in and have a close up killing thrust, underhanded and into the gut. He kept his distance.

"Come on," the man growled, waving Spur forward. Spur waited. The big man grew impatient.

"Who hired you, asshole?" Spur spat. The man snorted, drove in when Spur had only one way to go without dropping overboard. As Spur dodged that way the big man changed directions. Spur countered the opposite way as the bearded one charged forward.

Spur was cleanly out of the way until he stepped back and pushed out one foot, spilling the giant into a coil of rope on the deck. The man rolled and came to his feet quickly.

"Lucky bastard," he snarled. "Won't be lucky next time."

"Luck has nothing to do with knife fighting. It's skill. You're too big and clumsy. Should I kill you or just slice you up and push you overboard?"

The words angered the large man. He charged in again and Spur started the same movement, stopping it as the man corrected and drove his knife four-inches into the heavy man's right shoulder.

The man wailed in pain. Spur drew out the blade and saw the other man drop his knife. He looked at Spur a moment, then went to the rail and dove cleanly over the side. A moment later they saw him in the soft light of a cloudless sky as he stroked strongly toward shore 30-yards away.

Some of the watchers clapped. Others complained because it was over so quickly.

Spur wiped the blade on some freight stacked on the deck, pushed the knife in his boot and went back to the cabin. Lillian sat on his bunk, her legs crossed, her skirt covering them. She watched him come in, close the door and lock it. When he looked at her, she lifted the six-gun with both hands and aimed it at him. She wasn't smiling.

"Sorry about this, McCoy. I just follow orders. Doug left me a letter telling me what to do if you tried to follow him. Bruno was supposed to solve the problem. Now it's up to me."

"You always do what Doug tells you?"

"Damn right, especially when he leaves me five twenty-dollar bills. I'll explain that you lured me in here and tried to rape me." She pulled her blouse open and tore her camisole so one breast showed. "That should do it."

"One problem," Spur said.

She laughed softly and looked up. "I figured you'd have something to say. What's the problem."

"The Colt has the safety on, you can't fire it that way."

"What?" Lillian looked down at the six-gun and frowned. When she looked back up, Spur had lunged forward and closed his big hand over the cylinder preventing it from firing. He pulled the gun out of her hands and pushed her back on the bed.

"Lillian, what am I going to do with you? You're supposed to be a killer, and here you fell for the oldest trick in the lawman's book. That's a revolver, stupid. It doesn't have a safety. There is no way you can put a safety on a revolver. Rifles have safeties."

He kept the Colt in his hand as he stared down at her. She grinned and pulled her blouse all the way open and lifted the torn chemise to show her breasts.

"You like my titties, McCoy. Eat a little. Graze on me. They like it, too. We might as well be friends. We've still got a long way to go before morning. Just because I tried to kill you twice, is no reason we can't get friendly enough to have some good sex. Come on, Spur, let's fuck up a storm and worry about Little Rock tomorrow."

"Maybe I'm getting bored with you, woman. I just had you this morning, remember?"

"Yeah, you teased me like wild. I loved it. Let's do that again. You make me want it so much I'll do anything to get your big whanger inside me."

"Maybe I don't want to."

"You know you do. You're getting a hard-on just watching my tits jiggle. Admit it."

"Maybe you can bribe me with some more information about good old Doug Chandler. He can't hurt or help you now. What else do you know about him that you can use to pay me off?"

"Plenty. He's planning on killing his father-in-law just as soon as he can find the right time. The old man had a stroke, he's in bed. Doug was going to do it with a pillow that night but they threw him off the place."

"He kill the rich man, Lowell?"

"Don't know. He didn't say. Might have. The bearer bonds missing?"

"All but one. I think it got lost under a ledger."

"That's enough, let's get to it."

"Not enough. What's Doug going to do in Little Rock?"

"You know. Team up with that pussy slut Amy Hellman and run off to New Orleans."

"He paid you a hundred dollars and you try to get me killed. You know how much he's made off this scheme?"

"Fifty-thousand?"

Soiled Dove

"Closer to a hundred and fifty-thousand."

She sat up. "That much? That cheap bastard. He could have given me a thousand and never missed it."

"You work cheap. Are you a cheap whore, too?"

"Not a chance. I go five bucks for a half hour. Twice what the soiled doves in the cat houses downtown get."

"You were cheap enough for me. When is Doug going to leave Little Rock?"

"He left on the ten o'clock boat. Put him into Little rock about sixteen to seventeen hours later. He won't even be in town before about two in the morning. He probably won't be able to contact slut Amy before mid morning, maybe ten o'clock. You're only about four hours behind him."

Spur put his hands on her breasts and began to caress them. "How does he get in touch with her?"

"Oh, that's nice. Yes, keep petting me that way. He'll have a kid take a letter to her at the governor's mansion."

"You know where they meet?"

"Not even a wild idea."

Spur bent and kissed her hanging breasts and she murmured. "Now that I like. I think we're going to have a good fucking night after all."

"Depends on what else you can tell me about Doug Chandler. Oh, you also have to promise to testify against him when I bring him back for trial."

"Sure, no problem."

Spur frowned. "Why did you agree so quickly."

She shook her head. "I know Doug better than

263

you do. There is no way he's going to be caught. If he is, then he won't stand trial. Doug would rather die today than stand trial and get hung or go to prison. Believe me. This is one man you won't bring back alive. You might bring his body back. But that's the only way you'll ever get him back into Fort Smith."

Chapter Seventeen

Doug Chandler arrived on the river boat at the Arkansas state capitol of Little Rock a little after three A.M. There had been a delay up the river. He went to the hotel he and Amy always used, the Algonquin, but she wasn't there under the name of Amy Chandler. He took a room and slept until something awoke him in the morning. Amy lay beside him, watching him. She had tickled his nose to get him awake.

"Hey, pretty lady, good to see you. Guess what I brought?"

"Some money for us to spend?"

"More than that. Let me show you." He climbed out of bed, pulled on his pants over the short underwear he slept in and took out the packet of fancy certificates.

"The bearer bonds. Good as a hundred dollar bill. We have ninety-nine thousand dollars worth." He let his voice rise with his emotion. "Do you understand just how much money that is for the two of us?"

"A hell of a lot more than I've ever seen. It's a huge bunch. You say these can be cashed in by anybody who has them? You can take one to a bank or stock salesman and sell it to him for cash?"

"That's right. They aren't registered by name. That means, anybody who has them can cash them."

"That enough cash money to take us all the way to New Orleans?"

"Baby doll, that's enough to take us to London or to Paris, France. Enough to take us around the whole fucking world."

"Now there's a great word, fucking."

"Hush, and think about the money. We have enough cash and bonds to last us the rest of our lives. We can live like a king and queen."

"Cash money, too?" she asked.

He opened his traveling case and took out the stacks of bills. He threw the covers up on the bed and sprinkled the money, new and used, on the bed until it covered the fabric and changed the bed into a blanket of green.

"Jump on it and wiggle around a little," he said.

"I've got to be naked to enjoy it." She stripped out of her clothes quickly and fell on the bed wallowing in the money. Her eyes sparkled and her hips humped up at him. Then she held out her arms as she lay on her back, her knees came up and opened showing him what she had for him.

"Do me right now, lover. I need you deep inside me. This money and you make me so hot I could fuck a big dog. Come on, right now."

He dropped his pants and went between her thighs. "Hey, remember the first time I fucked you?"

"Always remember that. You were gambling at that charity ball here in Little Rock and dressed to kill. I came up behind you as you played poker. Then I sat down and you got one hand under the table where nobody else could see and you diddled my clit until I exploded right there at the poker table. I had to rush to the ladies' powder room before I leaked all over."

Doug rubbed her big breasts and grinned. "Yeah, and then later that night we found a vacant bedroom and locked the door. We fucked the rest of the night."

"But we do better now. Like on all this money. Come on, get inside me."

"I want to go slow, to enjoy it, make it last."

"Damnit, Doug, do me right now."

"Beg me."

"Damn, no. I don't have to beg. I learned that a long time ago."

She pushed him to one side and reached her finger down on her clit and strummed it. "Fuck, I don't always need you, spoiled little boy." Her finger whanged her clit back and forth and her breathing quickened and her face distorted. With her other hand she rubbed her breasts, then began tweaking her nipples.

Doug watched her in surprise.

Before he could even try to help her, Amy gasped and then shivered. She shook and closed her eyes, panting and shaking and growling and then her hips began to hump upward, slowly at first, then faster and faster. Her hand moved lower and she put three fingers together. She pumped them in and out of her well lubricated cunt.

"Oh, damn!" she crooned. "Oh, yes!" She wailed and moaned and pumped harder and harder until she broke into another climax, screeching this time and braying with delight. Her eyes were still closed as she wailed and humped and at last broke over the edge and eased down until she was quiet and still on her back. One hand held her crotch and the other cupped a breast. She hummed softly to herself.

After a minute or two she opened one eye and looked up at him. "See, I don't always need you. Now I can say I fucked myself on top of fifty-thousand dollars."

"Hell, anybody can rub herself off that way. So what? When are we leaving downriver? We'll need some disguises. You should get a dark wig of some kind and some dark glasses and a big floppy hat."

"Can't go right away. In three days we're having the Debutante Ball. This is the year I'm coming out. Hell, I have to be here or my mother will have a fit. She can be tough when she's really furious."

"Three days? Not a chance I can wait that long. By then there could be cops and sheriffs and Federal lawmen all over this town hunting for me like wild. We got to get out of this damn town early tomorrow morning."

She sat up and her breasts bounced and jiggled delightfully. "Not a chance in hell I can go tomorrow. Three days, then I slip away right after the big dance."

"In the meantime I get nailed by that Secret Service guy or the local sheriff. He must have twenty wanted telegrams about me sent out all along the river by now. Look, I got to leave tomorrow morning."

She pushed him gently back on the bed and played with his beginning of an erection.

"Baby, you always think better after you've been sucked off. You want me to do a mouth job on you right now?"

"No. Not yet. Get on your hands and knees, woman, and spread them just a little."

"Oh, glory, he's gonna do a doggie. Yeah. Love it."

She dropped on her hands and knees on the bed and Doug went behind her. A moment later she moaned in delight and almost at once she climaxed again.

"Love it!" she shouted, then they both fell forward and he kept working until he climaxed quickly and fell on top of her in total exhaustion.

He rolled away and gave a big sigh before he fell to sleep. She knew how he was after a good one. Slowly Amy nodded, then she eased off the bed, pulled on her clothes and made sure he was still sleeping. She thought of taking his clothes, but he had a whole bag full.

She went to the dresser top and looked at the bearer bonds. It took her only a moment to decide. She scooped them up, arranged them in one neat stack, then pushed them inside her blouse and around to her back. She made sure her blouse was tucked in well and buttoned securely, then she eased the door open and left. All she had to do was hide out somewhere until the police caught him. Maybe he'd get scared and decide to go downriver today.

Amy grinned. Now let her father try to boss her around. He always had held her allowance over her head. Now she had more money than he did. She scowled for a minute.

"Damn, I should have taken that thirty-thousand of my ransom money as well."

She shrugged, and walked across the street. She knew exactly where she would hide until poor Doug got out of town or was caught by the police. He'd never find her there.

Back in the hotel room, Doug Chandler woke up five minutes after Amy had left. He reached for her, then his eyes snapped open and he sat up. Her clothes weren't on the floor where she had thrown them. She wasn't in the room. He leaped off the bed and checked the bearer bonds on the dresser.

Gone, all of them.

"Damn that bitching whore!" he shouted. He quickly picked up all the bills off the bed and stuffed them into his traveling case. Then he dressed and found his door key.

Soiled Dove

She had stolen the bonds from him. How did she think she could get away with it? He knew her better than she knew herself. He had been thinking where she would go. There was no chance she would go home. The governor would control her then. He grinned. Yeah, he had it. He knew exactly where she would go. It would be the last place that she would think he would look for her. He was certain she would be there.

Ten minutes later, Doug stepped into the office of the Shrine School of Our Lady of Grace. It was one of the best schools in Little Rock. Even though Amy wasn't Catholic, her father had sent her to the school to help him pull in the Catholic vote. Doug had been there once before when Amy took some presents to her ex-teachers. This was the one place in the whole state where she could feel safe.

Sister Mary Benedict came out smiling as always. Her pale white hands were folded in front of her habit and she nodded.

"Yes, sir, what might we do for you today?"

"I was supposed to meet Amy Hellman here. Has she arrived yet?"

"Oh, actually she has, just a few minutes ago. She's talking right now with Sister Mary Utley. Why don't you come down this way."

The nun led him to a door that had no name or number on it. She nodded at the door and walked briskly away, confident that she had done the right thing.

Doug opened the door and grinned. Amy stared at him in disbelief. The nun had her back to him.

He motioned to Amy who stood and smiled at the nun.

"Sister Mary Utley, I have to go now. I'm glad we had a chance to have this little talk. I'll see what I can do about that new slateboard you need for your classroom."

The nun nodded and smiled at Doug who waved.

He caught Amy's arm and propelled her out of the room, down the hall and out a side door. "Neat. Where do you have the bonds?"

He saw the bulge at her back and touched her blouse there. He could feel the heavy paper bonds.

"Good, little girl, but not quite good enough."

"Yeah? What am I supposed to get out of all this? Just your big prick poking me now and then? You haven't even given me my fifteen-thousand, my half of the ransom money. I left you all fifty-thousand. You should have been happy at that." She looked at him and saw the anger on his face. "Where the hell we going?"

"Down by the river, where do you think. You stole from me. I'll put up with almost anything else. I know you got dicked a lot by my three robbers. That I don't worry about. They can't break your body. But nobody steals from me. Nobody."

"Hey, you get the bonds back. Look, I'll get them for you right now."

She started to unbutton her blouse, but he stopped her. He turned her around and lifted her blouse from her skirt and took out the bonds. He slid them inside his open shirt and then buttoned it.

"Now the bonds are in a safe place."

"So, we're even," Amy said, backing away from him. They were on a side street with only two stores on it and a few houses. It ended half a block down at the water. There was no dock here.

"Not quite even, little girl. You stole from me. That's unforgivable."

"So what? You stole from my father, from old man Lowell, from the railroad. You're no better than me."

"I didn't steal from you."

"You did. You stole my fifteen-thousand. You weren't going to give it to me."

Doug grinned. "Yeah, forgot about that. Yeah, I stole your fifteen-thousand, so sue me."

"I should kill you, you bastard. You never intended to take me with you, did you?"

Doug stopped when they came to the edge of the water. There were some small trees and brush growing there. He pushed her into the brush until they were nearly out of sight of the nearest house.

"Actually, I did plan on taking you with me to New Orleans. I wanted to show you off, show off your big tits. But now, I can't do that. You stole from me."

"So leave, go by yourself."

"You have to be punished for stealing from me." He hit her with his fist right on the side of her jaw. She cried out in pain and surprise and fell to the ground. He dropped beside her, his knee on her chest, pinning her to the ground.

"You stole from me, Amy, unforgivable. You've got to be punished for that."

He saw the fear in her eyes, and clamped his hand over her mouth so she couldn't scream. Then he took a knife from his boot and cut her blouse open. The blade was sharp. He made a three-inch slice across her right breast from the base up to the nipple.

She surged against his hand, screaming, but the sound came out only a gurgle.

"You must be punished with blood," he said.

He sliced the other breast, deeper, watching the blood gather and run down the side of her soft white belly. He cut her again, down the center of her chest, between her breasts all the way to her navel. She bit his hand and he yelped and drew it back.

Amy screamed as loud as she could. She screamed four times before he got his hand over her mouth again.

"You shouldn't have done that, Amy. After all we meant to each other. I was gonna take you with me. I was gonna give you the fifteen-thousand. You just got greedy. Your little cunt got greedy and wanted lots of cash to be free of your father. Well, you're gonna be free of him in a few minutes."

Her eyes went wider with fear.

"Amy, you know you shouldn't have stolen those bonds, don't you?"

She nodded.

"You know you've been terribly bad stealing them and running away where you figured I'd never find you. You admit that, don't you?"

Amy nodded.

274

"Now, Amy, did you tell the police where I was? Did you tell the sheriff or anybody?"

She shook her head side to side.

"Don't lie to me, Amy. I can hurt you a lot more."

Tears streamed down her face and made it hard for him to hold his hand over her mouth.

"Can you be good now that you've been punished for lying, Amy Hellman?"

Amy nodded.

"Oh, Amy, you're lying to me again. You know that if I let you go now, you'll run straight to the sheriff's office or the Chief of Police and tell them exactly where I am, what I'm going to do and what I did to you. You'd do that wouldn't you, bad Amy Hellman?"

She shook her head side to side.

"Quit lying to me."

He let go of her mouth and slapped her so hard it slammed her head to the side. Before she could scream again his left hand covered her mouth and this time her nose. She struggled to breathe.

"Amy, Amy. I'm sorry about this, but there's just nothing else that I can do."

He put the knife against her neck and in one quick slice pulled it sharply across her left carotid artery and her jugular vein. Her eyes glittered with pain for a fraction of a second, then dulled and went dark as the blood spurted from her carotid ten-feet across the brush and trees, pulsating out each time her heart beat.

He sat there on his knees watching the blood spurt time and time again. Each time it came, the arc was shorter until at last the rich red blood simply dribbled out of her neck. Her head rolled to one side and he heard a long, last breath gush from her lungs.

Doug Chandler sat there on his knees next to the blood splashed body and cried. He put his hands over his face to block out the view. She had been so great in bed, always ready for a good time. Always came when he called. She had given him a lot of pleasure and fine nights of lovemaking. Now she was gone. The fact that he had killed her wasn't important.

He stood, slid the knife back in his half boot and wiped his hands off on the grass. He didn't have a drop of blood on him. He turned and walked out of the brush.

As he did, a man came out of the house nearest him. He was older, but spry and sharp.

He waited as Doug walked toward him.

"What happened to your girl friend?" the man asked. "I heard her scream."

Doug tried to draw his six-gun but remembered he had left it in the hotel room.

"None of your business," Doug barked and ran past him up the street toward his hotel.

Now he had to get out of there. Get out of town before the police did find him. Now they had a new charge and one they might be able to prove. He stopped and looked back at the old man. He could kill him easily.

Doug changed his mind and ran on up the slight hill toward the rest of town and the hotel.

In back of him, the old man shuffled down to the brush and pushed into it. He came out a moment later, rushing as fast as he could on his bad leg. He went right past his house and to the next block, then over one more to the County Sheriff's Office. Inside, he told them what he had seen, gave a description of the man and the direction he had headed.

Spur McCoy had been talking with the County Sheriff and the Little Rock Chief of Police.

"This the same man?" the sheriff asked.

Spur turned to the witness. "Was the girl a young blonde with short hair, maybe 21 and slender?"

"Yep, sounds like her."

"Was the man short, maybe five-four or so, a little overweight, with brown hair?"

"Sounds like him. Yelled at me and hurried past."

"I can identify the girl," Spur said. "If she's Amy Hellman, the man involved is probably Doug Chandler."

"Amy, the governor's daughter?" the sheriff asked, his eyes wide in surprise.

"The same. It's a long story involving a fake kidnapping up the other side of Fort Smith. You must have heard about it. A lot of money was involved.

"Sheriff, I'd suggest you put a man at the railroad station and at the dock and livery stables. Don't let anyone who fits the description of Doug Chandler leave town. I'll go with the witness and confirm that the girl is Amy Hellman. If she isn't, I'll let you know quickly.

"Doug Chandler is wanted on several other

charges as I was telling you earlier, including a double murder."

Spur looked at the witness. "Now, sir. If you'd take me where the body is, I'd appreciate it."

Spur, the witness and two deputy sheriffs hurried along the street toward the river.

The moment Spur stepped into the brush near the Arkansas River, he knew that the dead girl was Amy Hellman. He covered her breasts, growled when he saw the slash marks on her body and the final slash across her throat. It had to be in that order. If she were already dead the cuts on her breasts would not have bled since her heart had stopped beating and there would be no blood pressure.

If it was Doug Chandler who killed the girl, he must have been out of his mind with anger to make her suffer so much before he killed her.

Spur set his mouth in a firm line and walked away from the site eager to get on the trail of this madman and bring him to justice. Now it seemed certain that Doug Chandler was the linchpin that held this whole series of robberies, swindles, murders and kidnappings together.

Chapter Eighteen

Knute Safire figured that Little Rock was far enough to run. He knew the man who set up the train heist was on the same boat he came on, but it didn't worry him. He knew that Doug Chandler would be moving on down to the Mississippi shortly and then all the way to New Orleans. He had told him so.

All Knute had to do was look out for himself. He'd been to Little Rock before. The place was growing like a spring cabbage. Must be ten-thousand people in and around the town. Booming, some said. He'd had a woman here for a while.

At the moment he was in the Red Ox Saloon where he had spent most of the first day in town after the river boat had arrived early in the wee small hours.

He'd slept on the way downstream on a bale of burlap bags. Now he finished the beer and wondered if he should have another one. He needed a place to stay. He thought of the rooming house where he lived the last time he was in Little Rock: Mrs. Grundy's Boarding House.

It was all right. The food was good. Damnation, could that woman cook! She was a widow, maybe thirty-five or so. Not bad looking with a nicely cushioned body. Knute grinned thinking about that one night she came to his room late and knocked. He was in his pants and bare to the waist.

He opened the door and she pushed inside and closed it. She had a glass in her hand and was either half drunk or pretending to be. She hadn't made any pretense about what she wanted. She put the glass down and took off her blouse. Then she had pushed her bare tips up against him and kissed his mouth.

They spent that night together, and two more, before he had to go downstream to do a small piece of work for a man. He hadn't seen her since.

Knute wiggled his toes thinking about the fifty-dollars he had in each sock. Yeah, good place to hide money. He had taken Doug's advice and kept his cash out of sight. He'd broken a dollar bill to buy his brews. Nothing unusual about that. If he'd flashed a twenty the barkeep might have signalled a tough to beat him up and take his money. A lot of crooked aprons worked on a 50-50 split with the mugger.

He tipped the beer bottle again, but it was empty. Better see about somewhere to stay. He figured on a bath, then a new shirt and a new hat to spruce up his appearance, and then maybe one of the soiled doves. Hell, it had been almost a week since he did Amy.

He snorted thinking about sexy Amy. She's the governor's daughter but she sets up her own kidnapping to get some of her old man's money. Strange. She was absolutely wild about sex. He wondered if Doug would poke her all the way down the river. Probably. He didn't worry abut Amy. She'd make out fine wherever she landed. She was that smart.

He pushed away from the table and walked out the saloon door.

Uta, that had been her first name. Uta Grundy at the board and room place. For just a minute he thought of settling down, poking Uta once a week or so to keep her happy, and do little odd jobs around the boarding house and let her support him.

He thought about it as he turned toward her place. It was about half-a-mile from the main part of town. Not easy to get to, but worth it for the suppers. Damnation, but that woman could cook . . . and fuck! She went crazy in bed, but never until she was stark naked. Nothing was too wild for her. If you could think of it, and it didn't hurt, she'd do it.

On his way, Knute passed the county sheriff's

office. He usually went on the far side of the street past any sheriff or police office, but this time he merely pulled the wide brim of his tan hat down a little more. Just before he got there, three men burst out of the county sheriff's door.

"Down at the end of Taggart Street?" the largest of the men asked. A deputy sheriff with a silver star on his shirt nodded.

"Yes, sir. That's what the witness said. That government man checked it out. He said no two ways about it, she's the governor's daughter all right. Throat slashed. Blood all over the body."

Knute edged up against the store front next to the sheriff's office and leaned heavily against the siding. Amy dead? Who the hell would do that? Doug? He could get hellish mad sometimes. Not much control of his temper. Damnation, gonna be hell to pay around here. He best get to Uta's place fast and settle in for a day or two until all of this murder business was settled.

The lawmen were gone down the street. He passed the office, then walked a little faster. Yeah, Uta's would be good. She took the newspaper. There'd be a story about it tomorrow, all the gruesome facts. He walked faster and didn't notice anymore the way the fold of greenbacks in his socks scratched his leg.

The boarding house was just as he remembered it. He might fix it up a little. Maybe some new paint and a trim. Hell, he had enough money.

He went up the plank sidewalk from the street, mounted the two wooden steps and started to knock. Then he grinned, turned the knob and pushed the door inward. It was about three in the afternoon. Uta would be getting things ready to start supper.

No one was in the hall or parlor. He saw the dining room table set for six. She wasn't full of boarders, good.

He went down the hall to the kitchen and caught the wonderful smell of fresh baked bread.

The moment he stepped in the kitchen, a woman turned and looked at him.

"Hi, Uta. Knute is back."

Uta was thick waisted with large breasts, heavy arms and a sour, pinched-in face. Her eyes were close together and she had her dark hair pulled in back and tied in a bun. She wasn't nearly as pretty as he remembered her. Uta stared at him a minute.

"Yeah, Knute. I remember you."

"You should, Uta. We were good together in your big bed."

Uta grinned and he saw the gaps in her front teeth. "Oh, yeah, that Knute. You back to stay?"

"For a time at least. You have my old room?"

"Nope, but there's another one. Bed don't make no noise when you bouncing on it."

Knute rubbed a growing erection behind his fly. "Uta, you have time right now?"

"Here in the kitchen in front of my pots and pans and celery stalks?" She giggled. "Not now. Got to make supper. You move into room eight, then I heat you up some water and you have a bath. I like you best all clean."

Knute nodded and turned. He wanted to jump

her right there, but he'd best take it slow. If this was going to be a hideout for a while, he'd have to take it soft and easy.

He went up the stairs, passed his old number six room and down to the end of the hall to number eight. It was half again as big as his former room. The bed was newer, had two chairs, a dresser and a small writing table.

He opened his blue carpetbag and took out some different clothes. The brown shirt was clean. Yeah, now that he had money, he'd buy some new clothes. Was he trying to impress this woman? Hell, yes. The dance hall hookers didn't look any better and she was a lot cheaper.

When he got down to the bathroom on the first floor, Uta had one bucket of hot water there and said she'd bring another one.

"Got me a new stove with coils in the fire box for the water to run through from the tank on the side. Gets water hot and keeps it hot in the reservoir for a long time."

She stood there as he poured the water in the tub. When she came back with the second bucket of water he had his shirt off.

Uta paused for a minute and giggled again. "I best not get my juices all riled up watching you take off your pants. I'll wait for the good part till tonight."

She tossed him a bar of store bought soap. "Get washed up. Supper promptly at six-thirty, case you done forgot."

"Hey, woman, I ain't forgot." He slid his pants down and watched her. Uta grinned, turned promptly and left the room before he could get his underwear down.

After a long bath, Nate put on his clean clothes, buffed his boots the best he could with the towel, and took his other clothes back to his room.

By the time he got downstairs again, there were three men and a woman waiting in the dining room. He recognized two of them who had been boarders when he was here before. Knute nodded at them and stood by the window looking outside.

He hadn't heard anything more about Amy Hellman which was fine by him. He wanted all of that trouble to go away. He'd been thinking about what to do next. He was just a year past thirty and he didn't want to go on robbing trains the rest of his life. He figured he'd been lucky on this one. He heard that Russ Dolan got himself killed over in Indian Territory.

Russ damn well couldn't enjoy that money he'd stolen. Ten thousand dollars. How did he have nerve enough to try that? He knew that Doug Chandler would track him down.

Five-hundred dollars and Knute had earned every dollar. He still had most of it. He figured he'd spent about ten dollars so far including his ticket on the boat. He had the rest of the cash in his small carpetbag upstairs far back under the bed. It couldn't stay there long. Tomorrow he'd have to put it somewhere. Where could he hide it? He thought of a bank, but wouldn't they ask him where he got so much money? Maybe not in a big place like Little Rock.

Two more men came in and at the same time

Uta carried in a tray with fried chicken, mashed potatoes and two kinds of vegetables in large serving dishes.

Before they sat down, Uta introduced him to all the people at the table. She gave them his name, then went around fast. He didn't try to remember any name except the woman's, Priscilla something. They sat down and ate.

Knute had forgotten that supper in a boarding house wasn't a time for polite or any other kind of conversation. The serving bowls came around the table. People helped themselves and then ate. Now and then there would be a request for the salt or butter or maybe to pass the chicken.

Knute sat beside one of the men he had known there before, a clerk in a store downtown somewhere. They nodded and ate and when the dessert came, bread pudding with whipped cream topping, they finished it and both stood about the same time. They went into the parlor where the men were allowed to smoke. Cigars or pipes were the favorite. The man Knute had sat beside offered him a long thin cigar that was nearly black.

"I get them in from New Orleans," the man said. "I think they come from Jamaica. Case you forgot, I'm Ben Upworth."

He held out his hand and Knute took it. "Yeah. I'm Knute Safire. You still at the store?"

"Yep. Probably die right there in the hardware section counting out some half-inch long by one-eighth inch stove bolts."

They both chuckled.

"You here for a time?"

"Yep, near as I can tell. Finished a project. Now I'm hunting something new."

Ben took a long pull on the cigar, tried to blow a smoke ring and failed. He shook his head. "Never could do that. Looking, huh? You take to clerking in a store?"

"Hardware store? I . . . I don't think hardly."

"Nice steady work. Know I'm gonna have a job. Get paid regular. Not a lot, but enough to get by."

"How much is the pay?"

"Boss said he'd pay a man starting work nine dollars a week. That's for six days, nine hours a day, eight in the morning to six at night."

"Sounds like one hell of a lot of work."

"Get used to it. I got no family to worry about or plan for. What the hell, it's interesting."

"Hardware, huh? Hell, I might give it a try. Why don't I let you know in a couple of days? I need to kind of settle down after my river trip."

"Sure, no problem. Boss ain't in a rush. I'll tell him you might come see him."

They sat on the worn green sofa and talked about this and that. The woman in the group, Miss Priscilla something, passed through quickly, smiling and fanning away the smoke as she went down the hall and they heard her go up the stairs.

She was in her thirties, Knute guessed, slender with big breasts and long brown hair. She had a sweet face, about twice as pretty as Uta.

"School teacher," Ben said when she was out of sight. "Right nice looking woman. Smart as a buggy whip, that Priscilla. I mean, yes sir, she's a smart one. Has been to college for two years she told us one night. Right nice too, not uppity or snooty. Now that it's summer and no school, she's working in a book store downtown somewhere. Told you she was smart."

"She ever . . . I mean, is she friendly with anybody here?"

"Nope. Friendly, but not like you mean. She had a gentleman friend once, but I hear he left town sudden. I figure she'll be married inside of a year, before school's out next spring."

The men finished their smokes and some drifted upstairs. Two headed out for a card room. Knute excused himself and took a walk around a couple of blocks. When he came back, no one was downstairs. He went to the kitchen and pushed the door open.

Uta turned and grinned when she saw him. "You look a lot better all cleaned up," she said.

"Getting some new clothes tomorrow."

"Good. Those are getting ratty."

"You still have your three rooms in back here?"

She grinned and she glanced down at his crotch. "Still do. Why you asking?"

"Do your bed springs still squeak?"

She laughed softly. "Does your pecker still go soft so damn quick after you get him shot off?"

"Yeah, but he's just resting, waiting for the next go-round."

She turned back toward the stove and fumbled with her hands at her chest a minute. When she swung around, she had opened her blouse showing him both her naked breasts.

"Like my little friends?"

Soiled Dove

"Oh, yeah. Right now?"

"No." She turned back and buttoned the blouse. "About ten o'clock after everyone is settled down. In my place, where it don't matter a fuck if the bed springs squeak or not."

Knute chuckled and started toward her, but she held up her hands. "Not now, about ten. You got a watch?"

He pulled out a battered pocket watch tied to the belt loop of his pants with a leather thong.

"Good, see you there about ten. Now scoot before somebody comes. I got my reputation to preserve."

He left and realized he had the start of an erection. Glory be, it hadn't been that long. He rubbed it gently and went up to his room. It was a little after 7:30. He had two-and-a half hours. Idly, he wondered which room the school marm lived in. No way to tell. Now there would be one good one to get all bare assed and waving them tits at him. Oh, yeah, nice.

He lay on the bed and remembered Uta. She liked it best when she got to be on top. Hell, didn't matter to him. What he needed was a short nap to get his strength up for a wild fucking night. He laughed and closed his eyes. He'd wake up well before ten o'clock.

It seemed only a few seconds later when Knute opened his eyes. The room was dark. He found a match in his pocket and struck it on the wooden floor. His Waltham pocket watch showed nine P.M.

He held the match and lit the lamp on the

dresser. An hour more? Things seemed quiet in the place. He opened the door and could hear nothing. Knute walked softly down the hall and then back to his door. The only sound he heard was someone snoring in room four.

He went back in his room and sat on the bed for a moment. All he could think about was Uta's massive breasts. They were as big as small watermelons. He'd never seen such big tits in his life. She wouldn't mind if he was a little early. He'd slip down there and surprise her. Yeah. Some women he'd had liked to pretend that he was raping them. They'd wail and scream and run away, and then when he caught them, they'd wind up practically raping him.

He slipped down the hall and took the steps one at a time, stepping on the part near the wall where they wouldn't squeak as they used to do.

Knute eased through the kitchen without a sound and went down the short hall to the door that led to Uta's back apartment she had built so she could rent all the rooms upstairs. He put his hand on the knob, wondering if he should knock.

He shook his head and turned the knob. It was not locked. Knute eased the door inward and saw that a light was on. It was burning low on a table next to a soft, new looking couch. He knew where the bedroom was.

Knute paused. Should he go in and surprise her? Maybe she was having a bath or something. No. She knew he was coming. She'd be ready. He was just a little early.

He grinned and walked the dozen feet to the

bedroom door that opened off the parlor. Just before he reached for the door, he paused. A sound came from inside. He didn't know what it was. A low cry? Maybe a moan? He frowned. Had she started without him?

It was a door that had a keyhole and a lock. He bent and looked through the keyhole. Knute couldn't remember ever doing anything like this before. He adjusted his good right eye and focused on the other side of the room.

He could see the bed. Someone lay on top of it. He saw naked legs. Then, to his surprise, he saw another set of naked legs. She was screwing somebody else? Couldn't she wait for him? He was about to push the door open when a woman's back, shoulders and head came up from the bed so she was in a sitting position. It wasn't Uta. He looked closer.

Damnit, it was the school teacher, Priscilla. She was naked and bouncing around, moaning, and had her head thrown back. He saw hands come up and caress her breasts. Then Uta sat up beside the schoolmarm and they kissed, mouth to mouth. Open mouth to open mouth.

My God! He'd heard about women who made love with women, but he'd never seen it before. What did they do? How did they do it? Rub each other off? Finger fuck each other?

He watched as the two women sat on the edge of the bed side by side with their legs spread. They pushed their hands down to each other's crotches.

Hey, he could solve their problem in a rush. He could do two of them. He stood, knocked, pushed the door open. He grinned at the two naked women.

"Ladies, looks like I arrived just in time. I'd say you have a real need here, and I'm the man who can fill that need in both of you. Oh, one at a time, of course. But in days like these, don't you agree that people should share with each other?"

"Get the hell out!" Priscilla snarled. She held her hands to cover her breasts.

"You big, dumb ox, I told you ten o'clock," Uta said, a small grin on her face.

The school teacher looked at Uta in shocked surprise. "You mean you were going to . . . to . . . with him?"

"Sure, Pris. You knew I went both ways. You're fun, but I miss a real good poking now and again. You never had one?"

"Of course, I just prefer the gentler, softer approach of another woman." She stood. "Well, it doesn't matter. I'm entirely out of the mood now. You two go ahead and have your games. I'll just slip into my clothes and go back to my room. I am disappointed in you, Uta. I didn't know that you'd ever been unfaithful to me before." Big tears streamed down her cheeks.

She didn't turn around, just stood there letting Knute stare at her naked breasts and the swatch of black fur at her crotch. Then she pulled on a skirt and a blouse and shoes and hurried to the door.

"We'll have to talk about this, Uta. I never let anyone else share my partner. I thought you knew that." She didn't wait for a reply. She turned and hurried out the door which she closed softly.

Uta shrugged.

"Silly little bitch. She never said anything about not fucking anybody else." Uta shook her head. "I guess she just assumed that she could have me all to herself. I know she doesn't fuck men anymore. Too bad, really. She's a good looker. Could have all the men in my place here the same night if she wanted them. I've seen them watching her. She flaunts those tits of hers every chance she gets. Nicely formed, ain't they? Course, they're not as big and beautiful as mine. Maybe she likes to tease men a little, just so she can tell them 'no' when they ask her."

"Maybe," Knute said. "Sorry I busted in. You and her were. . . . "

"Making love, yes. Not the way you and I do. More gentle, a lot of rubbing and talking and feeling and touching."

"Yeah, I saw a little through the keyhole. Is kissing her different than kissing me?"

"I don't remember. Come here."

Knute sat down on the bed beside her and bent in and kissed her lips. They came open and he parted his. Before he knew it, he was panting and so was she.

She had his shirt off the minute after their lips parted and then knelt in front of him and pulled open his pants.

Neither of them heard the bedroom door open. They looked up to see Priscilla standing there, a big revolver in both hands aiming it at them.

"Damn both of you," the woman screamed.

Before Knute could move she pulled the trigger. He had been about to rise when the heavy slug hit him in the shoulder. It spun him half around. He regained his balance and leaped up and rushed the woman with the gun. She cocked the hammer and pulled the trigger again. This time the round caught Knute full in the chest from four-feet away, drove him back on the bed, covering Uta who crouched half under him.

The woman with the gun fired once more, this time at Uta but she missed wide. Then Priscilla turned and fled out the door as Uta heard voices and sounds from the other tenants coming to see what the shooting was all about.

Chapter Nineteen

The moment Spur left the side of the Arkansas River where Amy Hellman's body lay, he knew he had a nearly impossible task. Little Rock was in no way a small place. How could he find one man in this town of probably more than 10,000?

First he jogged to the river landing where the passenger boat docked. He found out the next boat downriver would leave in two hours. The next boat upriver was four hours away. There were two city police there watching the ticket window and they would be on hand for the next boat departures.

There was a train spur up to Little Rock, but not on to Fort Smith. The train that came in here was a part of the Union Pacific network of rails that went to the Mississippi River and eventually all the way to New Orleans.

The killer could leave on the train. He could also rent a horse and ride downstream and get on the boat at another dock, or at the next train stop south.

Spur checked at the train station and found two deputies and Little Rock policemen patrolling the ticket office and the train about to leave. They had checked the train for any suspicious passengers.

"You don't know him," Spur said. "I do. Let me take a look."

Spur hurried through the three passenger cars but agreed that none of the people on board could be Doug Chandler unless he was a wizard at costuming and makeup.

By the time Spur McCoy hurried back to the sheriff's office, the county's top lawman stood there shaking his head. "I don't know what's happening in this town. The governor's own daughter cut up that way, slaughtered. We want to find that bastard, if he's the one who did it."

"Chances are mighty good he did. If you had just killed the girl, how would you try to get out of town? Train, boat? How?"

The sheriff hooded his eyes with heavy brows and scratched his cheek.

"Wouldn't try the boat or the train. Too easy to check them. If this is Chandler, no chance he's going upstream back to Fort Smith and his troubles there. So, I'd hire myself a horse and ride downstream to the next boat stop or train station."

"Good. Yes, sounds reasonable. How far is the

next boat stop downstream?"

"About five miles. Little village that has a big sawmill back in the timber. Ships logs and lumber out of there. Place is called Bayview."

"How far is it to the first train stop down river?" Spur asked.

"Tougher there. There's a flag stop long 'bout seven or eight miles. But for that he'd have to go in and buy a ticket and make himself conspicuous. First one with a station and platform and all is near fifteen-miles east and south along the river."

"So it looks like the boat. How many livery outfits in town?"

"Four. Yes, I'll send a man to each one to hang around and wait for a guy who looks like this Chandler."

"Give me a list of them and where they are. I want to check all four for the next few hours. If I were Chandler, I'd get out of this town as soon as I could. He should have enough cash on him, something like fifty-thousand dollars."

Spur walked to the first livery, the closest one. There was a sheriff's deputy there talking with the owner. No one had rented a horse all day. Spur rented one with saddle and all set to ride.

"Watch for anybody who wants a mount. Check them out good. But remember that Chandler could have a belly gun by now, or a .45. Be careful."

Spur rode the bay mare out of the barn and a quarter-of-a-mile north to the next livery. They didn't have saddle horses to rent there. He got instructions to the third one and found it on the other side of town. A city policeman was already there. Spur waved him over as he talked to the merchant.

"Yep, rented four single mounts today. Two to women, one to a barber who thinks he's a wild west cowboy, and the last one to a guy about half an hour ago. Seemed nervous and in a hell of a rush."

"Can you describe him for me?" Spur asked, an eagerness in his voice.

"Not too tall, maybe five-four or so. A little on the heavy side, but not, you know, real fat. Clean shaven. Maybe twenty-five to thirty."

"Sounds like my man. How did he pay for the rental horse?"

"Said he'd need it for a week, so I charged him for a week. Two dollars a day. Fourteen dollars. He gave me a twenty."

"You know where it is? You didn't get it mixed up with the rest of the cash?"

"Mister, I only took in one twenty-dollar bill in the last week. Know it's the same one. Just a second."

He went into a small office and came out with the bill. It was brand new. Spur checked the serial numbers. It was one of the stolen new bank notes.

"This is a stolen bill, sir. I'm giving it to this policeman, he'll turn it in and ask his chief what to do with it. Officer, also tell your chief and the sheriff that I'm sure that Chandler is mounted and heading down river." Spur turned back to the livery man. "Did the rider you described say where he was going?"

"Not a word. Talked as little as possible."

"Which way did he start out when he left here?"

"Took off to the east and some south. Only road down there is the old river road that we used before the railroad went in."

"How far away is that?"

"From here about two miles, maybe less."

Spur kicked the mount in the flanks and galloped down the street the way he hoped that Chandler had taken. The stolen bill tied it. Now all he had to do was catch up with the rider.

Spur pushed the mount for a quarter-of-a-mile at the gallop, then let her simmer down to a walk for a half-mile and lifted her to a canter. The canter would produce six miles in an hour. The next downriver boat wasn't due to leave Little Rock for another hour-and-a-half. It would take the boat a half hour at least to go downstream five miles. Should be plenty of time.

Twice along the way he checked the river road for hoof prints. He found several, but none he could identify. He had nothing to use for comparison. A mile out of Little Rock he found new prints. They were laid down over wide-wheel wagon tracks and seemed fresh, no bug marks across them.

The horse had been walking along here, but soon he saw the little puffs of dust at the back of the prints and where the front had dug in a little deeper. The animal was at least cantering.

Four miles later, Spur rode up to the small village of Bayview. He could hear a sawmill buzzing away in the distance. The whine of the big saw

screamed through the otherwise quiet countryside. It was easy to find the steamer dock.

The town's one street led straight to the river
and the dock with its piling driven into the Arkansas River mud bank and a small structure to serve
passengers and ticket sellers. He checked out the
area first. He saw a horse to one side that looked
on the tired side, but no chance he could identify
it as the one Doug had ridden here.

Where was he? Spur loosened the six-gun in his
leather and walked the last quarter of a block to
the steamship building. No one lurked outside. He
glanced through a window but saw only two people inside, a woman and a young girl. He pushed
open the door and went in. The man behind the
counter said the boat would be along in about
twenty minutes.

"That is, if she's on time and if that new pilot
we got misses the Siwash sand bar. He hit it on
his first trip down and it took them an hour to get
unstuck."

Spur bought a ticket to the next stop and
strolled outside to wait. If Doug Chandler was
here waiting for the boat, he was well hidden.
Spur walked up the street half a block and sat
down in a captain's chair in front of the hardware
store. He leaned it backwards against the shiplap
and pulled his hat down on his forehead until he
could just see out under the brim.

Not much moved in the village. A man went
from one store to another. Somebody rolled up in
a farm wagon pulled by two ragged looking mules.

Soiled Dove

When the driver stepped down, he looked about as tattered as the mules.

Five minutes later, he hadn't seen the fugitive. The whistle of a steamboat came then and he looked upriver and saw the small craft coming around the bend. It was no more than eighty-feet long, not the huge stern wheelers that plied the Mississippi. This one had an internal propeller of some kind, not showing a side or stern wheel for power.

The craft came along the dock, tied up and half a dozen people got off and three got on. None of them was Doug Chandler. Then as the crewman called for any last passengers and started to untie the boat, a man came out of some brush near the side of the boathouse and stepped on board.

Spur had been moving toward the boat since it had docked. Now he ran the last 50-feet and jumped on board just as the crewman let go of the last line. He gave the surprised crewman his ticket and looked around for the man he was sure was Doug Chandler. He was about the right size and he carried a small carpetbag.

The man wasn't in the main cabin where the other passengers were seated. It had benches and chairs fastened to the deck. Spur frowned. He went back on the deck and walked around the ship. Nowhere did he find the fugitive. The pilot house?

Spur retraced his steps to the ladder that led upward ten-feet to the door of the pilot house. Signs warned away passengers, indicating this was off limits and for crew only. Spur hurried up the ladder and looked through a small window in the door. He saw Doug Chandler standing beside the pilot who had the ship's wheel. Spur drew his Colt and eased the door open.

Neither man noticed him at first.

"That's right, the river is a little tricky here, but we stay in the middle channel and since we only draw ten-feet we have no problems. Now if we was one of them flat bottomed boats with a stern wheel, we could coast through three-feet of water and not even scrape our bottom. On down another 200-yards, we swing in close to the shore 'cause that's where the channel is."

"Interesting," Chandler said.

Then a gust of air through Spur's held-open door made Chandler look that way. He brought up his own six-gun and pushed it against the back of the pilot's head.

"Nothing to worry about, Captain, just keep doing your job. McCoy, you at the door. Lay down your six-gun easy on the deck or this sailor gets a slug through his brain."

"You wouldn't do that, Chandler. Because then I'd shoot your body full of five holes. Give it up. The chase is over."

"Not even started. Put your gun down now, or I'll kill this man."

"You've killed enough before, you just might. But I don't know how well you swim and the boat would undoubtedly smash into the shore somewhere. Can you swim?"

Chandler seemed confused for a moment, then he looked at the far side of the pilot house, saw another door and darted for it, snapping a shot at Spur as he went. Spur had eased around the side of the door and the round missed but it was too late for him to get a shot at the killer.

Instead of going through the pilot house, Spur dropped down the ladder and ran around the passenger cabin expecting to find Chandler on the far side of the ship. It was the side nearest the shoreline. They had pulled close to the shore here, not over 60 or 70-feet where the current had dug out the channel in a gentle curve.

Spur didn't see Chandler anywhere.

A woman ran up who had been standing at the rail.

"A man just fell overboard," she shouted. "See, there he is swimming for shore."

Spur swore, took off his hat and climbed over the rail, then dove the four-feet into the murky waters of the Arkansas River. He came up blowing out water and felt the current sucking at him, dragging him downstream. He stretched out in a strong crawl stroke and splashed water as he worked his way against the current toward the green grass and tree covered shoreline.

After 20 strokes he felt the current easing and his progress increased. He saw Chandler come out of the water 100-yards back upstream. Another two minutes of strong stroking and he felt his feet hit the bottom. He surged upwards and ran through the foot of water to the shoreline and wiped the water out of his eyes and smoothed back his hair.

Now, to find the little bastard.

He reached down to adjust his six-gun but came up empty. The weapon had fallen out of leather sometime during his dive or swim. He'd have to make do without it. He still had on his boots. He sat down and took them off and poured Arkansas River water out of them, wrung out his socks and put them back on. He squeezed water out of his pants and took off his shirt and wrung it out, then donned it again.

Dressed once more, he moved into the brush 20-feet to get out of sight and stopped, listening. He was too far away from Chandler. The man could be moving through the damp riverside country and making almost no noise. He had to get closer to him.

Spur went away from the river figuring there should be a road along this side of the water. He found one and looked both ways but didn't see Chandler. He eased back into the brush and ran forward upstream, hoping to find the man. After 30-yards he stopped and listened but heard no movement.

He ran another 30-yards with the same result. Only his soggy pants made noise slapping side to side. Spur gave a little shiver as the evaporating water on his clothes cooled his skin to the point of a chill. Where was Chandler going? Would he head downstream? Probably. Then why hadn't Spur seen him? They were no more than a mile from the small town they had just left on the boat.

Spur sniffed. Yes, wood smoke from ahead. Smoke could mean campers, rawhiders or a farm house. He moved quickly toward the smoke, tracking it like a beacon. It led him out of the brush and to the road. He paused before crossing. Ahead a quarter-of-a-mile he saw a log cabin and a barn. Smoke came from a smoke house just behind the well.

Spur watched but could see no one around the buildings. Chandler had been a lot closer to the smoke than Spur. Had the man smelled it or seen the cabin and rushed over there? Or had he seen Spur leave the ship, charged across the road into the woods on the far side and rushed downstream?

A moment later he heard a scream from the house, then a gunshot. Spur ran through the light brush upstream until he was directly across from the buildings. He paused, watching the place. He still had seen no one. There had been no more gunshots. The front of the house had two windows. He could see the side. It had only one window, up high.

Spur ran upstream another 30-yards, then came out of the brush and sprinted for the blind side of the cabin. He arrived with no challenge. Either Chandler had not seen him or he didn't have a clean shot.

Spur edged around the side of the building and looked at the front. He could see no one. He hunkered down and crawled to the first window in the front and slid upwards so he could see inside the cabin.

His view showed him part of the kitchen. A woman sat in a chair. A man sat near her. The man had been tied to the chair with rope. Doug

Chandler stood there watching them, holding a six-gun. Was it his own or one he took in the cabin? A six-gun worked just as well after a water dousing as it did dry. Nothing much mechanical to go wrong. The rounds fired just as well. He'd even fired his Colt once under water.

Spur eased down from the window considering the situation. Chandler was armed and had two hostages. He had no weapon. He could check around the place for an axe or a hatchet. The Indians used their hatchetlike tomahawks to good advantage. How much daylight was there left?

A look at the sun told him it was about three o'clock, maybe four. His watch had stopped due to its swim. His pants were still soggy but his shirt was drying. He should dry out before the chill of the evening. His pants would take the longest to dry.

He moved back around the cabin and ran to the barn. Inside he found a three tined pitchfork, an ideal weapon for close-in fighting, but not against a six-gun.

He found a hatchet sticking in a chopping block in the near side of the barn. He hefted it. Yes, sharp and well balanced. He could do a lot of damage with that close-in.

Spur carried the hatchet and looked out the barn door at the cabin. Smoke came out of the chimney now. Maybe the woman was getting supper. He ran back the way he had come and slid up to look through the front window.

The movement at the glass must have caught Chandler's attention. Spur found himself looking directly into the eyes of Doug Chandler. The fugitive swore, lifted the six-gun and sent a shot through the foot-square pane of glass just after Spur jolted his head downward for the protection of the thick log construction. Two more shots came through the window, then Spur heard a wail of pain.

He lifted up and looked again. The woman had just drawn back a butcher knife that showed red with blood. Chandler's gun hand hung empty at his side, a long bloody gash on his forearm.

Spur ran for the doorway. He pulled it open just as Chandler dropped to his knees to retrieve the six-gun. His right hand reached for the weapon. Spur was ten-feet away. He threw the hatchet with almost no backswing. The weapon turned once and the flat back of the hatchet head hit Chandler in the forearm driving his hand away from the gun. The woman dove to the floor and skidded the hand gun farther across the floor.

Chandler looked at Spur and must have realized he had no firearm. He held his forearm to slow the bleeding and turned and ran for the front door, sidestepping Spur's frantic grab at him. A second later he was out the front door and running.

Spur rolled over and ran for the front door. He paused. "Sorry about this, ma'am. He's a wanted killer, and I'm a lawman chasing him." He saw the six-gun, grabbed it off the floor and ran out the door.

Chandler had vanished.

Spur heard sounds in the barn. He ran that way, cocked the six-gun and stepped inside the door. A thrown pitchfork bounded harmlessly beside his feet but missed him.

In the dimness of the barn he could see a horse. Chandler would be trying to saddle it.

"Enough, Chandler. I've got the gun now. Come out slow and easy and you'll live to stand trial."

"Why, and let Judge Parker have the pleasure of hanging me? Not a chance."

Spur saw it coming out of the gloom almost too late. The horse screamed in pain and bolted straight ahead. Spur had to dive to the side to get out of the way of the thundering hooves. When Spur rolled and came to his feet, he heard the horse pounding away to the front and saw light where a door flapped at the rear of the small barn. Spur ran that way.

He spotted Chandler running hard toward the trees 100-yards away. Spur followed at a jog. Chandler would wear himself out at that pace and soon have to walk. Spur could jog at five miles an hour all day.

As Spur jogged toward the trees, he opened the hand gun and took out the four fired shots. He checked the brass and grinned. They were .45 caliber. The rounds in his belt loops would fit. He loaded the weapon with six cartridges and slid it into his holster. He snapped the safety strap and ran on.

Twenty-feet into the woods, Spur jogged past a big tree and suddenly Chandler jumped out from behind it and swung a two-inch branch at Spur. The weapon came so quickly that Spur had no time to draw, and could only drop to the ground.

He surged forward, hoping to pin Chandler before he got away.

When Chandler saw he had missed with the club, he darted away into the brush and trees. Spur came to his feet and gave chase.

For the next half hour the two men charged through the trees, with Chandler hiding once hoping to elude Spur, but the old tracker instinct saved the Secret Service man. He dug Chandler out but couldn't get a clean shot at him. The chase was on again.

They came to an upgrade and soon were on the top of a small cliff that looked out over the river. Chandler was almost across the bare spot when Spur came into the open.

He put one shot past Chandler and called out. "Not another move. I've got five more rounds and one of them will kill you, Chandler. Give it up and come back with me."

Chandler looked around for some way to escape. He could always jump off the 100-foot cliff to the rocks below. He shrugged.

"Guess it's all over. Damn knee hurts." He slumped down near a barren spot and rubbed his knee. Spur came up slowly, watchfully, wondering what the killer would try this time.

"Put your hands behind you, Chandler. I'll tie them and then we can get back to that last boat dock." Chandler growled but put both hands behind him. Spur moved toward him, paused three-feet away and shook his head.

"You had me going for a while, Chandler. I guess I didn't expect somebody as young and as lazy as you could set up the whole robbery and kidnapping."

Chandler shrugged, then both his hands came from behind him and he threw dirt and ants into Spur's face. The dirt clogged his eyes, the ants bit him on the face and went down his neck and bit him again and again. He clawed at his eyes to get them clear.

Chandler made a dive for his gun hand, but Spur held onto the six-gun. He pulled it away, then shot at the sound, but heard no cry of pain. He listened, then fired once more at the retreating sound of running footsteps.

Spur used his neckerchief and wiped the grime and dirt out of one eye, then the other. He took off his shirt and dusted the last of the pesky ants off him, then put it back on and reloaded the two spent rounds as he moved forward on Chandler's trail. The little bastard was more resourceful than Spur gave him credit for. He slumped down right beside the ant hill so he could use it.

So, Chandler was on foot, he was 100-yards or so ahead. Where could he go? Downstream? How good a woodsman was he? That might be the final telling factor. Spur settled down to tracking the fugitive through the woods. It was simple, like he had left a trail of brightly colored beads.

Spur moved slowly, cautiously, so he wouldn't get caught in another ambush. It was close to dark now. He couldn't track after dark, but neither could Chandler move fast. He might just give up until morning. Twice the trail had crossed the road that ran near the river. It didn't get much use now except by locals. Spur hoped that Chandler wouldn't waylay a farmer and steal a horse to try a getaway.

His clothes were nearly dry now. Spur edged forward another 20-feet, following the tracks in the soft mulch of the woodsy floor and then gave up. It was getting too dark. He had a decision to make. He could stop here and track in the morning. Or he could get back to the road and walk down two miles and wait there hoping that Chandler might be on a night walk himself.

Spur chose the walk in the moonlight. He ventured what he figured were three miles down the river road, then sat down in a dry spot near the road in a clump of willows to wait out his quarry. He just hoped that Chandler wasn't ahead of him.

Chapter Twenty

Maybe it was the still slightly wet clothes he wore, maybe it was a sullen wind that sped through the willow thicket. Whatever it was, the cold awoke Spur about midnight and he thought he'd frozen to death.

He stood and did a hundred steps running in place. Then he did what his father used to call side straddle hops, jumping out with his feet three feet apart and at the same time swinging his arms over his head until his fingers touched. Out and back, out and back. He did 50 of those and his legs began to burn.

At least he was awake, and warm. He had forgotten to get a blanket at the livery when he left. There was not a chance that he would start a fire and draw attention to himself. This section of the river in Arkansas was lightly settled. Much of it was overgrown with small hardwood trees of not much value except as fenceposts. He didn't know what the sawmill cut back up the river.

He at last got warm and kept walking around to stay that way. He wished he had brought a jacket of some kind, but it was far too late for that now.

By the time dawn came he had dozed off two or three times after sitting down by a tree. Light revitalized him and he remained entirely still trying to hear any approaching man or beast.

His watch was still waterlogged so he had no idea what time it was. He figured the sun had been up an hour when he heard the first sounds coming from upriver. A slight turn in the road just upstream from him masked the approach of anyone. He waited and at last he saw a man walking toward him. He limped slightly on his left leg and had no hat.

At first sighting, Spur figured the man could not be Doug Chandler, but as the form grew closer, he changed his mind. At 50-feet away, Spur knew for sure the walking man was Chandler. How to handle him?

Spur drew the six-gun, spun the cylinder and cocked the hammer. He would not shoot the man down without warning, even though he was a mad dog who deserved to die. His personal code and that of the department precluded any such action.

He would warn him, give him an ultimatum and if he did not comply, or made some threatening move, then Spur would shoot. He waited until Chandler was 20-feet away and slightly upstream from him before he called out.

"Freeze right there, Chandler. Don't move or you're dead."

Quicker than Spur thought possible for any man, Chandler jumped, dodged, dove to the ground and came up running a zig-zag course toward the river. Spur fired twice, then twice more, and each time he missed. He'd never seen such a jittery, herky-jerky target in his life.

He charged after him when he was only 30-feet away, but the young man sprinted like a running track star. The moment he entered the brush, Chandler was no longer a practical target. The smallest branch or leaf could deflect a .45 slug.

Spur sprinted after him and was only 20-feet away and gaining when they came to the edge of the river. There was a 10-foot bank here and Spur could hear the sound of white water ahead as the river narrowed. It was still 300-yards wide, swirling deep and strong from the recent rains upriver.

Chandler never hesitated or looked back. He hit the edge of the bank in stride, flattened out in a racing dive and entered the water cleanly and was at once swept downstream. He surfaced and came up swimming away from Spur.

For 100-yards, Spur ran along the bank trying to match the speed of the flood tide that swept downstream. Gradually he fell behind. He could see Chandler swimming ahead of him in the direction of the rapids where the river narrowed and increased in speed, but was still plenty deep enough for navigation.

Spur put the revolver back in his holster, fastened the hold down strap securely and jumped into the water. He tried to stay near the shore, but in seconds he was pulled into the current and swept downstream with a force that at once frightened and amazed him. He had never felt such a tremendous force from anything before as he did from the water.

He went under, came up, headed for a large rock in the side of the channel but maneuvered around it kicking and swimming for all his worth. Now and then he could see Chandler ahead of him maybe 50-feet.

The water battered them both for a quarter-of-a-mile, then the rough water was behind them and the flow of the river deepened and spread. Both men struck out swimming with what little energy they had left.

Spur couldn't do the crawl. He worked a makeshift sidestroke, floating on his side for as long as possible with each stroke before his head went under water. He surged upward and checked for Chandler. He had made it to shore, on a sand spit that extended out into the current. He crawled up and fell on his back exhausted.

By the time Spur made it to the same sand spit, he was so drained he could barely drag himself out of the water. He collapsed on his back on the warm sand with his feet still in the muddy Arkansas flow.

Spur felt his eyes close and jolted them open. He'd heard something. He looked up just in time to see a large rock over his head. He screeched and rolled to one side.

Chandler had used all his strength to lift the ten pound rock. It smashed down into the sand a moment later. It would have smashed Spur's skull like a summer ripe watermelon.

Slowly Spur drew his six-gun and aimed it at Chandler. He sat sagging forward almost falling on his face.

"Go ahead and shoot," Chandler said. "This whole damn thing went wrong from the beginning."

Spur tried to squeeze the trigger, but he didn't have enough strength. Or maybe he just didn't want to badly enough. He shook his head and let his gun hand sag. Chandler gave a little cry of surprise and delight, then fell slowly forward into the sand.

Spur wasn't sure how long he lay on the warm sand. He had pulled his legs out of the water at some point. He knew Chandler was still in front of him, sleeping or unconscious, he couldn't tell which.

He tried to sit up, but fell, then tried again and made it. What he saw made him think the ants were still in his eyes. A naked girl, maybe 20, sat 10-feet from them on the downriver side of the sand bar. She had long hair wet from washing, and she grinned at him without any modesty.

She waved a bar of lye soap and smiled. "Wondered if you two was agonna sleep all afternoon. Where you gents come from, anyhow?"

"Upriver," Spur said, surprised that he could still talk.

The girl looked at him, nodded and then

splashed her chest, washing the soap off her full breasts and flat stomach.

"You like what you see, big man?" the girl asked.

"You're a pretty girl," Spur said.

"Glad you think so." She pointed at Chandler. "He dead or something?"

"We're both beat up by the river. Didn't know it was so rough through here."

"Can get that way," the girl said. She turned and yelled. "Ma, they back to living. Y'all get down here."

"You live nearby?" Spur asked, getting his breath back and starting to get some strength in his hands and his arms.

"Here and there." The girl stood, washed soap off her crotch and her legs and turned toward him.

"Is this a sexy picture?"

"Damn sexy," Spur said. "What's your ma gonna say she see you like this with us?"

The girl laughed and it made her breasts wobble and jiggle. "Ma will be fit to be tied she didn't wait and take her bath," the girl said. "Oh, I'm June. You got a name?"

"Spur McCoy. This one is Doug Chandler."

"Funnin' down the river, huh? You musta busted up your boat."

"Right, hit a big rock."

"Dumb. Shame to waste a good man like you in the damn river."

A woman came out of the brush. At least Spur guessed that she was a woman. She was short, fat, and had hair that was dark and stringy looking as if it had never been washed. She wore a skirt and blouse that both were dirt-brown and would stand up by themselves if she wasn't wearing them. As she came closer, sloshing through the mud and water in a pair of knee boots, Spur could see that her face was pock marked and had six skin eruptions that showed purple and black.

"Ma, look who I ketched. Got us a pair of them and I get my pick. You promised last time."

The woman pulled a sawed off shotgun from a hole in her full skirt and aimed it at Spur.

"Get his iron, you expect me to do it all?" the mother growled.

"No, Ma. But I get to do this tall one. Ain't he a beauty? Not one you'd want to throw back."

Spur had a rule about never giving up his six-gun. Anytime a peace officer did that he was as good as dead. In this case, the same could be true if he didn't give it up. The old woman would probably blow him back into the water with the shotgun. He was sure she had double-ought buck loads.

He pegged them at last: rawhiders. The lowest of the low of prowling criminals who would kill a man for his horse and saddle. Who robbed and burned and raped and ruined anything they came in contact with. Fewer of them now, but they still roamed in the untamed parts of some states and a lot of territories and unorganized lands.

He felt the girl come beside him. She bent over and pushed one of her breasts up to his mouth.

"Kiss my tittie for good luck," she whispered. "I

won't let the old bitch kill you. Least not right away. Chew on me."

Spur chewed on the tender breast a moment, then let go. June took his six-gun and backed away.

"Now, get them up to the camp and tie them hand and foot. Don't want nothing going bad this time."

"Yeah, Ma." June said. She motioned to Spur. "Can you stand? You got to get your friend here up the bank to our camp. Ain't but about thirty-feet downstream."

Twenty minutes later Spur eased Chandler down on a blanket June had spread under the trees. A covered wagon of sorts harnessed to two sharp looking mules parked just of out of the shade.

A man Spur guessed might be middle-aged tumbled out of the back opening of the wagon, staggered a step and then fell on his face. He rolled over laughing. "Damn me, but I'm swished. Can't even fucking walk."

He looked at Spur from bloodshot eyes and nodded. "Damn me, but he's a young one. Looks strong as a billy goat after six she-goats in heat."

"Have a nap, Daddy, I'll take care of him. Ma gets the other one."

June sat down beside Spur. She hadn't put on any clothes yet. She picked up one of his hands and put it on her breast. "Pet me a little first, then I got to tie your hands together so you won't run away."

"Why would I do that with a sexy, naked woman

319

like you asking to get herself fucked?"

June grinned. "Oh yeah. I like your way. I'm ready just anytime you're ready. Guess we should get your pants off first."

"What about the others?"

"Hell, let them watch. Ma wants to get your friend into her bed inside. I'll help her, then we'll be out here in the sunshine. Pa's passed out again. I'll be back in a minute. Don't try to run. I've got your six-gun and I can use it."

The two women tugged Chandler into the trailer. He was conscious again but not in very good shape. Either that or he had heard it all and was faking it, planning something.

So was Spur.

June was in and out the wagon so fast Spur didn't have time to do anything. She held his borrowed gun as she came out and grinned. "Now, lover, I tie your feet together. Won't hurt your performance at all. And your hands will be tied and staked over your head. Yeah, that'll work. With me on top. I love the top."

She tied Spur's hands but didn't stake them down over his head. She forgot to tie his feet after she had pulled off his pants and his underwear. June grinned when his erection popped up.

"You're hot to go already?"

Spur snorted. "Woman, you running around buck naked, flipping them great tits around, making me eat them, tying me up while your tits swing, what do you expect?"

"Yeah, nice, huh. I don't have to get you all hot and ready to pop." She lay on top of him, then moved up and fed her breasts into his mouth one at a time. "I'd like to have you spank me the way my boyfriend used to. But they killed him. The old man did about a month ago."

"I thought he was your father?"

"Him? Nah . . . They killed Freddie and told me they would kill me if I didn't come with them. Since then the old man does me once a day. The old woman is the worst."

"Why do you stay?"

"No way to get out safe. They'd track me down and kill me for sure."

"Maybe not. I could help. Don't tell them but I'm a Federal lawman, that Doug is a killer I'm chasing."

June grinned, lifted her breast away from him and lay beside him playing with his erection.

"Sure, sure, and I'm the Queen of the May." She frowned. "You think you could help me get away free?"

"Absolutely. Play along with me. Untie my hands so it just looks like they're tied. Then let's not waste this tender moment."

She undid his hands so that with a quick pull he'd be free. She moved down and lifted off him, then lowered her delicious body toward his and he impaled her until she screeched in delight. She began at once to lift and fall on his erection. The pressure built and built and before he was ready, June bellowed out a scream and climaxed, jolting and trembling and crying, ending it with a long high keening sound that chilled Spur.

Spur waited for her to recover a bit. "Where's that six-gun?" he asked.

She shook her head.

"It's the only way. Can the old woman drive the wagon?"

"Yep, usual she's the one."

Spur looked over and the old man had come to and sat up. He looked at June.

"The gun, now," Spur whispered. She had it on the side where the old man couldn't see it. June hesitated, then she groaned.

"Oh, God, anything to get out of here." She pulled the six-gun toward Spur.

He jerked his hands free of the loosened ropes, grabbed the revolver and turned toward the old man who was on his knees now watching them. He snarled when he saw the weapon aimed at him and dove to one side toward his shotgun.

Spur fired three times. The second round caught the rawhider in the chest and flopped him backwards three-feet where he skidded on the grass and dirt and lay still.

June had rolled away and crawled as far as she could get from Spur. She came up running and darted into the brush. Spur heard screams from the covered wagon and looked for cover. He found a tree ten-feet away and ran bare assed and boot-less toward the tree.

Another scream erupted from the front of the wagon. Spur glanced at her just as he stepped behind the foot thick tree. The shotgun in the old woman's hands exploded once, sending a rain of buckshot into and past the tree that shielded Spur.

He started to look out, then pulled back just as the second barrel exploded.

It was double-ought buck that jolted through the brush and trees and into his protection this time. Eleven or thirteen slugs as big as a .32 caliber bullet.

When the rain of death had swept past, Spur stepped out and aimed the six-gun at the old woman.

"Drop it, woman, or you'll join the old man in hell," Spur called.

The woman wavered, then opened the breach and extracted the two spent shells. She had just reached for more rounds in one of the pockets sewn into her skirt, when a fist from inside the wagon powered down on the woman's hand holding the shotgun. It tumbled out the back opening of the wagon to the ground.

Then the woman was pushed from behind and she half-climbed, half-fell, out of the box that sat three-feet off the ground. A moment later, Spur heard sounds from the front of the wagon. By the time Spur ran where he could see the front opening, Doug Chandler waved a six-gun at Spur and darted into the heavy growth.

Spur felt naked and defenseless. He ran back to the blanket and pulled on his clothes, hoping that Chandler wanted to run rather than come back and get in range to shoot at him. He jerked on his boots and June came up. She had dressed.

"I'm going with you."

"You can't. I'm on a manhunt. He'd kill you to get at me. Not a chance. Can you handle the old woman?" She shook her head.

The girl looked up in terror. "Look out!" she screamed.

Spur dove to the left, the girl fell to the right. The old woman had reloaded the shotgun and fired from ten-feet away. The pattern of the double-ought buck hadn't had time to spread out much yet and Spur felt only one slug that clipped the heel of his boot. He rolled and knew there would be a second shot. He had reloaded the six-gun after using it and drew it as he rolled and came up shooting.

His first round startled the woman, and even though it was unaimed and missed her, it kept her from pulling the trigger for that vital half a second. Before she aimed and got her finger back on the trigger, Spur had fired twice more. Both rounds slammed into her chest. She powered backwards, a look of shock and disbelief on her dirt caked face. She looked up at the trees, then gave a long sigh and died.

"Oh, damn," Spur said. He hated killing a woman, even an evil, murdering, ridiculous excuse of a woman like this one. June came back and stared at the body, then she turned away and threw up.

Spur took her by the shoulders when she stood and stared at her.

"June, it's up to you now. Drive the wagon out of here, back on the river road and turn north. There's a little town up there that has a steamboat landing. It's maybe three or four miles. You can go by boat on up to Little Rock. You don't need to say anything about these two. Just get out, sell whatever you can from the wagon and get back to your home. You must have some relatives."

"A brother, up by Little Rock."

"Good. Get some money and go up there. I've got to go find a killer."

He reloaded the revolver as he spoke, then ran into the woods and looked for the trail that he knew Chandler had left in his haste.

He found the trail five minutes later. Chandler was trying to find the river road. They were still on the Arkansas side of the river. Ten minutes later, Spur found where Chandler had walked into the road and moved south. His footprints were plain in the dusty road. Spur began to jog to catch up with the fugitive.

He had been counting on Chandler not having a long range weapon, only the six-gun he must have taken from inside the wagon. He'd jogged on the far side of the river road in and out of the small brush to get out of the best range for a revolver. He could pull into the brush at any point and set up an ambush.

Chandler must still have the bonds and the cash. How? An oiled paper envelope or wrapping with oil paper to protect the bonds and money from the water. Maybe.

Spur stopped and stared ahead. A quarter-of-a-mile down the road he saw a horse and two men. Were they arguing? Was one of them Chandler?

Spur dug down and drew on all of his energy as he ran forward. He shot his weapon in the air once and saw both men turn and look at him. They stayed in the road and went on talking. As he ran forward, Spur thought that the talk ahead of him looked like an argument.

Both men stood on the ground near the horse. Spur thought he could see one man reach in his shirt for something and give it to the other man.

By the time Spur was 50-yards away the men shook hands and the shorter of the two stepped into the saddle. The man on the ground shook his head and now Spur could hear some of the talk.

"No, no. I've changed my mind. I can't part with Marybelle here, not even for the two-hundred dollars. I'll give it all back to you. No deal." The man on the ground grabbed the mount's bridle and hung on.

Spur charged faster, his weapon held ahead of him. He fired once more over the men's heads. Then he saw the man on the horse take out a six-gun and fire point blank at the one who held the bridle.

It had to be Chandler. Spur tried a shot from 50-feet at the big target, horse and man. He could get lucky. He sprinted now, the revolver cocked and ready. At 30-feet he fired again and saw the horse take the round in the head and go down.

Chandler spilled off the mount and Spur stopped running, waited until Chandler got to his feet and then fired the last four shots in his six-gun. He saw three of them rip into the killer, who was thrown backward by the force of the heavy lead slugs.

Spur took in the scene with one glance. Chandler down, the horse kicking its way into death, the other man in front of the horse moaning and trying to sit up. Chandler hadn't moved since he went down. Spur thumbed out the spent rounds and put in new ones until he had six more shots.

He was 20-feet from Chandler now and wondering why the man hadn't moved yet. He had seen one round hit Chandler in the shoulder and another buckle his right leg. The other round he wasn't sure of. Those two hadn't killed the man, Spur knew that.

With a shrill scream, Chandler lifted up, the revolver in his hand and in one swift motion he aimed and fired at Spur McCoy.

Spur's round left his gun slightly before Chandler's did, but there was no time to move or duck or dodge. Spur's round centered on Chandler's heart, drilled through it and dumped him dead in the dirt near the side of the road.

Spur took Chandler's round in his left arm. He grimaced at the pain, pulled off his neckerchief and wrapped up the arm to stop the flow of red blood. The round had passed all the way through the flesh leaving two wounds.

Spur heard a cry from the man behind him. He turned and saw one final feeble wave, then the man collapsed and died. Spur rested. The sprinting run had sapped what little energy he had left.

Five minutes later, he lifted up and dragged the bodies both off the road. He couldn't move the horse. He sat down and examined Chandler. Inside Chandler's shirt front he found the bonds wrapped in oiled paper. They were dry but most had a bullet hole through them. The bulges in

Chandler's pockets revealed the bundles of Federal notes, wet but still good. The money had been split into four bunches for his four pockets. Somehow it didn't look like enough.

Spur pulled off one of Chandler's boots and found another wad of money tied around his ankle. The other ankle produced more cash. Spur pushed the money and cash inside his shirt, made sure his shirt tail was tucked in well and then began walking north. He couldn't be more than five miles from that little town, Bayview, where they both had taken the boat for a short ride down river. He'd get there with time to spare before it grew dark.

Chapter Twenty-one

Nate Emerson rode into the Triangle T ranch and unsaddled his mount himself. He rubbed the mare down, gave her some oats and then put her out in the corral. He was stalling. He'd been stalling about having this talk with Father Teasdale, Louisa Mae and Emily ever since he found out that Doug was involved in the whole train robbery mess.

He couldn't put it off any longer.

At the kitchen, he opened the door and found Dylan Teasdale sitting in a chair at the table, sipping a cup of coffee. It was the first time he'd seen his father-in-law out of bed in the several days since his stroke.

"Hey, you look to be feeling better," Nate said.

Teasdale sniffed, sipped the coffee and put it

down. He had a big cookie on a plate nearby. "Feeling better, yes," he said. The words came a little slow, but easy to understand.

"That's great, I knew you'd whip this thing if we let you have some time." Nate poured a cup of coffee from the warm pot on the wood range and sat down at the table near the ranch owner.

"Father Teasdale, you know how hard I have been working lately. I'm trying my damnedest to learn all about ranching. I think you know that now. It didn't start out that way."

Nate shook his head. "Damn, I can't understand how dumb I was five years ago. You had me figured right. I liked Louisa Mae, she's a fine woman, but I also looked at who she was and what you had here at the ranch. I ain't never told nobody this before, but I guess I married Louisa Mae as much for the ranch as for her."

Teasdale nodded. "Figured that," he said and looked up. "Don't matter now."

The old rancher spoke slowly again, choosing his words carefully. He moved his right hand and warmed it on the cup.

"But, Father Teasdale, it does matter, to me. I want you to know that I'm truly sorry for those first four years. I wasn't much help around here. Didn't learn much. Just wasted money and lived a soft easy life in the house you built for me and Louisa Mae. Ain't much I can do about that now."

Louisa Mae rushed in from the door to the living room. She put her arms around Nate where he sat in the chair and kissed his cheek. "I heard what you told Pa, Nate. I'm just so proud of you that I could bust."

He turned and kissed her lips lightly. "Meant every word of it, Louisa Mae. Love you more now than I ever did. Trying to make up for them four lost years."

"Now you hush. Look how well Pa is doing. He walked out here with just me to lean on a bit. We figure within a month he'll be taking walks outside with no more help than a whittled cane."

"I'm thankful, Father Teasdale. Just so pleased. Wish things could be the way they was, but nobody can get that no matter how much we pray. So I'm real proud of you the way you're getting better."

"Keep my girl happy," Teasdale said.

"I'll try with all my heart and strength, Father Teasdale."

"Help me," the old man said.

Nate helped the frail old man stand, then he put his forearm under the old arm right up to his shoulder and held the hand in front to help him walk back to his temporary bedroom on the ground floor where the guest room used to be. It was fixed up for easy living for the patient.

Emily saw them coming down the hall and helped. Soon they had the old man safely on his bed and he settled down for a rest.

Emily went back to the kitchen with Nate. He sipped at his coffee, poured one for Emily and then looked at her.

"I've got some bad news," he said.

"You just come from town," Emily said. "It's

about Doug, ain't it? Couldn't be any good news about him. He played me for a fool for so long. But once he touched me, started to move his hands over me." She took a long breath. "Oh Lordy, but he was good making me feel so loved."

"Right, Emily, the news ain't good. Sheriff says it's all but certain now that Doug planned and set up the robbery on that train. The one where the sales contract for the ranch was stolen from the mail. Also stolen was twenty-thousand dollars in new bills. And he arranged for a fake kidnapping of the governor's daughter. He got some bearer bonds the Sheriff says are just like cash and are worth a hundred-thousand dollars."

Emily shook her head, then held it with both hands, her elbows propped up on the kitchen table. "My Douglas always was a man who thought big."

"There's more bad news, Emily. Doug is missing and two men in town got themselves shot dead during the night a couple of days back. Anyway, they think Doug is the one who did it. He took off downriver and that Federal guy is chasing him."

Tears seeped out of Emily's eyes and ran down her plain cheeks. She didn't try to stop them, just sat there crying without making a sound.

"I'd say that Doug won't ever be back to the ranch. Leastwise, not for a long time. If he gets away he might come back years from now when nobody remembers what happened. If he gets caught, he might decide to fight it out, which means he could be killed or have a trial before Judge Parker."

Louisa Mae went to Emily and held her shoulders. She glared at Nate. "You didn't have to be so sudden about it. Bad news goes a long ways."

Nate drank some coffee and nodded. "Know I ain't the best with words. Figured it had to be said. I best get along. Check with the foreman and see how things are moving. We ain't planned the fall roundup yet. Time we get to doing some figuring."

"Nate Emerson, don't you dare go out that door and leave us like this," Louisa Mae said sharply. "We got to figure something for Emily. You go wash the trail dust off your face and put on a clean shirt. Then we'll talk again."

Nate looked at his wife. She usually knew what to do at times like this. She was a year older than Emily and had been a mother to her most of her life.

Nate stood and nodded. "Reckon I could do with some washing up and whatever. Be back here soon."

When he left the room, Louisa Mae sat beside Emily, had one arm around her shoulders and their heads were close together. They were talking, cooking up something. He figured they'd been doing that since they were just little girls.

When Nate came back a half hour later, the two women worked over the stove making a batch of biscuits. Nate frowned. How did they get from tragedy, maybe widowhood for Emily, to baking?

As soon as Louisa Mae saw Nate coming, she left the stove, handed the hot pad to Emily and walked up to meet Nate. She took his hand and turned him toward the door.

"You and me need to take a little walk. Got some things to talk over."

Nate frowned. "Things to talk over?"

Louisa Mae looked back at her sister and shushed him as she pulled Nate out of the kitchen.

Outside, he stopped and stared down at his pretty, slender wife. "Don't understand you at all. We just talked. What else we got to talk over now?"

"Important things. We need to decide something, you and me. We always talk about important decisions, right?"

"Well, sure. I don't think that I own you the way some men do. It's more of a partnership with us, equal shares, equal work, like that."

"Good, then we'll talk about it."

He watched her, knowing that Louisa Mae would get to the point when she was ready. She was the smart one in the family. Had been keeping all the stock records and the account books for years. Her pa wasn't much inclined that way.

They passed the pump house and went up a little incline and then down the other side to where a small feeder stream chattered its way toward the Arkansas.

Louisa Mae found the right spot and sat down, spreading her skirt over her legs and patting the ground beside her. When he sat down she leaned in and gave him a serious kiss, licking his lips and urging him to open them. He did for a minute and then eased away.

"We gonna do it right here, Louisa Mae, in broad daylight where anybody could walk up the slope and see us?"

She laughed. "No. I just want to tell you that I'm proud of you and so pleased that you fessed up about part of the reason you married me. And I want to be sure that you want my body again and again. But not right now."

Nate scratched his head. "Sometimes you're a total puzzlement, Louisa Mae Teasdale Emerson. I do swear."

"It's Emily I'm worried about. She is a highly emotional person who likes to have . . . I mean, she is passionate, she enjoys being with a man. She likes to get poked. It means the world to her."

Louisa Mae looked at her husband. "Now don't laugh or titter or make funny faces. This is serious. Here is Emily who hasn't slept with her husband for the past six months, and now she finds out he's probably going to get killed or arrested and spend a long time in prison or be hung by Judge Parker's court. She's miserable and I don't blame her."

Louisa Mae punched her husband in the ribs. "Don't know what I'd do if I didn't get some loving from you every few days. Six months. God, she must be going crazy."

"Emily ain't exactly a woman to attract a lot of suitors, say if'n she is gonna be a widow," Nate said. "She just don't have many prospects for getting remarried, especially with three young'ens."

"We talked about that. She knows it. We discussed it for some time. Then I did the only thing that a loving, honorable, concerned person could do for her only sister."

Nate frowned and looked at his wife. "What's that?"

"We figured that if the Mormons can do it, we can. I want to share you with Emily."

Nate scowled. "Don't understand no way. You want to share me with Emily? That means I got to split her wood and take care of her house and. . . ."

"What it means, Nate, is that I want you to share her bed with her, say once a week, give her a good poking."

Nate leaned back. Surprise, then disbelief broke across his face like a thundercloud. "Share!"

"Yes. Why not? She won't use you up. She won't give you no disease. You'll still be making love to me two or three times a week just like always. Maybe even some Sunday afternoons." Louisa Mae hurried on now, not wanting to let him think too much about it.

"Oh, it won't be legal or nothing. You won't marry her, just kind of service her once a week and keep her happy. You got to figure out just when so she don't get pregnant again, but we got some ways to help along that line. We talked about it."

"You talked to her about me fucking her?"

"Hush, you know I don't like that word. But, yes, we talked about it, and I convinced her that it would be all right. She needs a man real bad, and won't hurt you. You told me once you could poke me twice a night all summer long if'n I wanted you to. Well, now here's another want I got for you. Now that you heard the idea, what do you think?"

Nate shook his head. "Five years ago I would have jumped at the chance. Now, I'm older. I don't know. I can see how it would be a help to Emily." He reached in and kissed his wife's lips, then bent and kissed her breast through the fabric of her dress.

"Just don't want nothing to come between us. You wouldn't get jealous of me popping your sister regular?"

"Not a bit. I know what it'll mean to her. In the meantime, we have some parties, get some young men out here to dance with her and get to know her. We go to church every Sunday in town and stay for the socials. We try to get her a beau. This is all supposing that Doug gets dead somehow. Pardon my saying it, but he's a rat and a skunk and a robber and a killer I'd think from what you said. I'd just as soon he was dead."

They sat there looking at each other. Slowly their lips came together. The kiss was soft and gentle and when they parted, she had a smile on her face.

"Louisa May Teasdale Emerson, you are the finest woman I've ever heard of or read about. A woman who would share her husband with her sister is a truly marvelous human being. I've never heard of anything so loving and giving before in my life."

"Then you'll do it?"

"Just until we can find out about Doug, and then

if he's dead, until we can find her a beau of her own."

"That could take months."

Nate grinned. "When I was seventeen I once had me a different woman every night for a solid week. Damned near killed me. It was a bet. But—" he held up his hands, "since I married you, I've never parted the thighs of another woman, not once, so help me God. If we do this, it's with your urging, right?"

"Right." Louisa Mae reached in and kissed him. Her hand pushed down to his crotch and rubbed around until she found the start of a hard place. "Oh, I wish I could have you right here, right now. But I promised Emily if you agreed, that you would go upstairs to that spare bedroom and she'd be waiting for you."

"Oh, damn, right now?"

"Darling husband. It's been six months for her. Just as a trial run, a practice. We'll see how it goes."

"Nobody is going to know about this but the three of us, are they?" Nate asked.

"Absolutely not, no one," Louisa Mae said. "I'm not about to share you with all the widows in Forth Smith." They both laughed.

When they got back to the kitchen a few minutes later, Emily was not there. They went up the stairs and to the far bedroom.

"I want you to come in with me," Nate said. "So we all know what's going on. Then I'll want you to leave. No peeking."

Louisa Mae smiled sweetly. "Darling husband,

I know every trick of lovemaking that you have ever used with me. You just be sure to satisfy this nice lady."

Nate knocked softly and he heard a voice behind the door. He went in first and Louisa Mae came in close behind him. Emily lay in the big bed with covers up to her chin. There was a question on her face.

"It's all settled, Emily," Louisa Mae said. "At least for now, and if something has happened to Doug, then until we find you a new husband."

Emily let out a held in breath. She pushed back part of the handmade quilts. She was fully dressed.

"I'm not taking off all my clothes," she said. "Not at first. I was three months wed before my husband saw me without any clothes on. Something a man has to earn."

Louisa Mae went to the bed, leaned down and kissed her sister on the cheek.

"I'm sure everything will be just fine." Louisa Mae turned and hurried out of the room before she started to cry. She wasn't sure if they were tears of joy or wonder or pleasure or what. She knew it was the right thing to do for her sister.

They were all strong and could work through it. A year from now she hoped and prayed that her widowed sister would be happily remarried. After all, she had done it once. A woman with a dowry of half of a $750,000 ranch shouldn't be too hard to find a husband for.

Chapter Twenty-two

Spur McCoy made it back to Fort Smith almost a full day after he left the two dead men on the road downstream from Bayview. He hated to leave the men on the road, but he didn't have time to bury them.

It had been a long wait for the boat after he arrived at the tiny village with the sawmill where he and Doug had boarded the riverboat. A deputy sheriff stationed there took Spur's report and his eyes widened as he looked at Spur's credentials. He said he'd take a wagon and go bring in the bodies.

Spur arrived in Fort Smith a little after noon, had a good meal, then went to see Sheriff Booth Grimm. The local lawman listened to the story and twisted his face into a wry grin.

"Damn, I was hoping you'd kill that bastard Doug Chandler. County don't have much money for trials. Ends it, far as I'm concerned. He killed three people in my county, now the case is closed."

"Except for the money, and that Railroad Express clerk, Clancy. I still think he was in on it."

"Some gent came in from Kansas City with a registered letter receipt that matched the one the post office had here. They authorized me to release the nearly nine-thousand dollars the man said he'd sent along as a down payment on the Teasdale place. So I guess that's all settled.

"He said he wouldn't think of buying a ranch in an area that had as much crime as we have here. Left this morning on the train."

Spur began pulling the stacks of money from his pockets. Some of it hadn't dried out yet. The sheriff stared.

"Be damned. You are a rich man."

"Don't I wish," Spur said. "First we count it, every soggy dollar bill. Better get a witness in here. Then you give me a receipt for it."

"Then I can turn it over to the governor's man and the new stuff to somebody from the Railway Express, I'd imagine. I'll do some talking and find out the right procedure. It all here? The fifty thousand?"

"Don't imagine. Figure Chandler spent some of it. Most of the new bills probably here. Let's get a deputy in here and start counting. Be nice to have a table or something where we can spread out the wet money to dry."

It took them the rest of the afternoon. The wet

bills stuck together like they had paste on them.

The deputy said he'd fallen in a lake once and his cash money stuck together. He let it dry before he took it apart. It wouldn't work. He had to soak it all again and get it wet to get the bills to separate.

"So looks like we better finish working before it all gets stuck tight," Spur said.

Only sixty dollars was missing from the new bills of $20,000. When they at last had a count on the money sent for ransom of Amy Hellman, they could find only $27,470.00.

"Little over twenty-five hundred missing," the sheriff said.

"Figure some of it could be floating down the Arkansas and the Mississippi by now," Spur said. "Then he spent some for his passage and I don't know what else. Best we can do." Spur had the sheriff sign a receipt for both amounts of cash and had the deputy witness it.

Spur headed for the best eating spot in town and had gone only a few rods away from the lawman's office when someone fell into step beside him. He looked over and found Lillian, the hotel maid, part time whore, and spy for Doug Chandler.

She looked over at him, a frown clouding her pretty face.

"You heard," Spur said.

"Yes. You didn't have to kill him."

"You weren't there, you don't know. You want me to charge you with conspiracy to rob a train and to do murder and pitch you into jail?"

Soiled Dove

"No, but I don't think you'd have enough evidence to do that even if you tried."

"I have all that evidence. You told me about what Doug said."

Lillian grinned. "Oh, that. Just some strange woman's fanciful imagination. It would be your word against mine. You can't prove I did a damn thing."

"At least you didn't get me killed. If you had, I'd be really bitched out about it."

She looked up quickly and saw him grinning. Her smile came back. It was an extremely interesting face. He saw the pure white blouse she wore that stretched tight over her breasts. White blouses like that had been his downfall time and time again. The white ones with peekaboo lace were the worst of the man traps.

"You had your supper yet?" he asked.

"No."

"I could buy. I still have a couple of dollars of expense money left."

"You mean it? You ain't whiffed-off at me?"

Spur chuckled. He could afford to relax a little. He had only one small problem to clear up. Tomorrow would be time enough for that.

"Lillian, if whiffed-off means mad at you, I'm not. I'd have to say you're just a working girl trying to make a few bucks. So how about supper?"

"Where we going? One place won't let me in the door."

"Hey, if you're with me, you can get in any place. What one tries to keep you out?"

"The Arkansas Royal Cafe."

"That's where we're going."

Spur opened the door and let Lillian walk in a step ahead of him. He saw an officious head waiter move toward her. Spur caught him in mid-stride and tapped him on the shoulder. The smaller man turned and the frown on his face relaxed into an expression of pure duty.

"My friend here and I would like your best table," Spur said in an icy tone that could bring a chill to the toughest gunman in the land.

"Yes . . . yes sir, Mr. McCoy. I heard you tracked down that Doug Chandler."

Spur didn't comment, just held out his hand pointing the way into the dining room.

They ate the best roast beef dinner on the menu and sipped a moderately dry, red wine.

Lillian giggled at the heads turning toward her. "This is so much fun," she said. "And all those old biddies over there are shocked right down to their fat bellies. This red wine is good. I always forget if it's red wine with meat or with fish."

"I don't remember either," Spur said. "But tonight I wanted red wine, so we have red wine."

They finished the dinner with large pieces of cinnamon apple pie covered with the new topping the whole town was talking about, ice cream.

Spur left a 50 cent tip on the table and they strolled outside. Lillian had caught his arm and stared back at any of the matrons in the room who were brave enough to glance at her.

"Oh, that was delicious," Lillian said. "Just to see their faces. They think whores aren't people, they really do. I've heard them talk when they didn't know I was listening."

They stopped on the boardwalk. It was dark out by then. She held his arm tightly so it pressed against her breast.

"If you don't have nothing special planned, be proud to invite you to my place. I've got some good sippin' whiskey and a fine soft bed. I figure I owe you an all-nighter for you taking me to dinner with all them damned snobs."

Spur smiled down at her in the semi-darkness cut by the spill of light from the restaurant's windows.

"That's real good sippin' whiskey?"

"Damn good. I paid four dollars a bottle for it in Little Rock."

"The bed is good and soft?"

"Featherbed, none better." She paused, then leaned close to him and whispered. "Course, the fucking is first rate, six times at least I'd say by the way you're pushing your arm against my tit."

Spur chuckled. "Might be that I could do with a little relaxing at that. Why don't we continue on to your small abode."

A few minutes later in her house, Lillian scratched a match and lit a coal oil lamp she had left near the door on a small table. She pulled the blinds, then lit another lamp in the living room. Lillian set Spur down in a big soft couch, moved a foot stool out for him and grinned.

"Be back in a minute with the good stuff."

When she returned, she had a tray with a bottle of whiskey, two glasses and a bowl of salted peanuts. She sat down beside him, then pushed over until she pressed against his side with her whole body. She snuggled against his shoulder and waved at the drinks.

"Give it a try. Best in the house."

Spur poured a small drink and tasted it, just a sip. He closed his eyes and smacked his lips.

"Lady, that is fine whiskey. I thank you." He put the glass down and turned to her. "Now, we finish with this and then we won't talk about it again. Did you know anything about the plans to rob the train, or to kidnap the girl?"

"No, nothing. Absolutely nothing. Doug was poking me now and then, but he never let drop one hint about the train. First I knew of it was when I heard about it on the street. Then in the newspaper."

"When did he sic you on me?"

"Same day you hit town, two days after the robbery."

"What did he tell you to do?"

"Find out why you were in town, which he already knew, and to find out what you knew about the robbery and about him and his family."

"Wasn't much to tell him, was there?"

"No, but he had to pay me just the same."

"You don't mind being a spy?"

"It's a living. A girl needs every dollar she can scrape up to keep her ass in motion."

Spur grinned. "Your grilling is over." He caught the glass and sipped at the whiskey again. He looked at her face, then pointedly down at her breasts still stretching the white blouse. "I'd say it's time we take the whiskey and glasses and test out that feather bed you're so proud of."

"First, a stand-up."

"A stand up? Have you ever tried one before?"

"No, but a friend of mine has. She says it's nothing too wild. It's like a real quick one where you don't even have to get undressed, not even your shoes. Just open your fly and whip it out." Lillian giggled. "Oh, yeah, I really want to try it. Unless you don't think you can."

"Done it before," Spur said. He grinned as she began to undress. The white blouse came first. He held her hands and did the buttons for her, caressing her breasts through the soft fabric, pleased when he saw she had nothing on under the blouse. He parted the fabric and caught both her big breasts.

"You can do all the encouraging you want to, lover. I enjoy this part of it the most."

Spur stepped back and let her get out of her skirt and two short petticoats. A minute later she stood there in front of him nude and posing. He could see that she enjoyed her work.

"Now, it's your turn," she said. She went to her knees in front of where he stood and opened his fly, then began to dig out his erection. She gave up and he did the job leaving his belt buckled.

"My gawd, I forget how big you really are, even coming out of your fly." She bent and kissed the tip of his penis and then stood. "I'm ready, I'm ready," she said.

Spur went to the door and leaned back against it. Solid enough. He turned.

"You put your hands around my neck and lace

Dirk Fletcher

your fingers together." She did.

"Now, jump up and wrap your legs around my waist. Hang on good with your hands so you don't fall on your head."

"Really? Jump up?"

"I can lift your legs if you're too old and decrepit to do it yourself."

She laughed at him, held his neck tightly and jumped upward. Her legs lanced around his back and Spur caught them and held her a minute.

"Now, can you cross your ankles, lock them?"

She could.

He turned slowly and let her back lean against the solid door.

"That makes it easier," she said.

He lifted her hips away from him, moved his erection so they would match and slowly drove into her wet and ready slot.

"Oh, damn!" Lillian shrilled. "Damn, damn. I never felt anything like that in a thousand times. How the hell you do that? That is so wonderful. Just—"

Before she could finish, she exploded in a climax that almost tore her body out of his. She surged and humped and bucked and snorted and her breath came like a steam engine. Her whole body racked with spasm after spasm that brought forth a long series of rumbling moans that finished in a shrill keening that echoed throughout the house.

She tapered off only to start again and go through the whole series of reactions, always end-

348

ing in the keening that pierced through the whole house.

Sweat formed on her upper lip and her brow. Her chest turned pink from the orgasm and she was panting and humping again and again. At last she gave one final thrust with her hips and quieted.

"I guess she didn't like it," Spur said.

Lillian couldn't talk. Her eyes rolled and she nodded that she indeed had enjoyed it as she tried to get her breath back and her whole body functioning again.

She opened her eyes and stared at him.

"Fantastic," she wheezed. "Marvelous." Then her eyes closed again and she gave a big sigh. Her inner muscles began to work on him a moment later, gripping and relaxing, gripping and relaxing. Spur gave an automatic humping motion with his hips and he was off.

He pounded upward, driving her against the wall and then lancing as deep as he could on each double push thrust. He set up a double timed rhythm and she opened one eye and squealed. "I'm coming again."

He couldn't wait for her or even feel her movements. He was too much involved with his own building passions. Again and again he thrust and she reacted. He drove again and then he knew that the end of the world had come. Stars exploded and galaxies spun off and merged and clustered and the sun roared at the earth at terrifying speed and vaporized the whole planet in one gigantic fire ball as the whole universe shattered and imploded and soon there was nothing left but one gigantic black hole that had swallowed up all matter, except Spur and Lillian who pounded again and again until they both sagged against the wall in total exhaustion.

Slowly Spur let his knees bend and Lillian slid down the wall. They both sat on the floor in a tangle of arms and legs he wasn't sure they could ever unjumble.

They soon tipped over and lay on the floor, separated, but clinging together trying to extend the thrill.

Spur moved first. He edged upward until he was sitting and stared at the naked form below him. She lay on her side, one delicious breast resting against his leg. Her knees were drawn up shadowing her crotch and one hand rested against his crotch and his shrunken penis.

Her eyes drifted open, then closed, then snapped open.

"Oh, god, what a dream. I thought you were exploding the whole world and the sun was coming at us." She looked up at him. "The sun didn't hit us, did it?"

He shook his head. "Weird, that's exactly the same dream I had about everything in the universe but us vanishing into nothingness."

"Strange, but wonderful. Amazing. I don't think that I've ever—" She stopped. "Maybe I say that too much. But this time it's true. It's never been as good as that time. Not ever. Not since my first time when I lost my virginity when I was fourteen."

"Fourteen? Why did you wait so long?"

"I was shy," she said, grinning.

"I bet. Where's that whiskey?"

They found it, then lay on the bed each with a glass. They sipped at the whiskey and then she put down her glass and gently removed all of his clothes. She sat over his naked body admiring him.

"I've never seen a man with more scars than you have. Bullet holes, knife slashes, you do live a dangerous life."

"Like that fresh bullet hole in my left arm?"

"Is that what that is? I figured I had bitten you when I was going wild."

"You did, but you bit me on the neck."

They laughed and sipped at the whiskey.

"You don't have to leave tonight, do you?"

"Nope. Oh, one more little business thing we need to talk about. One loose end to make it all neat, then no more talk about the robbery-kidnapping-murders. Did you ever see the trainman, Clancy Steffens, talking with Doug?"

"No. I don't know Clancy, he didn't come to the house when I was there. Nobody did."

"Now, think carefully. Did you ever hear Doug talk to the other men about Clancy. Mention the name, even?"

"The name does sound familiar. The more you say it. The first night I went there was the day you came to town. He sent word to me. He was talking with the three men who had evidently been back from the robbery the day or so before. Yes, I remember. He talked to the big one."

"Knute Safire?"

"Yes, Knute. I remember Doug saying that he'd be right back, he had to go pay off Clancy. He turned back to Knute. Then he said, 'I just hope you didn't hurt Clancy. I promised him that he wouldn't get hurt.'"

"Yes, that figures. I had a hunch that Clancy was an inside man on this all along. They got in and out of that express car too quickly to get two locks open."

"So, you going to talk to Clancy?"

"Tomorrow. If he's still in town tonight, he'll be here tomorrow. Doubt if he'll be back on duty yet. The company might be investigating him right now as well."

Spur eased down on the pillows on the bed and sipped at the whiskey. Lillian spilled some spots of whiskey on Spur's chest and bent and licked them off. He nodded. She poured on some that ran down across his belly into his hairy thatch at his crotch.

She licked the whiskey off him, working lower.

"Keep going, darlin'. Just keep going on that whiskey trail," Spur said. She did.

Chapter Twenty-three

The next morning, Lillian fixed a big breakfast for Spur and herself and they lingered over their second cups of coffee.

"Don't tell me you have to leave town soon. I'm not ready for you to go."

Spur smiled and touched her hand across the table. "I still have to confront Clancy. I'm not sure how it will go. I don't think he'll break down and confess, which will make it a lot harder."

"Not much evidence against him?"

"Not with three of the four of the train robbery conspirators dead, the fourth one, Sully, in jail, and maybe he's decided not to talk after all. Sully could be a problem. Our evidence against him is weak."

"So Sully could get off?" Lillian asked.

"Could, but we'll come up with something to charge him with that will stick. You'll have to testify that you saw him in the hideout house here in town and that you heard him bragging about the train robbery. Can you do that?"

"Sure, why not. I heard him."

Spur grinned, drained the coffee and kissed her on the cheek.

"Thanks for breakfast and everything else." He grinned. "Now I better go see Clancy."

It took him ten minutes to find the right house again. Spur knocked on the door and the man's wife answered with a baby in her arms. She was a thin, waif of a woman who probably got pregnant if a man smiled at her. She was tall, with soft red hair, freckles and a pretty face.

"Clancy? He ain't here. Who you?"

"I came to see him the other day. Where can I find him?"

"Went to work, leastwise he went down to the station. Wants to get back to work, but they still investigating the robbery."

Spur thanked her and hurried to the train station. The stationmaster said Clancy was there, in the trainmen's rooms at the end of the station.

"I'll let you in this way, 'cause that outside door is always locked and you don't got no key."

The trainmen's rooms were locker rooms, and dressing rooms where they could get into their uniforms and a small lounge. Mostly the conductors and brakemen used the area. Spur saw Clancy sitting at a table playing solitaire.

"Clancy Steffens?" Spur asked standing over him.

He tried to stand. Spur put his hand on his shoulder. "That's all right, you can stay seated. I'll get a chair, too. I need to talk to you again. Remember when we talked the last time?

"Yes. I remember."

"Good. I thought you might have thought of something that would help us now that a week's passed. We have a prisoner, Scully Whisper. Do you know him?"

"No."

"Have you ever seen him?"

"Hard to say. I see a lot of people in my job."

"Clancy. May I call you, Clancy?"

The man nodded.

"Good. You must know that two of the train robbers are dead. The big one called Knute Safire, and the tall thin one by the name of Russ Dolan. The man who set up the whole robbery and kidnapping is dead too, Doug Chandler. Did you know that?"

"Didn't know about the one you called Safire. Big guy who came into the car and blew the safe?"

"That was the one. Before they died, the men told us some interesting facts. Some of them about you."

Clancy laughed softly. "McCoy, a big Government agent like you knows that dead men can't testify. Now if they had writ something down and signed it before a judge, that would be real evidence. I told you. I didn't know the three men who robbed me. I didn't help them. They knocked me

355

out, for crying out loud. I'm still trying to get my job back. I don't need you nosing around here."

"Oh, I don't think you should plan on getting your job back. Letting one man blow your safe without even a blast in protest from your shotgun, makes the company a little suspicious."

"The explosion on the outside door stunned me. I couldn't hear or see. Told you that. He was all over me before I could get my shotgun off the rack."

"I wonder about that, Mr. Steffens. Sully has been singing for us in jail like a mocking bird. Did you know that? He talks to a man every morning and he writes down what Sully says, with witnesses. He's told us just about the whole story of the robbery.

"He says you got fifteen-hundred dollars for your part. Not bad. That must be three years pay for you, I'd say. Is that about right?"

Clancy shook his head, stood and walked around the chair. He sat down again. "Told you, I didn't help in the robbery. I didn't get any part of any payment. If I had a thousand, five-hundred dollars in real money, you think I'd stay in this hell hole?"

"Sully tells it different. Oh, we'll give him a lighter sentence for his testimony. I'd say you're in big trouble."

"His word against mine. No jury would convict me on that kind of evidence."

Spur smiled, took out a fresh brown cigar and bit off the tip, then licked it all over and lit it. He puffed on it until it was going well, then blew out a mouthful of smoke.

"We've got a second witness. A person who saw you in the hideout house here in town with the other two robbers and with Doug Chandler. This witness will testify that you bragged about your part in the robbery. How they couldn't have done it without you."

"I never was at any hideout house." Clancy snorted. "Hey, Mister Hotshot Detective, that's still just somebody's word against mine. You don't have any kind of a case against me."

"Sully will see that you spend at least ten years in prison. He's our ace in the hole on this hand. Better think it over."

Clancy stood again and stared hard at Spur. "I knew that you'd try to scare me. I ain't done nothing, so I don't admit to nothing."

A trainman came into the room, looked around and walked over to Clancy.

"Hey, got a wire in for you. Looks like it's from your boss."

Clancy took the envelope, shot a glance at Spur, then tore it open. The folded wire that came out was a full page long. Clancy read it quickly, scowled, then read it again more slowly the second time.

"Damn it!" he bellowed.

Spur grinned. "Damn, Clancy, you get some bad news?"

"None of your business."

"Oh, but it is. Your employers are not happy over the fact that they would have been liable for

357

a hundred and twenty thousand dollars in losses from that robbery. I know they've been carrying on their own investigation."

"The bastards."

"Yeah, true. A lot of people get upset when they look at a loss of a hundred and twenty thousand dollars."

Clancy turned around and walked out of the room. Spur followed him into the station. Clancy went to the station master and talked a minute, then headed for the door. Spur cut him off and held up his hand.

"Clancy, we can go on talking here or through the bars of your jail cell, which do you want?"

Clancy turned, sweat beading his forehead. "Told you all I'm going to tell you. Arrest me if you want to. I'm going right now to find a lawyer to talk to. He'll stop you bothering me."

"Good, I'll see you later either in court or in jail."

Spur turned and left the station. He went directly to Judge Amos Parker's court. The judge was in his chambers during a recess.

"Judge Parker, I need a search warrant for Clancy Steffens' house. He's the Railway Express agent on board that robbed train. Some of the cash is missing and I think he was the inside member of the gang."

Judge Parker asked Spur two questions, then filled in the blanks on a document from his desk and handed it to Spur.

"Good for 48 hours, no more. I hope you find what you want. That case seems to be winding down."

"Yes sir. Only one man in custody but three of the perpetrators are dead. Now I need this one last man."

Spur took the warrant and showed it to the sheriff who accompanied him to the express clerk's home. When the sheriff showed it to Mrs. Steffens, she began to cry. "Told Clancy he could never get away with it. Told him so, I told him so. He said it was fool proof. Said he'd pulled it off and nobody would ever know."

"Mrs. Steffens, do you know where he hid the money?"

"No, he wouldn't tell me. But he didn't get the five-thousand he was promised. He only got fifteen-hundred. He hid it somewhere in the house, I know. I asked him what happened if the house burned down and he said it would still be safe."

Spur frowned a minute. "Do you have any kind of a steel safe in your home?"

"No, not that I know of."

Spur shrugged. "This order from the court authorizes us to search your house, Mrs. Steffens. We'll be careful not to make a mess of things."

The sheriff, one deputy and Spur went to work on the house. The place had no basement. Spur checked the first floor. He started on the floor boards with a small hammer, but found none that were loose. There was no throw rug over a removable panel to a cave below. The sheriff took the second floor and the deputy checked outside the house.

After two hours they met and shook their heads. "Safe. Clancy told his wife the money would be safe even if the house burned down."

Spur looked around, then grinned. There was a small shed in back that protected a horse in bad weather and from the sun. It fronted a small corral. Spur went inside the door and looked around. Room for two horses. There was one saddle, some tack, a big feed bin that he found contained oats and a small stack of hay at one end. He used a pitchfork and stabbed it through the hay, but found nothing. He opened the grain bin. It was three-feet square and almost that high. The slanting top covering it leaned upward against the rear wall to allow easy scooping up of the oats for the horse.

Spur plunged his hands into the oats. He found nothing. He brought the pitchfork over and began systematically to dig into the loose oats that were 30 inches deep. On his thrust into the far corner, he hit something. It took him several tries to bring up the item. When he had it surfaced, he grinned.

"I'd say you've found something there," the sheriff said from the doorway.

Inside a small leather satchel, they found three stacks of money, all one and five dollar bills. Spur bet that it would count up to nearly $1500.

"How many lawyers in town?" Spur asked the sheriff.

In the next half hour they checked at five different lawyer offices. In the last one they found Clancy talking seriously with a young lawyer. Clancy didn't resist when the sheriff arrested him for possession of stolen money and participation in the train robbery.

Soiled Dove

"Looks like you have a client after all," Spur told the surprised lawyer. He took one look at the satchel filled with money and then at Clancy.

Spur stood outside the Sheriff's office and hooked his thumbs in his belt. He had given a deposition for the trial on both Sully and Clancy. He was free and clear. Next stop should be the telegraph office to report in to the general.

He changed his mind and hurried to the livery.

It took him nearly two hours to ride to the Teasdale's Triangle T ranch. Nate saw him coming and met him, handed the horse off to a ranch hand and led Spur into the house.

"Father Teasdale is coming along remarkably well," Nate said. "He heard about Doug's death and took it well. He half expected it, and so did Doug's wife, Emily. Father Teasdale can talk almost naturally now.

"The doctor says he should be up and walking in a week or so, but he'll have to take it easy around the house."

In the kitchen, the two sisters sat over coffee. Spur nodded to both of them. The plain one, who he knew was the widow, did not look at all in mourning or grieving. Maybe that was over already.

They went through to the front screened-in porch and found Dylan Teasdale in a rocking chair moving back and forth.

The old man stopped when he saw Spur.

"The detective." Teasdale held out his hand. "Owe you a lot, Mr. McCoy." He paused and took several deep breaths. "Please sit."

Spur dropped into a chair near the rocker and smiled. Teasdale had his color back, he had a sparkle in his eyes, and his hands moved in nervous little gestures that told more about impatience and boredom than about sickness.

"Glad you're feeling better," Spur said. "Sorry about your son-in-law, but I had no choice."

"Don't worry about him. I've got me the best of the two. Nate is coming along just fine. Don't tell him I said that."

Teasdale looked up at Nate and smiled. "Don't want to sell the ranch now that I got somebody to leave it to. Nate is gonna be a damn fine rancher one day."

They talked for half an hour, then Spur saw that Teasdale was getting tired. He said goodbye to the rancher, wished him well and he and Nate went back to the kitchen.

The two women sat at the big table close together and had been whispering. When Spur came in they both stopped and watched him. He nodded and Nate got him a cup of coffee and some crab apple jam and biscuits. They sat down.

Louisa Mae nudged her sister, who took a deep breath. "Mr. McCoy, you ever thought of being a rancher?

"Mrs. Chandler, I've never given it much thought."

"If you have, I can make you a good offer. The triangle T here is the best in the state. Last year we was offered a little more than eight hundred thousand dollars for it, land, cattle and buildings. I own half of it, or will when Pa passes on. All you need to do to be a rich man is marry me and wait a few years."

Spur looked from one woman to the other. Both were deadly serious. Spur sipped his coffee and glanced at Nate.

"No help here. When these two decide to do something, it usually gets done. I'd say you better be cautious about what you say next." He was grinning.

Spur smiled. "Emily, that's a tempting offer, but I have a contract with the United States Government that I can't break. I'm bound in their employment for another ten years. Now if you're still free at the end of my contract. . . . "

Emily shrugged. "Afraid not. This has to be done soon. I figured you'd be a good man to practice on. Who knew, I might have been struck by lightning."

They all smiled then and Spur finished his coffee and got on his way back to town. Nate saw him off. Said indeed they did want to find a husband for Emily, but they'd try to do it a little more diplomatically and more romantically.

By the time Spur got to town and put the horse in the livery, it was starting to get dark.

He headed for the telegraph station and Lillian met him halfway there with a big smile.

"See, good things come to those who wait. I been waiting for you for three hours."

"Glad you found me. Want to help me send a telegram?

"Not if it says you've finished this job and are ready to take another one and race out of town."

"Then you best not come."

She grabbed his arm and pulled it in tightly against the side of her breast. "Well, maybe I could walk part way. I was hoping for supper at that fancy eating place again."

Spur looked down at her. He took a deep breath. He was finished here. He could take a day or two to relax, and then wire the general. He didn't have any definite time schedule. When was the last time he'd taken a vacation?

He turned away from the railway station and headed for the cafe.

"I think some pheasant would be nice for dinner tonight. Have you ever had pheasant cooked in a good wine sauce?"

Lillian said no, reached up and kissed his cheek.

"After supper we can test out that feather bed again?"

"Sounds interesting."

As they walked to the cafe, Spur looked forward to the meal and the evening. But he was starting to get that itch again. The itch that gave him a wonderment and a curiosity and a yearning to know just what his next assignment would be as a United States Secret Service Agent, and where it would take him.

"Hey," Lillian said. "Quit thinking about work. This is fun time, now and for the next three or four days."

Spur grinned and opened the door to the restaurant, eager to stare down the snooty head waiter one more time.

GIANT SPECIAL EDITION **SPUR**

DIRK FLETCHER

TWICE THE LEAD, TWICE THE LOVIN'— IN ONE GIANT EDITION!

Wilderness Wanton. Everything comes bigger in Montana's Big Sky country—the rustler's rustle more; the killer's kill more; and the lovelies love more. So the Secret Service has to send its top gun to clean up the territory. Spur McCoy has hardly set foot in the region before robbers set upon him, dollies fall upon him, and a rich S.O.B. puts a price upon him. With renegades after the bounty on his head, and honeys after the reward in his bed, McCoy will have to shoot straight to wipe out the hard cases, then wear out the hussies.
_3624-X $4.99

Klondike Cutie. A boomtown full of the most ornery vermin ever to pan a river, Dawson is the perfect place for a killer to hide—until Spur McCoy arrives. McCoy knows the chances of mining gold are very good in the Klondike. And to his delight, the prospects for golden gals are even better. With the help of the local Mounties, Spur is sure to get his man sooner or later. But when it comes to getting the ladies, he will strike the mother lode quicker than a dogsled driver can yell mush!
_3420-4 $4.99 US/$5.99 CAN

Dorchester Publishing Co., Inc.
65 Commerce Road
Stamford, CT 06902

Please add $1.75 for shipping and handling for the first book and $.50 for each book thereafter. NY, NYC, PA and CT residents, please add appropriate sales tax. No cash, stamps, or C.O.D.s. All orders shipped within 6 weeks via postal service book rate. Canadian orders require $2.00 extra postage and must be paid in U.S. dollars through a U.S. banking facility.

Name _____
Address _____
City _____ State _____ Zip _____
I have enclosed $_____in payment for the checked book(s).
Payment <u>must</u> accompany all orders.☐ Please send a free catalog.